THE BRIDGE TO MURDER

ALSO BY FRED LICHTENBERG

The Hank Reed Mystery Series

The Art of Murder

Murder on the Rocks

The Edge of Murder

The Bridge to Murder

Murder by Chance

THE BRIDGE TO MURDER

A HANK REED MYSTERY, BOOK 4

FRED LICHTENBERG

Released June 2024
ISBN: 978-1-664457-260-3

ePublishing Works!
www.epublishingworks.com
Phone: 866-846-5123

To the Real Whitestone Boys

"I have reason to bless the breeze that wafted me to Whitestone."

WALT WHITMAN

ACKNOWLEDGMENTS

Thanks to Sharon Menear and George Bernstein, from my critique group, who have helped me immeasurably throughout my writing process. Thanks to my editor, Nadja Hansen, for her help putting the pieces in place. Thanks to Patti Roberts, the best cover designer one could ask for. A big thanks to my front-line editors, my dear wife, Sonia, my sister, Margaret Kelly, and my free mental health advisers, Mark Lichtenberg and his partner, Marla Berger. And to Bob Marchant, a Whitestone boy, for his help in police matters. Thanks to Anthony DuBois for his insight into the world of firefighting. And to Andre Goncalves, director of the Sé Boutique Hotel in Fungal, Madeira, Portugal.

And finally, to my publisher, Brian Paules, and his crew at ePublishing Works! Thank you all.

PROLOGUE

Whitestone, New York, July 6, 1996

J ust past sunset, the majestic Bronx-Whitestone Bridge displayed a spectacular chain of dazzling lights over the East River, of New York City, connecting two of its five boroughs—Queens and The Bronx. Folks on the Queens' side referred to their bridge as the Whitestone Bridge.

It was hard to believe the beauty of the bridge, lighting up Francis Lewis Park below, created anything less than a romantic haven for lovers.

About a quarter of a mile away from the bridge stood Fillmore's, a tavern built in the early fifties, where fishermen hung out after a day at sea. Today, it was more a gathering place for the locals. The older residents came to drink; the younger generation, to hang out mostly on weekends.

That night, Hope O'Brian was among the younger generation. Only she wasn't there to drink or converse; rather to pour her heart out to Annie Baxter, her best friend. Hope was crestfallen.

And blindsided. She and her fiancé were inseparable. For three years, Mike had been attentive to her every need and desire as she was to his. They were soulmates, planned on marrying, and led a carefree existence, traveling as often as possible to Europe and lingering in their beloved Italy.

Hope, twenty-five, was dressed in washed-out black jeans and an ivory linen blouse and arrived at Fillmore's just after 8 P.M. She found a stool in the corner, away from the other patrons, looked around, and took a breath. The bartender approached and asked for her order. She waved him off, telling him she was waiting for a friend.

The bartender, a forty-something with short brown hair, smiled.

"Sure, let me know when you're ready."

She checked her watch, then the front door. Annie was ten minutes late. "Come on girl," she breathed.

Returning to her misery, Hope obsessed for the umpteenth time. The last time she saw Mike was at their favorite restaurant, Nona's, on the water near the Whitestone Bridge, overlooking the East River. She'd been sipping her favorite merlot and watching Mike, who had been pensive since they arrived. He'd already downed several Dewars and water, which she found odd. Like her, Mike usually drank only wine when they dined out.

Odd, also because Mike was never at a loss for words, and his sullen expression concerned her. He finally gazed up at her, his eyes moist. "I have to tell you something."

Hope's heart raced a few beats. Not a good sign. She was guessing the booze provided courage.

He looked away. "I'm having an affair."

Hope's temper flared. Had she heard right? "Having or had?" she demanded.

Mike swallowed hard and met her angry gaze. "It just happened."

She glared. "It just happened?" she repeated. "What the hell is going on? And who is she?"

He coughed. "A co-worker."

"Co-worker?" she said. "You work only with men." She stopped. "Oh, my god, please don't tell me—?"

He put up a hand. "No, of course not."

"Then who is she?"

"Rebecca Daugherty," he blurted.

Hope's eyes widened. "The boss's daughter? Hell, she just graduated from NYU. She's what, not quite twenty-one? You're almost thirty." She shook her head, pictured Rebecca, or Becky for short.

"She's so ordinary. Your words, Mike. And has short hair. You hate short hair on women. You said you loved my shoulder-length auburn hair. And it wasn't that long ago, you admitted, *she* has zero personality."

Hope stopped, as a light went off in her head. "You son-of-a bitch, you don't love her; you want a partnership in her father's insurance agency."

———

Sitting at the bar, still waiting for Annie, now thirty minutes late, Hope pressed her obsession into high gear. Their breakup was three months ago, and she still couldn't shake it off. She stewed in her misery, alone, in her apartment. Every morning struggling to catch the Q-15 bus in Whitestone to Flushing, where she worked for a small construction company.

Her anger and dejection festered. Since the breakup, Annie tried drawing her out of her funk. "You need to get out, Hope. Let's go for a drink and talk about girl stuff."

Annie meant well, and to appease her, Hope finally relented.

"Okay, one drink."

"Great, I'll meet you at Fillmore's Friday evening, eight o'clock. And don't stand me up," she said with a chuckle.

Hope steeled herself and was getting dressed when Annie called.

"I met a guy," she said with excitement. "At Louie's Candy store of all places. I stopped for ice cream. You know I can't get enough French double chocolate. He was ahead of me standing in line and we got to talking. Anyway, we're gonna hang out a bit so I might be a little late. I'll tell you all about him later. Please don't hate me."

A little late! That was over an hour ago, and Hope was seething. Now when she finally agreed to get out, her friend disappointed her. She felt like a fool.

Her eyes searched the dimly lit bar, which buzzed with excitement. At that moment, she got fed up and was about to leave. "No more rejections," she breathed.

But then, a voice entered her space. She turned and gazed up at a tall, athletic type guy with short black hair and a sweet smile.

Hope placed a hand to her ear. "Sorry?"

He moved closer. "I asked if you were waiting for someone?"

Not anymore. "Long story."

"I'm a great listener," he said still smiling.

Hope hesitated.

"I'm Julian."

And I'm pissed. She could go home and sulk or chat with this guy, Julian, who wasn't bad-looking. She noticed his green collar shirt matched his eyes.

She took a breath. What the heck. "Hope, hi." She realized she'd stuck out her hand, and Julian took it. He had soft skin like he was a white-collar worker. Not that it mattered.

"Can I buy you a drink?"

Julian wasn't pushy, just friendly, and nice. And handsome. Mike was handsome and look where it got her.

"Okay."

He called the bartender. To Hope, Julian asked, "What's your preference?"

"Merlot."

He repeated her request and ordered a Bud for himself. When

the drinks arrived, Julian paid. He looked around and pointed at a small table in the back of the bar. "It's quieter there. What do you think?"

She nodded. Easier to talk. Hope followed Julian and wondered if she was too impulsive.

They toasted to life. Hope hadn't had a real conversation in a bar for years and let Julian start. He was an interesting guy and funny. He made her laugh at his jokes.

They ordered another round, and after two merlots, Hope felt at ease. Soon, they were deep into conversation, pausing only to order another drink. She glanced at her watch occasionally but, after a few hours, gave up on Annie. Let her enjoy herself.

Julian claimed he'd been through a rough relationship and hadn't been actively seeking to meet anyone. Hope swore she wasn't either. He regaled her with tales about his travels. He loved sky diving, parasailing, heck, anything in motion. They compared notes.

After three or four glasses of merlot—who was counting—Julian moved in for a peck on the cheek.

Goosebumps.

Around eleven, he asked if she'd care to go for a walk to the nearby Whitestone Park.

She smiled. Locals called Francis Lewis Park the Whitestone Park and shaved off the Bronx in the Bronx-Whitestone Bridge.

The park was known as a lovers' meet-up spot. Some couples parked; others walked to the bridge's landing. She wondered where this *walk* might lead. The last thing she needed was a rebound from Mike. But Julian seemed like a decent guy. He offered to drive and drop her off later at her car.

She took a breath, considered the risk, then agreed. He paid the bill, and they strolled out to the parking lot into his late-model Lexus.

Exiting the car, they entered onto the path leading underneath the bridge. Hope felt the cool breeze against her face and smiled to herself. Must be the wine, she thought. Cool, friendly, delightful.

Julian stopped near the water and pointed to a group of teenagers frolicking under the bridge. "Too noisy over there."

"Looks like they're having fun."

They changed paths, this one leading to the back end of the bridge. Outside of the thump-thump from the cars above, the wooded area was quiet, dense, away from everything.

He stopped and turned to her. "I really like you, Hope. I'm glad we met." He drew her into his arms and their lips touched tentatively. Julian wanted more and before long, with each lingering kiss, their mouths got wilder, their tongues fencing.

She stepped back. "It's been a while for me, Julian. I haven't kissed another man except my ex in…years. I'm not ready for this and need to take it slow. Okay?" She searched around and felt a chill. No one in sight.

Julian muttered. "Of course." But he didn't stop. He pressed his mouth against hers again, this time getting a little free with his hands.

"Dammit, Julian, I said I wasn't ready."

"Come on," he said, his voice taking on an edgy tone. He reached in again, but she slapped his face.

"I wanna leave. Now." She pushed free and started back toward the park entrance, picking up speed. But as her pace quickened, Hope felt his stale beer breath hot on her neck. She glanced up. The damn park lights were at least a hundred feet away.

Now what she thought as the path split up ahead. Confused, she chose the one on the right hoping it wouldn't dead-end.

"Hell, I bought the drinks," Julian growled.

Childish.

Hope began to sprint but stumbled over rocks and roots and realized she had taken the wrong path. In fact, the lights were now farther away than before.

He grabbed her arm and spun her around. "What the hell is wrong with you?"

She was out of breath, but with one last bit of energy, Hope pushed him back, forcing him to loosen his grip. As she turned, Hope tripped over a root and landed onto a mound of earth. Julian stood hovering over her, and she became terrified. She stiffened and started screaming, spitting out loose dirt.

Julian reached down, touching her leg. Hope screamed louder and swatted him away. "Leave me alone," she cried. As she pushed herself up, her eyes locked onto a shadowy mass not more than five feet from her. She fell silent, fixating on it. Hope rubbed her eyes with her sleeve. Was that blood? She lifted her soiled hand and pointed. "What is that?"

"Where?" Julian huffed. "I don't see anything."

Hope shifted her head to get a better look. It was a woman, face up and still. She was wearing a blue blouse with hearts. Her friend's favorite top.

"Oh, God, that's Annie!"

ONE

S itting back in my leather office chair, I'd been reflecting on a recently solved missing person's case when a familiar knock interrupted my thoughts. In walked my mail carrier, Jakub Mazur.

"Morning, Hank." His face creased by his usual friendly smile.

"Hello Jake," I said, grinning back. "What's in your goody bag for me today? A check or two, maybe?"

"Don't know about a check," he said with an accent that hadn't diminished since arriving from Poland twenty years ago. "But this one," he said, waving a letter in the air, "has a lovely fragrance. Jasmine, I think." He handed me the letter. "Enjoy the day."

"You, too." I waved and watched him leave before taking a whiff. Definitely jasmine. I didn't recognize the sender's name or address and took another sniff before slicing the letter open.

"Dearest Hank,"

My heart quickened a beat, and I sat up.

"You're probably wondering who I am, and why I addressed it *Dearest*. A hint. Twenty-five years have passed since we last saw each other. Where has the time gone? I hope you are well and happy. Maybe married? 😊 As for me, life is okay. Mom is getting up in age and starting to forget. Another hint. Too bad Mom and Bobby were only friends when Luca disappeared. No more hints. Are you smiling yet?"

I stopped reading and indeed, produced a smile. Lisa Falcone, my teenage girlfriend. In the past, I too, had wondered if we would take our relationship further. Back then, Lisa was the love of my life.

I sighed. It had been twenty-five years since her brother, my good friend, Luca, vanished under circumstances that still baffled me.

Had Lisa become nostalgic as Luca's disappearance approached its twenty-fifth anniversary? That was a crazy night. A young woman named Annie Baxter was stabbed to death under the Whitestone Bridge, around the same time Luca and his friends were celebrating his eighteenth birthday.

The police concluded Luca was responsible and took off. My friend had remained missing all this time. I was certain he wasn't the killer, despite the investigators finding Luca's knife near the victim's body. Both his and her DNA were on the blade. Case closed.

My hands shook slightly as I drew the envelope to my nose and again inhaled the jasmine. Lisa Falcone had become Lisa Pisano of Stamford, Connecticut. While my first girlfriend's past remained a mystery to me, her choice of perfume hadn't changed.

I opened the lower desk drawer, fumbling around and retrieving ancient junk. I flipped through the file until I found a faded *Whitestone News* article dated July 8, 1996. One I knew by heart. It began with Annie Baxter's murder and ended with Luca Falcone's disappearance.

It mentioned Luca had been celebrating his eighteenth birthday with four friends. Their statements were weak because the teens were impaired by booze. No one knew where the birthday boy had ventured off to. Hence, Luca Falcone became a suspect.

My take, since I wasn't at the party due to a stomach flu, was the real killer remained at large, and my friend also became the victim of foul play. I swiveled my chair and glanced out the office window. None of it made sense at the time, nor now.

A white 1969 Pontiac Firebird passed by and stopped for a light on Main Street. My father owned one of those beauties, and it brought back fond memories. I waited for the light to change before returning my thoughts to Luca. Or rather Lisa.

I suspected her letter became an opportunity to connect through the tragic event. But as I continued reading, Lisa's tone had changed. No longer was she giving funny hints and adding smiley emojis; she needed my help about the past. She'd discovered I was a private investigator and believed I was the only person she trusted to handle a sensitive discovery.

She ended with 'PLEASE CALL!'

That got my attention, and I was quick to call her. Lisa included her cell number and email address, so there'd be no excuse not to respond. Not that I wouldn't. I gathered my thoughts, including her *Dearest Hank* greeting, and punched in her number, remembering she was married.

Her voicemail message greeted me. It was the same mellifluous voice I'd remembered and left a brief message. "Look forward to hearing from you."

Ten minutes later, Lisa texted me, apologizing for not taking the call. She was in the classroom and asked if I was available tomorrow night at Fillmore's.

Tuesdays are quiet and private.

I liked privacy and intrigue, and texted back…

Look forward.

My godfather Bobby, who lived near Lisa's mother, had mentioned years ago that Lisa was married with two kids. Sounded perfect. My life was not quite as fortunate: divorced for years and though I'd had a few romances, most turned out brief and messy.

Fillmore's was a neighborhood bar owned by Finn Mulcahy since the sixties. Finn's passion was drinking and schmoozing with his patrons, so I suspected if he was still breathing, he'd be bartending.

I'd first stepped into Fillmore's when my dad and Bobby surprised me for my twenty-first birthday. They—sorry Mom, men only— introduced me to my first legal drink. Fillmore's was one of those bars where patrons stopped by for a drink, to socialize, not for the décor. Being a neighborhood tavern, it reminded me of Cheers, where everyone knew your name: familiar and friendly. Though I recalled my godfather telling me about two guys who got into a pissing match over a woman. Chairs flew in every direction, one shattering Finn's iconic Guinness Draught mirror. Both drunks were banned for life, but the woman they fought over got a pass.

I parked in the lot and entered the bar, adjusting to the dim lighting. The place hadn't changed. The same dark and dingy atmosphere. The Guinness mirror, still shattered, looked like the remnants of a heroic soldier.

As Lisa suggested, Fillmore's was quiet. Two old guys in flannel shirts sat at one end of the bar chatting with the bartender. It wasn't Finn, but rather, a younger Finn—his son Conor. When he saw me looking around, he approached, looking friendly.

"Hi, what can I get you?"

He obviously didn't recognize me. I hoped it was the lack of lighting rather than me aging. Back when we were teenagers, Conor Mulcahy was too young to work the bar, and contributed to his father's operation by schlepping kegs of beer from the cellar while attending Queens College. Conor hadn't aged much, a few grays around the temples, and he spent some time in the gym, judging from his bulging muscles straining through his short-sleeve shirt.

"Say, Conor. It's been a while."

He leaned closer. "Hank?"

I smiled. "Me."

"What a surprise!" He extended his meaty hand and squeezed. Definitely worked out. "Damn, what are you doing here? I mean, were you visiting someone in the neighborhood?"

"Actually, I'm meeting a friend, someone you know." I let him guess.

He frowned. "Here?"

I nodded. He searched the front door, and his confusion switched to a wide grin. Perfect timing.

"Lisa?"

I was afraid to turn. Worried, she might not recognize me. My heart fluttered, and I just stood there waiting...for what?

Hank, this isn't a date.

I turned and beamed. God, Lisa was gorgeous, dressed in jeans and a light gray top. She stood at five-four, with dark brown, shoulder-length hair. Her eyes were almond-shaped, which drove me crazy, along with her sexy smile. I fell in love with that smile. Time stood still.

"Hi, Conor." A wave.

She then ambled over to me, but I couldn't move. "You look frozen, Hank. I know it's been a while."

I managed to restart my heart and opened my arms. We embraced, both bodies trembling. Lisa offered me a kiss on the cheek, then leaned back. "You look great. Not a day over eighteen."

That caused more hugs before Conor interrupted. "What about me, Lisa?"

After they hugged, Conor said, "This is a crazy surprise. It's been—"

"Twenty-five years," Lisa said. "At Luca's memorial service."

Her mother had held one, still praying for her son's return.

"God, yes, of course. You look…great." He gave her another squeeze.

"You were always sweet, Conor. Thanks."

We stood wondering who would break the silence.

"Hell, this is a bar. What are you guys drinking?"

Lisa glanced at me. "I was too young to drink back then, Hank. What do you drink these days?"

I turned to Conor. "A Peroni."

"Sure. Lisa?"

"A house cab."

While Conor left for our drinks, we kept staring at each other. I know what I was thinking. Somebody was a lucky guy.

"Thanks for meeting me." Her eyes swept the bar, then back to me. "How about we sit at one of the tables in the rear? It's private."

Conor brought over our drinks, and we chatted about the past. I recalled Conor being a flabby kid despite lifting kegs of beer. He was still single and had inherited the bar, though his father spent a good portion of the day chatting and drinking with the old-timers. A pension perk.

"Bobby stops by occasionally, usually with his latest girlfriend." Conor winked. "He's brought several ladies over the years. He's gotta be what?"

"Old." I smiled. "I think Viagra helps him."

We laughed.

Conor turned serious. "I still can't believe it. Every time I go fishing near the bridge, it brings me back to that night."

"You were there?" I asked innocently. "I thought only the White-stone boys were invited."

"No, no," he defended. His face turned red. "I mean, it's what I heard."

I nodded. "Of course. Me too. I had a stomach virus that day."

Conor said, "From what I heard, the other guys were drunk and awakened by the cops. They freaked out about the murder, then freaked out more when told Luca disappeared."

Lisa added, "At first, the police thought the murder and Luca's disappearance were connected, that maybe Luca was also killed. But then they investigated and…it still haunts me."

I touched her hand.

Conor said, "Sorry I didn't mean to bring it up. I—"

"It's okay," she said dotting her moist eyes. To me, "At the time, your Bobby was the desk sergeant at the 109th and wanted to get involved in the investigation, but being too close to the family, the brass refused to let him." She scowled. "Things might have turned out differently."

Lisa wanted to believe that, but I doubt Bobby would have come up with a different conclusion. Meaning, to this day, the real killer got away with murder.

Conor shook his head. "I'm sure the real killer is still out there."

Lisa added, "It was a bad time for me and Mom. Dealing with Luca's disappearance and the murder…"

We paused the conversation to sip our drinks.

Conor said, "Did you know the murdered woman's girlfriend was here that night waiting for her to show up?" He nodded. "She met some guy, and eventually they went to the bridge. That's where she found her."

I nodded. "I'd heard that. I assume the police took her statement," I said, bringing out my cop Q&A mode.

He shrugged. "I would guess so."

"Do you recall seeing the friend here that night?" I asked.

He shook his head. "I was too young to work the bar. My father remembered a couple leaving but couldn't offer the cops any more help."

I assumed Finn was inebriated at that hour but kept that to myself.

Conor scanned the bar, then asked, "So really, why are you guys here? Don't get me wrong, I'm glad you stopped by." He grinned. "Are you a couple?"

That was unexpected, and I let Lisa answer. She met my gaze and stared lovingly for an instant, then blinked, and sighed. "Just friends."

Oh, well.

After a beat, Lisa sighed. "I asked Hank to meet me because a witness recently came forward regarding Annie Baxter's murder. This *person* was certain Luca wasn't the killer."

Conor said, "Okay?"

"And Hank's a private investigator."

That got my attention, and I asked, "How?"

Her gaze met mine. "I received a letter and thought about going to the police, but I don't trust them. Not after their conclusion about Luca's guilt. I assumed they wouldn't be interested in reopening the case anyway."

She paused, swirled her glass of wine, and continued. "As far as I'm concerned, their investigation was short and shoddy. They were eager to close the case, and since my brother wasn't around to defend himself, the detectives were satisfied he was the killer."

I kept my expression in check. A letter close to the anniversary sounded suspicious. Where was this person twenty-five years ago? But I didn't want Lisa to sense skepticism and nodded.

"You're probably thinking this is another person sending false hopes," she added. "Especially this close to the anniversary date." She paused. "Look, I'll admit, in the past, my mother and I have gone through our share of disappointments. This feels…different."

I didn't ask how different. That would be later.

Lisa turned to Conor. "That's why I'm asking Hank to investigate."

———————

"Can we see the letter?" Conor said, his nose nodding at Lisa's handbag.

She dug her hand inside her crocodile-embossed cross-body bag, then stopped. She turned to Conor, "Sorry, nothing personal, but I think Hank needs to read this alone. I hope you understand."

"Oh," he said, his voice flat. "Yes, of course." He gazed at her bag. "If you need another round, just wave. I'll be at the bar."

We watched Conor leave, his head craning in our direction.

"Such a character," Lisa said, then gulped her wine. She placed the glass on the table, removed the letter from her bag, and dropped it on the table. "I'll let you decide what we should do after reading it."

We?

My eyes drifted to the standard white envelope. I said, "It should probably be dusted for fingerprints, but I'm guessing the sender used gloves before mailing it. And anyway, the letter had to be handled by postal service people, including the mail carrier. And you, of course."

"Oh, God, I didn't think about it at the time. I screwed up—"

I smiled. "It's fine. Like I said, there are numerous prints on it already. What's important is the contents of the letter."

Lisa touched my hand. "Yes, of course." She peered at the letter, then with the tip of her finger, pushed it closer to me.

The letter was addressed to Lisa Falcone at her mother's address, so I assumed the sender had no idea Lisa was married and lived elsewhere. The postmark was stamped Flushing, the next town over, and dated a few weeks back.

"Mom received it a while ago and called me. She didn't open it, thank God. After I read it, I debated turning it over to the police. But like I said, I didn't trust them twenty-five years ago; why would I trust them now?" She paused. "The exception is your godfather Bobby, but he's retired from the force."

I nodded. "And happily, retired."

"I'm not naïve, Hank. It could be a hoax. In fact, the *Whitestone News* reminded its readers about the killing on its twenty-fifth anniversary. It could have been some nut trying to stir up trouble for us. And seeing Luca's name in the paper again brought back horrible memories." She closed her eyes and took a breath. "Sorry." She met my gaze. "But what if the contents of the letter are true?"

I removed the one-page letter and began reading. The anonymous scribe claimed a witness saw Luca confronted by a man inside Francis Lewis Park, close to where the dead woman was discovered. A few minutes later, Luca dashed out of the park toward the bridge, the witness following him. It was his belief the person who confronted Luca killed Annie Baxter, not Luca.

His. Was it a slip or had the writer purposely included the gender?

While the murder part was reassuring, what bothered me was where Luca wound up after being confronted. The writer claimed my friend took off to the bridge. That didn't make sense. The underbelly of the Whitestone Bridge was *inside* the park, where Luca's friends were hanging out and partying for his birthday.

I stopped. None of the Whitestone boys reported seeing Luca leave or return to the party, probably due to the alcohol consumed that evening. My guess: they were dead to the world at the time.

When questioned by the police, their statements were consistent. At some point, Luca disappeared, but no one recalled the birthday boy leaving.

I reread the letter. The writer hadn't mentioned a timeline of events, but if the witness observed Luca being confronted by the killer, it had to be before midnight. According to the police, Annie

Baxter's friend discovered the body around that time, so it was unlikely the killer stuck around after killing her.

Lisa was biting her lip when I looked up. I didn't want to disappoint her, but she needed to know my thoughts. The contents of the letter didn't feel right. The author should have known Luca was already in the park when he took off. Perhaps it was an honest mistake, or the letter was a fake. Either way, I'd be searching for a ghost.

"It's interesting," I started, "but I'm not sure I have enough information to follow up. I know it's not what you hoped to hear, but there are apparent conflicts in the letter."

"Oh." Her expression turned to disappointment.

I sighed. "Tell you what, I'll check the postmark, see if I can obtain other prints, and take it from there." I held off suggesting the sender might not live anywhere near the Flushing post office.

Lisa nodded. "Thanks, Hank. I didn't know if you'd come. I'm kinda nervous seeing you after all these years. We've taken different paths in life. And—"

I touched her arm. "I'm a bit nervous myself. I didn't know what to expect either."

"You are?"

"Nervous? Well, yeah." It's said your first love was forever, and while Lisa and I hadn't seen each other in twenty-five years, my feelings returned quickly. Still, I said, "Bobby told me you were married with kids."

She frowned, averted her eyes and nodded. "Yes." No smile.

"Sorry, I didn't mean to pry."

"Our marriage has had its ups and downs for years. But we have children together and…Hank, please don't get the wrong idea. I really want you to investigate. We're working out our marriage."

Good to know where I stand.

Lisa hadn't asked about my marital status, so I assumed she heard I was divorced through Bobby's grapevine.

Conor stopped by with a tray of salted peanuts. "Don't mean to pry, but you'll probably be here a while." He nodded at the letter. "What do you think, P.I. Hank Reed?" he said with a grin.

"I think we need another round."

Conor scrunched his nose and shuffled back to the bar. Definitely nosy.

"You said your mother doesn't know the letter's contents. That's probably a good thing. And I'm guessing that was the reason you wanted to meet me here."

A nod. "I was afraid she'd start asking questions about you showing up after all these years. Mom's not well." She sighed. "The early stage of dementia, but she's lucid at times. It could...damage her already fragile health."

My guess was someone was playing a cruel joke on Luca's anniversary, but I didn't want to upset Lisa. Instead, I asked, "Why do you feel hopeful this time around?"

She smiled wistfully. "The letter stirred up the past, and I thought of you, what you were doing with your life. That's when I discovered you were a private investigator. It felt like an omen."

TWO

I watched Lisa drive off and sighed. Had the past turned out differently, I was convinced we'd be together today. But fantasizing wasn't healthy. Right now, I needed to keep my feelings in check and concentrate on the mission.

My godfather's house was a few minutes from Fillmore's, and when I pulled into his driveway, just after ten, the living room light was on. Interesting. I figured, like many retirees, he'd be asleep by now.

I hadn't seen my godfather, Bobby Larkin, in a while, and he was thrilled when I told him I'd be staying the night. He and my father had become best friends during their tours in Vietnam. Bobby never had children—though R&R in Bangkok might have proved otherwise—so he took a shine to me. It was he who introduced me to Luca when I was sixteen. He'd been dating Luca and Lisa's mother, and I fit right in with both. But a year later, Bobby began dating someone else.

I still had a key and told Bobby I'd be arriving in the evening. Though retired, he kept his old service Glock 17 handy, so I'd better not surprise him.

There was no sign of him, so I turned off the living room light and tiptoed to the guest bedroom. Passing his bedroom, I heard the steady creak of bedsprings and chuckled. Lucky guy. Bobby might consider buying a new innerspring mattress.

The next morning, I woke around eight to the slightly caramelized aroma of coffee permeating my room. I dressed and entered the kitchen where I found a woman standing over a stove flipping pancakes.

"Morning," I said glancing at the stove.

She recoiled and swung around, a black spatula pointing at my head.

"I give up," I said, raising my hands and smiling.

"Sorry, you startled me," she said, then grinned and lowered her weapon to her side. "You must be Bobby's godson, Hank."

I sure hope so.

In her early sixties with tones of gray and brown in her closely cropped hair, she was dressed in jeans and a light-blue blouse under an apron that read, 'Get Out of My Kitchen.'

"I'm Mary. I hope you're hungry."

I looked at the frying pan. "I am now."

She smiled again. "Bobby should be out in a minute. He's slow in the morning. Aches and pains." She rolled her eyes.

Especially after an active night.

I settled at the table, and a moment later, Bobby strutted in like a kid. Bobby, mid-sixties—though he never revealed his age—was tall and thin, and reminded me of Clint Eastwood.

A grin creased his face. "Morning, Champ. Everything good?" Without waiting for a response, he walked over to Mary and sealed a kiss on her lips. "Morning, love."

She caressed his cheek. "You have a handsome godson."

He glanced at me. "Hank? He's okay."

"Pour the boy some coffee. The pancakes will be done in a minute."

"Yes, ma'am." He grabbed two mugs off the counter, each saying, 'I Love Whitestone,' filled both and handed me one. He winked. "This is my friend, Mary Costello."

"We met."

"Yes, of course."

She flipped her last perfectly round pancake and brought over a plateful. "Bobby has told me so much about you."

Don't they all say that? "All good, I hope."

She glanced at Bobby and winked. "Everything."

Mary centered the plate and waited for us to indulge.

"No one makes blueberry buttermilk pancakes like my Mary."

"Oh, Bobby."

"It's true."

I took a much-needed bite, followed by a gulp of coffee. "So how did you guys meet?"

Mary and Bobby exchanged looks. "You tell him," she said.

"Mary was my student at the academy. But it was only recently that we became reacquainted through a mutual department buddy. It was love at…*second* sight." He winked.

"It was for me, Hank," she said with a smile. "Though I knew Bobby had been around the block. Today, I keep him in line through his appetite."

"Not so, Mary."

She rolled her eyes. "I'm not thirty anymore."

Lovers.

After swallowing another fluffy forkful, I gave a thumbs up. "Great." I wanted to ask Mary about herself, but I was hungry. Besides, the way my godfather went through women, this might be the last time I'd see Mary Costello.

I met my godfather's gaze and said, "If you have time later, I'd like your input on something."

"Sure, kid. Does it have anything to do with last night?" He gave me a toothy grin.

"It does, but it's not what you think."

Mary had errands so Bobby was all mine. We took our coffees to the living room where a large bay window showcased part of Francis Lewis Park.

"So how long have you guys been dating?" I asked, taking a seat on the sofa.

"Oh, about two months. Mary's great. She could be the one, Hank," he said, taking a seat on the other corner.

Of course, she could.

"She seems nice. And her pancakes are to die for."

"Enough about me. Tell me about last night. I'm sure you noticed how stunning Lisa is."

"And married," I added. "With kids."

He nodded. "That too. But I heard through the grapevine that she and what's-his-name are having marital problems."

"Chuck. They're working things out. I'm fine, really."

He suppressed a laugh. "If you say so."

I shook my head.

"So, if it wasn't a romantic hookup, what was this get-together about?"

I took a breath. "Lisa wants me to investigate Luca's disappearance."

Puzzlement crossed his face. "I thought it was a dead issue." He stopped. "Sorry for the pun. Why would she suddenly ask you?" Then, "Ah, of course, the twenty-fifth anniversary. I still think she had an ulterior motive to see you."

That was my godfather, always looking out for me.

"Lisa received an anonymous letter. I read it. The sender swears Luca didn't kill Annie Baxter and was running from someone, who, if it's true, may have been the killer."

Like me, Bobby was suspicious of out-of-the-blue, anonymous letters. His mind was churning as mine had last night. He glanced out the window, then turned to me. "Gee, Hank, not to throw cold water on this revelation, but it sounds—"

"Flimsy, I know."

He scratched his pate and studied me. "You feel obligated, I get it, but do you have a plan?"

My hesitation suggested I hadn't. "I just found out. But I owe it to the family. Especially if the sender is telling the truth, whoever he is."

Bobby had put the murder and disappearance to rest years ago. As for me and Lisa, my living almost two hours away on Long Island compounded the problem. A month after Luca's disappearance, I headed for Stony Brook University, majoring in psychology. Following graduation, I joined the Suffolk County Police Department. A few years later, an opportunity arose, and I took a position as Police Chief of Eastpoint, the town where I grew up. Following that, I returned to Suffolk County as a Homicide Detective. That lasted a few years before I set up a private investigation business. Here I was twenty-five years later, divorced and helping my first love find answers.

Bobby said, "I know I'm rehashing, but the detectives combed Luca's bedroom and the rest of the house, searching for his Swiss Army knife, hoping the one at the murder site wasn't his, but it was nowhere to be found. What does that tell you?" He paused. "Besides, Luca's DNA was found on the blade they recovered at the scene. And then he disappeared."

Facts are important, but the entire incident didn't make sense. "He'd been partying with his friends. Was it possible Luca waited until his friends passed out from the booze, only to run into the woods where he found Annie Baxter, who he didn't know, stabbed her, and ran off? Totally out of character and absurd and you know it. The investigators should have stepped back and thought how crazy that sounded."

Bobby walked over to the window, mug in hand, and peered out. He waited a moment before meeting my gaze.

"I get what you're saying, and I agree with you. Do you know how many times Marie and Lisa came to the precinct begging *us* to continue the investigation? Us, Hank, and I was helpless because it wasn't my case. The brass forbade me from getting involved because I was too close to the family." He stopped, gulped down his coffee, then scrunched his nose. "Damn, it's cold."

Bobby took a breath. "I felt helpless." He waved his arm. "Sorry, I get fired up just talking about it. I don't know what Luca's knife was doing at the crime scene. Maybe he lost it before the murder. You know how dense that area is."

He stopped and sucked in some air. "The detectives filled me in every step of the way. But in the end, it was Luca's blood and knife that made their case."

Bobby paused and wiped his mouth. "And now, a fucking letter appears out of the blue. It's bullshit. Some creep is playing with Lisa's emotions, and she's falling for it." He paused. "Look, I'm not telling you what to do, but if Lisa and her mother are hoping you'll exonerate Luca, I'm afraid they'll be terribly disappointed. Nothing personal. And Marie's not in the best of health, so another disappointment could kill her." His hand holding the coffee mug trembled, and I let him settle for a moment.

I said, "Look, I'm not a miracle worker, and promise to end the investigation if I don't find results soon."

He averted his eyes. "You do what you think is best, son."

I said, "I recall you telling me something was off with Luca a few days before he vanished, like he was holding the world on his shoulders."

Bobby nodded. "I was his surrogate father, but he never told me

what was bothering him, and I didn't press. Maybe I should have."
He was about to continue but stopped.

"What?"

He shook his head.

"Bobby, don't hold back on me."

He ignored me and trudged into the kitchen. I watched him reach for a glass, his hand trembling. He ran the water and lingered, staring into space. He shook his head, then turned off the faucet and returned empty-handed, his face ashen.

I waited for my godfather to explain his hesitation, but he changed the subject. "Since you're set on pursuing the past, why not start with visiting Annie Baxter's shrine."

I stared up at him blankly. "What shrine?"

"I guess I never told you." He pointed at the living room window. "In the park. The murder site. Her parents set up a memorial site for her, and over the years, friends and family have left all sorts of things: cards, letters, and mementos. I've been there a few times when I walked in the area. You might as well start from the beginning." He paused. "And while you're there, say a prayer for her."

THREE

Whitestone 1988

The kid had been a problem since he was old enough to walk. He enjoyed torturing insects and small animals. His parents assumed it was a phase he'd grow out of. But his bad behavior continued in school, where he was identified as a troublemaker, like slashing bike tires for fun. He threatened anyone he didn't like, including his teachers, and by age twelve, he'd been kicked out of several schools.

His parents continued to believe his actions were temporary, that hyperactivity was the cause, and seeking professional help was unnecessary.

Like the kid, his father bullied his son mercilessly. No wonder the twelve-year-old was a sadistic bully. The only distraction that kept the boy quiet and content was video games. *Super Mario Bros* was his favorite.

That Saturday morning he'd been up since six, watching, playing, and kicking the hell out of his enemies. At ten o'clock, his father entered his basement bedroom, looked around, and shook his head.

"Hey," he said with a scowl. "It's Saturday and the lawn needs cutting. That's your job, so get your ass up and cut it."

When his son refused to acknowledge him, the father grabbed the headset off the kid's ears and started yelling. "I'm talking to you, stupid!"

The boy blinked hard. "What?"

"Are you deaf? I said cut the grass."

The son wasn't deaf or dumb. And the hatred in his eyes suggested a disregard for his father. "I'm playing."

The father tossed the headset across the room. "Not anymore. And you were late for breakfast, so after you finish your chores, you'll eat. Let's go."

The twelve-year-old stood, his fists tightening, slipped past him to the door. Outside, he cranked the Snapper propelled mower, looked around, and considered how he would approach the front lawn. He peered at the living room bay window, where the bastard stood watching him.

The lawn would take less than an hour and then he'd get back to Mario. Before starting at the edge, he gazed back at the window and smirked. Great, his old man was gone.

He took his time, cut the grass methodically, and when he finished, stood back and snickered. He returned the mower to the garage, went back to his room, locked the door, and continued his gaming. Ten minutes later, with the door locked, his father banged and screamed, adding in a few choice words.

"You smart ass," he ranted. "You think you're an artist? Get out here and remove the raised FU design you made."

The kid laughed, followed by an "FU dad," then returned to his game.

Like father, like son.

FOUR

Francis Lewis Park was named after an American signer of the Declaration of Independence, though many locals refer to it as Whitestone Park, and was located a few blocks from Bobby's house.

I arrived around ten that morning, the sun peeking through the clouds. Rain had fallen during the night, and the grass was still wet. Still, the park looked beautiful. I scanned the landscape where Lisa and I had walked hand-in-hand to the water, past the sloping lawn trees and shrubbery fronting the East River, with a bird's eye view of the Whitestone Bridge. My lips ticked into a soft smile. Wrong time for those memories.

Today, the park was active with joggers, dog walkers, and anyone you'd expect to see this time of day. It was probably too early for lovers. That was a night thing. I'd start at the entrance asphalt walkway and stop when I reached the flagpole. Bobby suggested I turn left and look for a narrow dirt path. There was only one.

I reached the path, which led to the underbelly of the bridge, then followed it about twenty feet before stopping. The East River was on my right, and I noticed something different from the last time I'd been here. Fishermen were now casting their lines away from the jetty, which had been a popular location underneath the bridge. My eyes swept the area—which appeared off-limits and fenced in. My first thought was 9/11 and the security required to stave off terrorists. Twenty-five years ago, the jetty was open to the public, and where Luca and the Whitestone boys celebrated his eighteenth birthday.

I imagined the boys drinking, partying, and having fun.

What happened, Luca?

On my left, maybe twenty-five yards away, was a playground with handball and basketball courts. As I continued, the path became overgrown with tree roots and rocks, but passable. As I made my way up a gentle incline about twenty feet later, I noticed another path. Bobby didn't mention two, but as Robert Frost might have suggested in his beloved poem, take the one less traveled.

But then I thought, more than likely, the mostly overgrown path would lead toward the water and away from the shrine, so I took the other. Sorry, Mr. Frost. Up ahead, past bramble bushes, I came upon a small circular clearing with a three-foot Christian cross at one end. The crime scene turned shrine.

Up close, the shrine was surrounded by square natural slate stones that had weathered over the years. At the foot of the cross sat greeting cards, and a personalized stuffed brown teddy bear that read, 'Miss you Forever.' A few flowers had been sown recently, including blooming forget-me-nots. Very apropos, considering it was Annie's twenty-fifth murder anniversary.

The spot reminded me of highway memorial sites, except this place had been a crime scene, not an auto accident area. What was Annie thinking that night as she approached this dark secluded area? Romance? Surely, not murder.

Huge silver maple trees had probably protected the shrine from storms over the years, but today the ground was soft, possibly from the recent rain, and I noticed fresh footprints leading away toward the bridge. A man's sneaker?

I followed the prints until they ended at a locked eight-foot gate, which hadn't been there twenty-five years ago. My eyes glimpsed to the right, and I noticed a runner passing along the bramble, parallel to the water. From the back, it looked like a guy, dressed in jeans, sporting a ball cap, and racing toward the park entrance.

"Hey," I called out and started after him. He turned quickly so I know I got his attention. But instead of responding, he picked up his speed and shot toward the parking lot. I sped up after him, cutting back to the path. My feet kept tripping over roots and rocks slowing me down. By the time I reached the park entrance, the guy had jumped into a black Ford SUV and shot out of the spot.

I bent over and took a much-needed breath. I was getting too old for this and admonished myself for not getting the plate number.

Back at the site, I snapped a few photos with my phone, including personalized cards, the names potentially helping my investigation. The sun peeked between two maple trees and inside the shrine. It was then I noticed additional footprints. Probably from the same guy who apparently visited the site.

The sun shined on a slender object extending from the dirt, near the cross. It caught my eye. Upon closer examination, it appeared to be a ballpoint pen. What the hell kind of memento was that? I used a handkerchief to pluck it up, then held it to the light. It looked new.

Jensen Law Firm was engraved on one side. Lee Jensen, the former city councilman? Why would he or a client plant it there? I pushed myself up and looked out toward the park entrance. Maybe the guy running from me put it there. Was he sending me a message?

I took one last look around, then, as Bobby suggested, said a prayer for Annie Baxter.

And for Luca.

FIVE

Whitestone 1991

As the years passed, the kid couldn't get enough video games. His latest, *Splatterhouse*, a beat 'em up arcade game, was bought with money he stole from his mother's purse. The game was considered violent, only not to this player. He got more enjoyment killing the enemies and called the antagonists Dad. The more he played and killed, the more complete he felt.

At fifteen, he'd been expelled from every school in the Whitestone/Flushing area, and as a result, his parents kept him home. By this time, the father and son hit a breaking point. Letting him play his games in his bedroom, to his heart's content, was the only way to normalize the situation.

And so, the kid, who called himself the hunter, filled his day killing off the enemy. The father stopped demanding his son cut the lawn or do any chores around the house, with the expectation that once he turned eighteen, he'd be kicked out permanently.

With his mother out shopping, it was just father and son. The old man on the roof, the younger locked in his war room. At noon, the kid grew hungry and went upstairs to the kitchen. He peered outside and noticed a ladder leaning against the wall.

He waited a moment, fantasizing, then quietly opened the kitchen door. The ladder was carefully placed, and his father stood firmly on an upper rung, singing along to whatever he was listening to on his Sony Portable AM/FM cassette player.

The son stood in front of the ladder and lightly shook it to get his father's attention. He peered down and their eyes locked. The kid waited until he saw fear on his father's face. He smirked, and with one hard pull, overturned the ladder, his father falling wildly to the concrete, his Sony player scattered. The kid waited until he saw blood before returning to his room, where he slipped on his earphones.

Another win.

SIX

As I entered Bobby's house, the anguished sound of muttering and swearing came from the living room, where my godfather was sitting at his computer, playing solitaire, and clicking the mouse furiously.

"You, okay?" I asked, suppressing a laugh.

He didn't look up. "In a minute. There's fresh coffee inside. Shit. Not you, Hank."

I let him stew over his game and stepped inside to grab some coffee. When I returned, he was still swearing.

"I hate computer games," he said, clicking off the computer. He peered up and, with a smile, I passed him a mug.

He took a much-needed gulp. "Thanks. I'd rather play board games."

"Yeah, but they're not as easy to shut off."

"Yeah, yeah." Bobby peered back at the blank screen, then at me. He must have sensed where I'd been and asked if I'd found the shrine.

I sat across from him on the sofa, swung one leg over the other, and took a sip of coffee.

"That park is still beautiful. Great memories," I said wistfully. "But to your question, yes, I found the site. It's very peaceful. You'd never have thought it had been a crime scene."

I paused. "I suppose that was the purpose of the site. Cards, mementos, and a teddy bear. Also, I found a pen stuck at the foot of the cross." I reached into my pocket and removed the handkerchief.

"A pen? Doesn't sound like a memento to me. Someone must have dropped it by accident."

"I suppose if it were lying around, but this was planted." I unfolded the handkerchief and extended my hand. "It could be evidence."

Bobby scrutinized it then squinted. "It's a pen from Lee Jensen's law firm. Well, it was. He retired a couple of years ago. Lives most of the year in Hilton Head. What I'm getting at is I don't see the connection between him and Annie Baxter."

Bobby leaned back in his chair and closed his eyes. He does that to help his thought process. A few moments later, he was back and met my gaze.

"Maybe Matt or Tara placed it there." He shook his head. "No, that doesn't make sense. They're Jensen's kids but were too young to know Annie Baxter. She was in her early twenties, and they were teenagers. What am I missing, Hank?"

I shrugged. "Nothing plausible. While at the shrine, I noticed wet footprints leading away from the site and followed them. There was a guy, at least I thought it was, running toward the park entrance. I tried getting his attention, but he only ran faster. I chased after him, but he was too quick and, when he reached a black SUV, took off. I didn't get a plate number."

Bobby sipped his coffee. "And it wasn't Jensen? Scratch that; you haven't seen him since you were a teenager."

"I'm guessing he was in his late thirties or early forties. I didn't get a good look. Maybe he stuck the pen in the ground."

Bobby walked over to the window, peered out a few moments,

then turned back to me. "How many people do you think know about the investigation?"

I uncrossed my legs and sat up. "Just me and you. I'm not sure if Lisa told anyone else except maybe her husband."

He nodded. "So, this whole pen thing could be a coincidence. If—"

"Conor," I said. "He knows. Lisa mentioned it last night at Fillmore's. He was curious. No, he was nosy. But I don't see a connection between him and Jensen. Do you?"

Bobby shrugged. "Honestly, other than Jensen stopping by for a drink, I don't think they're chummy. At the time of the murder, Conor was a teenager helping Finn. And for the record, they had alibis, not that they needed any."

"It's possible Conor told his father. You know how chatty Finn gets, especially under the influence. He could have told anyone." I paused. "Except, Conor, like me, only learned about it last night, and the place was dead."

"Jensen," Bobby breathed. "He was a piece of work. Probably still is. Besides his law practice, and some kind of factory business, he was a councilman for years. There were rumors about his dalliances, not to mention robbing Peter to pay Lee Jensen." Bobby shrugged. "Rumors were never confirmed, but he certainly had a proclivity for women. On the other hand, he did good things for the district."

Bobby added, "Jensen might have screwed around, but murder, I don't see it. Besides, he wouldn't have taken Annie Baxter to the park for a quickie. He was strictly a wine-and-dine guy, so if he were going to kill her, he would have done so in some fancy hotel room. And, as far as I know, Annie Baxter never worked for him."

I sighed in frustration. "You said he retired. I'm guessing his shingle is no longer outside his office."

Bobby shook his head. "The place is now owned by another law firm, a father and daughter: Berger and Berger. Nice people. They hand out their own pens." He grinned. "Tell you what, I'll have it checked for prints. At least, that should satisfy your curiosity." He paused. "It may take a while, but I still have connections."

"Thanks. And while you're at it, have them check the anonymous letter Lisa received. It's in the guest bedroom. I'm guessing there are too many prints on it, but who knows?"

Bobby said, "And since we're on the subject of Lee Jensen, did you know detectives dropped by his house the day after the murder?"

I shook my head. "What were they looking for?"

"Procedure. They were more interested in Jensen's daughter, Tara. She and Luca were dating. Actually, they were serious. The detectives asked Tara if Luca had his knife with him on the day of the murder. She claimed she didn't know, but he always kept it with him. It was a special birthday gift from his father when he was fifteen."

I frowned. "That certainly didn't bode well for Luca even if it were true. You'd think Jensen, being an attorney, and politician, would have shielded her from the Q&A. At a minimum, provide vague answers. Unless Jensen wasn't crazy about his future son-in-law."

Bobby waved me off. "Jensen liked Luca. He worked part-time for him and helped with his campaign. But you're right; he should have been more protective of Luca. Except..."

He paused and gave me a critical look. "There were rumors Tara was pregnant. Maybe the old man was pissed off and wanted to make an example out of the kid."

Another surprise. "I don't recall her pregnancy. The family must have hidden it."

"Oh, they hid it all right. Apparently, Tara went away for a while, gave birth, then returned home after the baby was put up for adoption. End of story. Years later, Tara married and had two kids. I haven't seen her very much since her parents retired."

Like me and Lisa, Luca and Tara were inseparable. We would have been one happy family had circumstances been different.

"She marry local?"

Bobby chuckled. "You could say that. She married another Whitestone boy: Jesse."

I blinked. "Jesse?"

"You look like me when I found out. It didn't make sense to me either. They're very different people. He drank, still does from what I understand. Maybe she lost her way after Luca disappeared. Or maybe Jesse was there to keep her from falling."

I liked Jesse, only not for Tara, and wondered what other surprises my godfather had in store for me. As for Lee Jensen, hearing about his less-than-stellar character, I hoped he hadn't sealed my friend's fate after learning his daughter was pregnant.

SEVEN

To get a better sense of how the original investigation concluded, I needed to review the cold case files, and asked Bobby if he could get access. "Both Annie Baxter's and Luca's," I said. "I'm hoping they'll provide some overlooked nugget." I shrugged. "Can't hurt."

Bobby nodded. "I still have contacts, but bear in mind, you might be disappointed with the outcome. A few years after the murder/disappearance, I reviewed the files. I'd been frustrated and wanted to satisfy myself that the detectives were thorough. I, too, was hoping to find an opening for them to continue. But in the end, I realized the detectives followed through on every lead." He sighed. "I became more frustrated afterward realizing there was nothing else to investigate. What I'm saying is you shouldn't expect much."

Bobby wanted to shield me from disappointment. Over the years as a homicide detective, I had my share and wasn't expecting miracles. Or maybe I was. I said, "I'm a big boy. Thanks."

"I'll make a call." When he left, I sat back on the sofa and waited, hoping his contact would come through, regardless of the outcome. A few minutes later, my cell buzzed. My mail carrier, Jakub Mazur.

I sat up. "Everything okay, Jakub?"

"I'm sorry to call, Hank, but I think someone's been in your office."

"You mean, broke in?"

"I'm afraid so. I knocked on the door like I always do. It was open, so I entered figuring you were inside. That's when I saw your office with stuff all over the floor."

"Files?"

"Papers, folders, a picture frame, all scattered about. And your desk drawers and cabinet files were open. Hank, it's a mess. Do you want me to call the police?"

I thought about asking Jakub if anything had been taken, but he wouldn't know. "No, that's okay. I'll handle it. I should be there in an hour. And Jakub, thanks for calling."

Bobby was on the phone in another room and laughing. I assumed shop talk. I needed to get to my office and sent him a text before shooting out the door.

He called as I entered the Northern State Parkway.

"What the heck's going on? Where are you?"

I gave him the abbreviated version. "I'll fill you in later."

The office was as bad as Jakub claimed. Someone had jimmied the lock and had a field day. I maneuvered around the scattered files until I reached my desk. Positioned neatly in the center was a newspaper article. The same one I'd taken out of the drawer recently: The 1996 murder headlines.

This was no random break-in. I'm no genius, but the posed article was a glaring threat. *Don't continue the investigation or else.*

I tightened my fists. The perpetrator made a big mistake. Never threaten Hank Reed with a *don't*. Maybe the pen at the shrine was a coincidence. Not this. Unfortunately, there was no CCTV coverage, so I'd have to find out the old-fashioned way.

My office was part of a two-story, stand-alone brick and concrete structure divided by a small yard and driveway. The upstairs tenant was a single guy living in a one-bedroom unit with a separate entrance. He was a roofer and drove a red pickup truck, which was gone.

I knocked anyway and gave him a few minutes. When he didn't answer, I slipped a note under his door with my cell number.

I returned to my office and called Bobby. "Sorry for the rush. My mail carrier called and reported a break-in. My files were dumped all over the place. What struck me was the bastard found an old newspaper article about Annie Baxter's murder in my drawer and placed it on my desk. It sounds like a threat, which, you know, I don't take lightly."

"You obviously hit a nerve. They were quick. The word hasn't even got out yet."

Right, the word.

"Whoever was responsible doesn't want me digging up the past. But what do they think I'm capable of discovering that the investigators missed? Heck, I should be thrilled if the perpetrator believes I might find something, but I don't like being threatened. The cold files should be an important start. Did you–"

"We're on," Bobby said. "Are you available tomorrow?"

"You bet. The sooner, the better. What time?"

"Tomorrow morning at nine at the District Attorney's Office on Queens Boulevard." He added, "I might be retired, sonny boy, but I still have friends in the Department. In the meantime, I can help you clean up if you need me."

I glanced around and took a breath. "Thanks, I can handle it. In the meantime, go ahead and invite Mary over. Maybe she'll cook you something special."

He snickered. "Oh, that. Not tonight. My friend Jane promised to make a pot roast. It's just an innocent dinner at my place."

Right, innocent.

"Enjoy. And don't forget, you have to get up bright and early."

"Smart ass."

―――――

A few hours later, with the office looking presentable, I headed home. I wasn't in the mood to chat, but Lisa should be made aware of recent events, and I punched in a text.

> How many people did you tell about my investigation?

Chuck and Tara.

I didn't think Lisa's husband, Chuck, was a threat, at least not with the investigation. Tara was Matt's younger sister, so I assumed she mentioned it to him. And for sure, she told Jesse, her husband.

Why?

> Curious.

Did something happen???

Lisa would probably haunt me if I didn't tell her.

> Are you free for a phone call?

EIGHT

When I arrived at the courthouse, Bobby was on the steps chatting with a middle-aged guy in uniform, his captain's bars suggesting he was Bobby's contact. He introduced me to John Delaney, an amiable guy with a friendly face.

Delaney walked us inside, and after we signed in and handed over our cellphones, led us to a small windowless room with fluorescent lights, blank white walls, and a metal table with two chairs, reminiscent of an interrogation room back in the day. He pointed at two sets of files on the table.

"The room isn't the Four Seasons, but it's quiet and you'll have access to whatever you need. Anything else, the officers up front can help." He turned to Bobby. "Sorry, but you'll have to memorize any information you come across that's important. It wasn't easy getting you access."

Bobby snorted. "I'll leave the memory to Hank." He lowered himself into a metal chair and grimaced. When Delaney left, he said, "There's no way my ass is gonna sit for hours without a seat cushion. How about you start? I'll come back with coffee and a few seat pads."

When he left, I peered down at ancient history. The files were thinner than I'd expected for a murder investigation. Then again, there wasn't much of an investigation. I sat and picked up the folder on the right: Annie Baxter's file. Judging from the paucity of the folder, we'd probably finish in a few hours.

I laid her file down and opened Luca's musty-smelling gray folder. I took a sniff. No surprise there after twenty-five years. Luca's photo had been stapled on top and probably taken a few months before he disappeared. He was standing on the rocks under the Whitestone Bridge, smiling. I was sure my friend wasn't smiling the night he vanished.

Underneath the photo sat the original UF61 complaint report and DD5 reports. I began reading the statements from Luca's friends. The boys couldn't remember when they'd nodded off, but Alex claimed he got up at some point to pee. He hadn't looked at the time, only telling the cops it was still dark. He didn't notice if Luca was among the boys.

I sat back and gazed at the ceiling. Annie Baxter had been killed around midnight. Outside of Luca's blood-stained knife that was recovered near the crime scene and vouchered, the investigators couldn't place Luca physically at the murder scene. That bothered me. For sure, I'd have to interview the Whitestone boys, particularly Alex.

Another DD5 from the Scuba Recovery Team investigation concluded after sweeping the East River that Luca probably hadn't drowned.

Bobby sauntered in with cushions under his arms and set two coffees on the table. He handed me a cushion and placed the other on his chair, before strategically working into it. I watched him sit, followed by an "Ah, much better," grunt.

I suppressed a laugh. "Do you remember Alex? Nice kid, shy as I recall. He woke up sometime during the night but hadn't noticed if Luca was missing."

"Right, I remember reading that." He took a sip of coffee. "Alex came from a tough home. His father was a tyrant, emotionally abusive, and an atheist. He refused to allow the kid to attend Sunday mass." Bobby shook his head. "Poor guy. Alex never returned home after college. His parents moved out of Whitestone years ago. I think the old man died."

I perched on my now cushioned chair and returned to the file. More interviews with neighbors, a few classmates at Flushing High School, Luca's parish priest at Saint Luke's, and Conor and Finn from Fillmore's Tavern. I studied Conor's whereabouts that night. He'd been working in the bar's cellar.

I rubbed my chin and recalled as teenagers, Conor taking us to the basement where Finn stored kegs of beer and boxes of liquor. The stench of foul beer permeated the room. There was a private door for deliveries that led outside away from the front entrance. It was also an easy access to the bridge, less than a ten-minute walk.

I glanced over at Bobby, who appeared to be looking for something.

"What's up?" I asked.

He searched the floor. "My phone. I think—"

"We had to hand them in. Remember?"

He glanced up. "Right. I'm losing it." He adjusted himself in the chair. "I just remembered Mary wants to come over tonight. What do you think?"

I smiled.

"What?"

"I suggest you get rid of the pot roast Jane brought over last night."

He slapped his forehead. "Damn, good catch, Hank. Mary knows I don't cook…"

"You'd have a lot of explaining to do."

"Right. Would you remind me to text her when we get out of here? I'll tell her tomorrow works better."

"Sure, if I remember."

He narrowed his look. "Wise guy." He thought for a moment. "How about we have pot roast sandwiches tonight?"

I snickered. "So, I can save your ass. Sure, I like pot roast."

Returning to business, my eyes stopped a few pages into the file that read Possible Witnesses. It mentioned two phone calls coming into the 109th Precinct the day after the murder from two different pay phones. The first caller, a male, claimed to be on Powells Cove Boulevard near Whitestone Farms' Market around two a.m. when he noticed a young male alone on the sidewalk. The caller said the guy was moving at a good clip. He didn't think anything of it until reading about the murder the following day. The witness wouldn't leave his name.

The second caller, also a male, told the dispatcher he saw a young man entering Little Bay Park around 3:00 A.M. The caller claimed to be walking his dog when he noticed the individual heading toward Fort Totten. He, too, called after hearing about the murder.

Walking his dog at 3:00 A.M.?

Like the first caller, he wouldn't leave his name. Asked if he had previously called, he claimed he hadn't.

I sat back and sipped my coffee. Two o'clock and then three. Had the witnesses sighted Luca? And if so, why was my friend heading toward Fort Totten? I shivered at the thought of him wandering aimlessly. Unless he had a destination in mind.

I gazed over at Bobby. "According to the letter Lisa received, the writer claimed Luca had been heading toward the bridge, so I assumed he meant the Whitestone Bridge, which didn't make sense at the time, since he was already there. But if he was on his way to Fort Totten, as the cold case files suggested, Luca would have passed the Throgs Neck Bridge, making the letter more plausible."

"Throgs Neck?"

I held up the file. "It's in the report. You read it years ago. I guess you don't recall the two sightings the night Luca disappeared?"

Bobby sat up. "Let me see that."

I folded the page and slid it over to him.

He shook his head as he read the file, then peered up, a dismayed look crossing his face. "Hank, I don't recall reading this. I was upset at the time and could have missed it, but…"

He continued reading. "It doesn't mention the detectives following up on the tips. Why the hell not?" He scowled.

"You'll notice the two calls came from different pay phones. One in Clearview, the other in Bay Terrace, both in the 111th precinct. Yet the callers chose to call your precinct."

Bobby nodded absently. "It could have been a coincidence. Remember, the murder happened in the 109th."

"Maybe," I said, not convinced, and crossed my arms.

"What's bothering you?" he said.

"You knew your precinct. What did you think of the detectives on the case?"

Bobby went back to the file and nodded. "Right, those guys." He frowned, then met my gaze. "Not my favorite duo. They did their job, but I never cared for them. They appeared at times to be … sneaky." He shrugged. "But as far as their work, I never had a problem with them." He stopped. "Jesus, Hank, I hope you're not suggesting improprieties. I kept the precinct in good shape—"

I put up my hand. "I'm not insinuating, but you have to admit, it seems odd they didn't follow through."

"I gotta take a pee," he muttered, and got up to leave. As I watched him trudge out the room, my hope was that Bobby was protecting his precinct rather than suddenly feeling doubtful.

I continued but gleaned nothing more from either file. I sat back frustrated that the two witnesses came forward after sighting Luca, or someone like him, heading away from the crime scene toward Fort Totten and that, possibly, the detectives on the case were negligent or worse. Before closing the file, I gazed at Luca's photograph.

Tell me, my friend, where were you going that night?

NINE

That night, I left Bobby's place around 1:00 A.M. My godfather thought I was crazy looking for Luca's ghost in the middle of the night. I wasn't delusional and quietly agreed with him. The real reason was emotional. I wanted to sense my friend's fear that night, assuming it *was* Luca.

Little Bay Park, where the second sighting took place, was less than two miles away. The streetlights helped lead the way, and as I passed Fillmore's Tavern, which was still open, glimpsed the cellar door illuminated by a streetlight. Had Conor slipped out that night? After hearing about my investigation, he seemed eager to help, but I chalked it up to being nosy. Now, I had to consider that Conor had witnessed the crime and was afraid to come forward at the time. Or, God forbid, he was the killer.

The street leading to the first sighting near the Whitestone Farms' Market, was quiet. The caller claimed a young male had been moving at a good clip, and that meant he was heading toward Little Neck Park. I surveyed the normally active street with shops on every corner. There were no bars in the area, so what was the witness doing at that hour? Walking his dog, like the second caller? I doubt it. He never mentioned it to the dispatcher.

The road leading to the park was residential and dark, the only sounds coming from the humming of air conditioning units. I picked up my pace and reached the park entrance twenty minutes later.

What was my friend thinking as he entered? Dread? I suddenly felt a chill up my spine. My cell phone buzzed, and my heart skipped a beat. An unknown number. I answered anyway, but the caller hung up.

Does somebody know I'm here?

I had a choice: continue or retreat. The park was dark, and, like the night Luca entered, the waning moon didn't provide much illumination. His only assistance would have been a flashlight, assuming he planned his trek. Cell phones hadn't become popular yet.

I entered the park, not activating my cell phone flashlight, and took a deep breath. Here we go. Patches of light guided me along the asphalt path. I'd hoped the walk would be quiet, but soon the wind kicked in, stirring the bay against the rocks. Dark and creepy. Before long, a hissing and squealing sound became louder, and I fumbled to flip the flashlight of my cell on, only to find a pack of rats darting about me.

Christ, I hate rats.

They dispersed quickly, and I picked up my pace again toward the jetty, where the second sighting took place. Arriving, I pointed my light ahead, stopping at the dimly lit guard house. Could Fort Totten have been Luca's destination? The fort was only open to the public during the day, so it was unlikely Luca entered at night. If he tried, he would have been confronted by the guard, unless he was meeting someone outside the fort.

Totten Road led to the fort from Bell Boulevard, an easy access from the Cross Island Parkway. A quick in and out. I trudged over to a gray weathered bench near the parking lot and sat, peering out into the darkness. I thought of Luca and the Whitestone boys. Life was so innocent back then. Until it wasn't.

Sorry, Luca, there's nothing here.

As I looked toward the parking lot, about thirty yards away, I glimpsed a shadow—a car. When I aimed my light at it, I heard a clicking sound behind me, followed by the car's lights and alarm activating.

What the hell!

I sensed a presence behind me and, as I turned my light, the last thing I remembered before going dark was a Mets ballcap.

My chirping cell woke me, and I grimaced touching my crown. Blinking into the early morning sun, I realized I was on the grass and felt around for my phone.

"Hello," I groaned.

"Where the hell are you, boy? I was ready to call out the troops." He chuckled. "I thought we'd have breakfast together."

"I think you better come and get me. I got waylaid. And bring Tylenol. I'll explain later."

Waiting for Bobby, I got back on the bench, rubbing my head. Whatever the bastard used to clip me wasn't around, nor was the car in the parking lot. No surprise there.

The sun was a temporary relief as I surveyed my surroundings. I then turned to the fort beyond the park. I'd have to check with the guard on duty last night. My arms stretched like a cormorant, my fingers touching a slight indentation behind the bench. I gave it a good rub before getting up and studying the markings. It was heart-shaped, with an inscription inside, the letters worn over time.

I leaned in and snapped a few photos with my cell, then enlarged the picture. My heart raced. Were my eyes deceiving me? The initials were crudely etched, but I swear they looked like LF and TJ., Luca

Falcone and Tara Jensen. I enlarged the photo to the max, fighting to confirm the initials. Below, inside the heart, was a date: 07-06-96.

The day Luca disappeared. How was that possible? Luca didn't have his knife with him; it was found at the crime scene. Unless he'd been scoping out the area that day, knowing he'd return later. And in the process, ruminated about his life, and memorialized his love for Tara.

TEN

Bobby exited the car, looked around, and when he saw me, waved. The parking lot was sprinkled with early risers, none of them heading in my direction. They probably assumed I was homeless.

"What the hell happened?" he asked, handing me a mug of coffee and two painkillers.

I struggled forward and pointed at my crown. "Pretty, no?"

"Good Lord." He sat down beside me, examined my skull. "On closer look, it's not that bad. If the bastard wanted you dead, you would be."

"That's comforting," I said, popping the Tylenol in my mouth, followed by a slug of coffee. "Some creep in a Mets ballcap slammed me. And I love the Mets." I attempted a laugh, but the pain held it back.

"You still have your wallet?"

I felt my pants pocket. "It wasn't a mugging."

"Hank, my boy, no more field trips. Whoever it was might not go so easy the next time."

I touched his shoulder. "This incident tells me I'm on the right

63

track. What I don't get is how he knew I'd be here. And he was quiet as hell."

Bobby looked around and shrugged. "If you decide to go on another hunch, I'm coming with you." He rubbed his stomach. "Now let's get out of here. I'm hungry." He got up and I tugged on his arm.

"Okay, but before we go, I want to show you something." I lumbered up and pointed at the heart-shaped engraving on the back of the bench.

"See it?"

He leaned in. "I forgot my glasses. What's it say?"

"Try this." I opened my camera and enlarged the heart. "How about now?"

"Christ, Hank, I need a magnifying glass. Just tell me already."

I did.

When Bobby's girlfriends weren't around, his idea of breakfast was coffee and burnt toast. I settled for the coffee. After applying a cold compress to my head, I texted Lisa, who I assumed was in the class-room. She got back fifteen minutes later.

> What's up?

> Where was Luca the DAY of his disappearance?

A moment later,

> Home most of the day. Spent a few hours with Tara. Why?

> Did they go to Fort Totten Park?

I don't know. Need to ask Tara. Why?!!!!

Call her now. Ask!

So mean. 😊 Okay, I'll get back.

Soon!!!

Ten minutes later she returned with…

Tara says she wasn'. Didn' seem in a good mood. Nasty with me. So what' with Luca and Fort Totten?

I texted her the photo.

OMG! What do you think?

Don' know yet.

Hank, this could be BIG!!

It would appear so, but I needed to dig further.

Keep you posted.

ELEVEN

The tall man with thinning gray hair and a Just-For-Men dark brown mustache was agitated. He stood in his bedroom peering out at the courtyard where his wife and her friends were engaged in a game of mahjong. Despite the sunny day, he fidgeted watching the women. Up until a minute ago—before the phone call —he was content living his life without a care.

The caller had changed that.

"What do you mean investigating the murder?" The man scratched his head, an involuntary act when he smelled trouble. "That case was closed years ago. Why the sudden interest?"

As he listened, he stiffened. He wanted details: the whys, the whats, and the hows. But the caller only provided piecemeal information.

"Someone from the department reopened the investigation. Based on what? The case against the kid was supposed to be airtight," he said, his voice rising.

"I'm trying to tell you it's not official," the caller corrected. "Just some private investigator sniffing around. I'm sure it's nothing, but I figured you'd wanna know, just in case."

"Just in case, what? Does this P.I. guy have a reason for opening the case? And how come the cold case unit isn't involved? Sounds like there are too many missing pieces. I don't like it." He stopped. "Who is this guy? The P.I.?"

"Hank Reed. Some guy who hung out with the teens back in the nineties."

More head scratching. "The name doesn't sound familiar. You sure about this?"

"He's from Long Island, but he spent weekends with his godfather, Bobby Larkin. You certainly know Larkin. He was the desk sergeant at the 109th."

"Right, Mr. Honest. I know him. Well, someone must have hired Reed. That's what P.I.s do. They investigate for a fee."

"I'm told it was the kid's sister. Seems she received a letter out of the blue saying her brother didn't kill the woman."

"That's it? For Christ's sake, the letter's probably a fake. Maybe Reed just needed the money and offered to look around. I wouldn't put too much credence in the investigation. He'll probably milk it for a week and quit." He paused and relaxed his shoulders. "And as for Luca, Reed's never gonna find him. End of story."

When the caller hesitated, the man said, "What aren't you telling me?"

"There's been a situation."

"What kind of situation? I thought you told me everything."

"Someone broke into Reed's office and made a mess of things."

"Yeah, so? It sounds like a personal problem."

"Except..."

"Christ, I hate this bullshit." He stepped inside the bathroom, flipped on the light, and stared at his sixty-five-year-old face. He looked younger before the phone call. Where did those lines come from?

"Whoever was responsible left an old newspaper article on Reed's desk."

"Yeah, okay."

"Wanna know what the headlines read?"

"Are you playing with me? Give me the fucking information."

"The Annie Baxter Murder."

The man winced and remained silent.

"You there?"

"You're sure about this?"

"Oh, yeah. I don't know what's going on, but somebody's threatening Reed. And it's not us. Who else would be interested in shutting down the investigation?"

The caller didn't wait for a reply. "If Reed's a capable P.I., he knows he's onto something and is not going to stop. But who...?"

Back to the bedroom, the wrinkled-face man trudged across the carpet and peered down at the women. They were still playing with the tiles. "How did you find out about this anyway? You said your sources. They gotta be retired or dead."

"Funny. It wasn't any of my sources. Someone sent me a text with a brief note and a photo of the article on Reed's desk. I don't know why he sent it, and that's disturbing. If he knows something—"

"And you couldn't figure out who sent it? What the hell, man, you were a detective. Did you suddenly get rusty?"

"They used a burner. I'm worried someone knows about the past and—"

"Not on an open line." He paced the room, seeking an explanation. He came back with, "You'll have to follow Reed around and find out what he's up to. If he starts discovering things..." He hadn't thought out the next part yet.

"I'm retired," he whined.

"So am I, and I want to remain that way. You have as much to lose as I do, so, stop complaining. I'd come up myself, but you know my situation. My wife will figure I'm up to something." He walked back from the window and plopped on the bed. "She doesn't trust me."

A snort. "Not with your history."

He was too upset to argue. "Just handle it. And update me. We both need burners. Call me when you get yours."

"Right," the caller said, deflated.

They disconnected and the thinning gray-haired man gripped the phone and swore. He heard women's voices below and walked back to the window. He hated mahjong. His wife glanced up and waved. He threw her a quick one then returned to the bathroom mirror. His thoughts turned dark. He had compartmentalized that incident years ago, and now it was coming back to haunt him.

Life was too good for the past to resurface, so there was no way he'd let Reed continue without consequences. That would be the end of him. He sighed. If Reed discovered who was responsible that night—he tried to stop obsessing, but that only made it worse. Obsession doesn't go away by itself. He needed to go outside.

Two things provided pleasure these days: women and golf. Right now, he'd have to settle for the second. He entered the garage, collected his golf bag, and took off in his Alpine White BMW 5 series, hoping the demons wouldn't follow.

TWELVE

Bobby's lack of cooking skills warned my stomach I needed to eat. So, on the way to my office, I stopped at a local bagel joint and ordered a toasted cinnamon raisin bagel with cream cheese.

The headache from the phantom who clipped me finally subsided after swallowing a few more painkillers, and I began taking notes of the last few days' events. What I needed was 'who told who' about my investigation. Bobby promised to check with chatty Finn at the bar, but that would probably lead nowhere.

One person stood out: Conor. Then there was my godfather's precinct. Why hadn't the detectives followed through with the eyewitnesses? For a fleeting moment, the thought of Bobby knowing about the sightings and saying nothing, concerned me. He'd never mentioned police corruption at his precinct, and I prayed he'd been truthful.

The day passed without meaningful answers, and as daylight faded, I flipped on the desk lamp. Within minutes, the sense of being watched created a tingling in my back, and I realized I made an easy target.

Gun shy, I ducked, slithered to the door, and opened it, my Glock at my side. A woman stood less than twenty feet from me and froze, staring at my weapon.

"Are you looking for someone?" I asked, now relaxed considering she held only a cell phone. I holstered my Glock.

She blurted out, "Hi, Hank."

I narrowed my eyes. "Do I know you?"

Her lips tweaked into a tentative smile. As she stepped closer under the streetlamp, her appearance became clearer: possibly forty, with shoulder-length black hair.

She stopped a few feet from me. "It's been a while," she said, her voice shaky. "You look the same, though as I recall, you were really skinny back then." A quick teasing glance.

She knew me. "I'm still at a loss," I said. "Can you be more specific? You know me from—"

"Whitestone," she said. "I'm Tara, Matt's sister."

I blinked. "Tara! What a surprise." We embraced then I pulled away slightly. "It's great seeing you, but what are you doing here?"

She glanced furtively down the street. "Can we talk inside?"

I ushered her into the office, shut the curtains, and motioned to the chair opposite my desk. "Are you okay? I mean, this is a bit odd. Odd, but nice," I corrected and sat down.

She fidgeted in her seat. Definitely not a social call.

"I apologize for showing up like this, but I didn't want to call or text."

I smiled to relax her. "Okay." She kept passing her cell phone from hand to hand. Her body language suggested she was far from relaxed. "It's okay, Tara. You can speak freely here."

She nodded, but she was clearly unsettled. I knew her as Tara Jensen. She had indeed changed from her teenage years. Back then, she wore braces. Her front teeth were now perfectly aligned and pearly white. Her straight black hair fell to her shoulders, and she wore little makeup. Not that she needed any. But it was her green eyes that set her beauty apart. Luca loved those eyes.

Tara peered down at her cell, probably checking the time, which was just past eight.

"Lucky I was here," I said. "Normally, I'd be home by now."

She nodded and gazed at the door. I followed her look and sensed she had second thoughts about popping in on me.

"You said you didn't want to text or call. I'm guessing it had to do with leaving a record." I nodded at the pink iPhone she kept squeezing. "Whatever the reason, I'm here to help. Whatever's discussed in my office stays here. Okay?"

A small nod. With a finger, she dabbed at emerging tears. I opened a desk drawer and brought out a box of tissues. At least the intruder didn't snatch them, though I swore once I caught up with the guy, he'd need more than tissues.

She took a few. "Thanks. You do look the same, Hank, honestly."

Tara was sweet. "You, too." I offered a smile and hoped she had more on her mind than discussing looks.

She held up her phone. "I didn't want anyone to see your number."

Anyone.

My brows arched. "Your husband?"

She nodded.

"Bobby filled me in on our group, so I know you and Jesse are married." I wondered if she wanted me to find him an AA sponsor but struck that down immediately.

"He's having an affair," she blurted.

I sat back. "Oh."

She caught my confused look. "Sorry, you probably thought my visit had to do with Luca."

"I did, but that's fine. Anything I can do to help."

"I thought maybe you could confirm my suspicions while investigating the murder." She must have realized how that sounded and stood. "Sorry, this wasn't such a good idea." She stood to leave.

72

I remained seated. "How long have you been suspicious?" I asked, pressing her to stay.

She hesitated, returned to her seat. "About a month. We've had problems over the years, but it's always been about his drinking. This is different. When sober, Jesse is loving and apologetic about his problem. He always promises to stop. Recently, he's been going out in the evening a few days a week, assuring it has to do with a client."

"And you think he's having an affair?"

"Wouldn't you, Hank?"

I wanted to stay objective and remained silent.

"Sorry. I know Jesse's a good guy and great father. The truth is when he returns from…a client, he appears relaxed and more loving. Probably out of guilt."

She continued, "We have a history, two girls, and…" She paused, glared. "But if he's fooling around, I'm divorcing him."

I waited for Tara to divulge the third party.

Tara scowled. "She was a friend."

Was.

I probably should be taking notes, but I didn't want to distract her.

Tara took a deep breath. "I miss Luca so much," she said, changing the subject. "If he hadn't…"

I moved the tissues closer to her.

"I recall Luca telling me your parents approved of you guys dating. Can I ask a few questions, all relevant to Luca and Jesse?"

She sat up. "Yes, of course."

"When did you and Jesse start dating?"

"A few years after…" She stopped. "I hope you're not suggesting I cheated on Luca. I would never."

I hit a nerve.

"I'm just gathering facts, Tara. Please, go on."

She leaned back. "Sorry, I'm a bit edgy." She looked at the curtains. "Jesse and I attended the same college. He was two years ahead. I guess I missed my friends back home, and he was there. One thing led to another, and he asked me out. It felt right."

"Your marriage must have been okay for a while."

She nodded. "In the beginning, I tolerated his weekend drinking, but then he continued during the week. He began losing jobs, and I begged my father to hire him. Dad was an attorney but also owned a manufacturing company. He hired Jesse until a few years later when he sold the business. The new owner wasn't interested in keeping him on." She shook her head. "I had to ask my father for help, again, which I hated doing, but I was desperate."

Tara plucked up a tissue and dabbed her eyes. "Sorry, Hank. I hated asking my father for anything. Fortunately, he had a friend in the pharmaceutical business and found Jesse a rep position. He travels a lot, which is fine with me." She looked away.

I nodded. "How's your brother Matt?" I asked, switching topics. "You two still close?"

She smiled warmly. "Very. He's not very fond of Jesse, never has been, except when they were teenagers. He's seen what he's done to my family."

I asked, "Does Matt keep in touch with the other guys? I heard everyone scattered for college that September following Luca's disappearance and never settled back to Whitestone."

She shook her head. "Sadly, no. Luca was the glue back then. Outside of Christmas cards, there doesn't seem to be much interest in the past."

"The reason I'm asking is I'd like to talk to the Whitestone boys about that night, including Jesse."

"Haven't heard that name in years, but sure, I'll tell Jesse you got in touch with me."

"Does he normally check your phone?"

"Oh, that. I guess I was just paranoid when I came here. He's cool."

Right, cool.

"And your parents, how are they? Your dad must be retired from his law practice."

Tara scowled. "I guess. We haven't spoken in a while."

I wondered if her pregnancy and the adoption had anything to do with their falling out. "Sorry, it happens in the best of families."

She sneered. "More like the worst." She stopped. "I'm sorry, I didn't come here to air out dirty laundry."

"It's okay. Like I said, our conversation stays here. By any chance, have you told anyone about my investigation? Besides Jesse?"

She shook her head. "I was going to tell my mother."

"Don't."

She raised her eyebrows. "Why not?"

"Nothing personal, but the fewer people that know, the better. It's a...P.I. thing."

"Oh, I get it. Sure. What about Matt? You wanted to get in touch with the Whitestone boys."

I smiled. "Yes, of course."

She waited a moment. "So, will you investigate?"

"Oh, right, Jesse. Of course. But it'll have to be part of my overall investigation. Are you okay with that?"

A hopeful nod. Tara opened her purse. "Can I pay in cash? Jesse and I have a joint bank account, and I don't want him knowing."

"Cash is fine, but I'm not going to charge you yet. And, of course, you'll get my friend and family discount."

She closed her purse and laughed nervously. "Thanks." She checked the time. "I better get back home." She got up to leave.

"Before you go, I need to discuss one more thing with you."

She sat back. "Sure."

"I had asked Lisa to call you. I wanted to know whether you and Luca went to Fort Totten the day he disappeared."

She scowled. "I told her no. Why?"

That was abrupt. I opened my cell to the photo app, found the photo I was looking for, and passed it to her.

Tara drilled into the picture. "Oh my God. And you think he might have carved this the day…?"

"Look at the date. It was the day of his party."

She continued staring, then sighed.

"I wasn't sure it was a good idea, you seeing this considering you're married to Jesse."

She ignored me and with her finger, drifted around the photo. She peered up, tears now flowing. "We were so much in love…why didn't he tell me something might happen to him?"

I had my suspicions but shrugged. "I'm sure he would have, had he known."

She held my phone tight. "Can I text the photo to my cell?"

When I hesitated, she begged. "Please, Hank."

I nodded and she followed through, her phone chirping the receiving sound. She stared one more time at the photo and sighed, then turned to me.

"I better get home. Jesse thinks I'm out with a friend."

I stood. "You wouldn't be lying."

When she reached the door, I said, "You never told me the woman you suspect is having an affair with Jesse."

Tara turned, her face twisting. "Luca's sister, Lisa."

THIRTEEN

J ust what I needed, a distraction from the investigation. And of all people, Lisa and Jesse. I sighed at the thought of following them around only to discover Tara's suspicion come true. Bad for Tara, and in some way, for me. It would stain a perfect image I'd kept of my teenage love.

After sleeping poorly, with dreams about infidelity, I entered my office around seven. My day would consist of contacting the White-stone boys: Matt, Kyle, Alex, and the possibly cheating Jesse.

Matt Jensen was a lot like his father: ambitious. He left White-stone two months after Luca's disappearance to attend the University of Pennsylvania and wound up marrying his college sweetheart. They had a son and eventually moved to East Island, in Nassau, Long Island, a peaceful and upscale community hugging Hempstead Bay.

He answered on the third ring and sounded genuinely happy to hear from me. We exchanged pleasantries and discussed our past friendship. He told me he'd heard from Tara about the investigation and wished me luck.

"I hope you catch the bastard," Matt said with unexpected anger. I guessed the wounds from his friend's tarnished reputation returned.

"I don't have to tell you, Hank, Luca didn't kill that woman or anyone else. How they found his knife at the crime scene is confounding. And then he disappeared. They killed him."

"They?" I asked, rising from my seat.

"I mean whoever did it. If you want my layman's opinion, Luca heard an altercation in the woods behind the bridge and checked it out. That's when he confronted Annie Baxter's killer." Matt paused. "That's where my theory goes cold. I assumed they fought, and the guy killed Luca, but only Luca's blood was found on the knife." He paused again. "And as far as what happened to…his body, is anyone's guess."

Matt's theory sounded logical, but he obviously wasn't aware of the sightings from the cold case file, so I mentioned it.

"Seriously?" He thought a moment. "So, Luca was alive and heading to Fort Totten. Why would he go there?"

"Good question. From the police report, the cops woke you guys up, and that's when you noticed Luca missing. Alex claimed he got up to pee at one point but, apparently, hadn't noticed Luca missing. According to the sightings in the cold case files, Luca had to have left the group sometime after midnight, so perhaps Alex woke up before then."

"I remember that. We were drinking heavily, so I wouldn't be surprised if he didn't notice Luca had gone. I woke up with the biggest hangover and finding out about Luca made it worse." He sighed.

"I told my old man what happened, and he couldn't believe it. Especially, that Luca was missing and a person of interest. He was happy that Luca and Tara were dating and sounded very upset. He then asked if the police treated us with respect. He was a councilman at the time, and the last thing he wanted to hear about was overzealous cops, especially dealing with his kid.

"I told him they had. The detectives took our statements and left. One of them said before leaving, 'Say hello to your father'. Yeah, dad had clout."

Right, clout.

I mentioned Conor wanting to be a Whitestone boy.

Matt snickered. "Haven't heard that name in a long time, but yeah, Conor wanted in. We weren't interested. He was a decent kid, but an odd duck. I think he sniffed too much stale beer in the bar's basement. Why do you bring up his name?"

"Just checking anyone questioned by the detectives. Conor told them he'd been working downstairs in the basement."

"A solid alibi being cooped up in the basement." He laughed. "I remember the time we ran out of there after his father caught us drinking. We were about fifteen. Finn was pissed."

He stopped. "I hope you're not suggesting Conor snuck out and killed the woman, then ran back to the bar? He might have been odd, but he never showed signs of violence. Only disappointment. I felt sorry for him. He never had many friends and, as far as I knew, didn't have a girlfriend. He runs Fillmore's now that his father retired."

"Poor Conor," I added and then asked about Matt's parents.

"I hear they're snowbirds. Guess you don't see them very often."

"They're doing okay, I guess," his tone flat. "My mother likes the change, don't know about my father. We haven't spoken in years."

"Oh." I feigned surprise. "Sorry to hear that."

"Yeah, well there's a lot of bad blood between us. I'll stop there. I probably said too much already."

I then asked about Tara, not mentioning our meeting concerning her husband, Jesse, and Lisa.

"That's another story."

When he didn't continue, I asked about the bedroom window stunt she pulled.

He laughed. "Oh, that. I got an earful the next day from my

father. He was upset, more with Luca, who was older and should have known not to entice an almost seventeen-year-old to make out under the bridge."

"But he was happy with their relationship."

"Oh, sure. But like most fathers with daughters, he was concerned she might get pregnant."

I went back to my chair and sat. "He actually told you that?"

"Well, not in so many words. But I knew. Besides, Tara told me he didn't want to be a grandfather anytime soon."

"And your mother, how did she feel?"

"Mom always deferred to my father. Still does," he added, his tone cold. "She liked Luca. But on one occasion, she had a heart-to-heart with him about babies, and he got the message."

I held off a beat. "There were rumors Tara was pregnant."

Matt's silence told me I hit a nerve. "I thought you were looking for a killer. What does Tara have to do with that?"

I pedaled back. "You're right, I'm sorry."

"Hank, that was a lifetime ago. My family went through hell."

"Do you think Luca knew about the pregnancy when he disappeared?"

"I hope you're not suggesting Luca skipped out because he didn't want to be a father. He wouldn't, okay," he grunted.

"I'm not suggesting anything," I defended. "I knew Luca, too. He would have taken responsibility for the child."

"Damn right." Matt quieted down. "My parents sent her to live with an aunt until the baby arrived, then took the infant to a Catholic adoption agency. Tara returned home, telling friends she had TB and had to recuperate upstate a few months. Everyone knew, or assumed, the real reason."

"And it was definitely Luca's baby?"

"Of course. Why would you even ask?"

"Sorry, Matt, I ask lots of questions for a living."

He said, "If you're suggesting it was Jesse's, you're wrong. They started dating a few years later."

"Thanks for clarifying."

"Look, I know you're doing Lisa a favor digging up the past, but I don't see a connection between Luca's disappearance and my sister's pregnancy."

"Sorry, our conversation stays with me."

"Good. Any further questions?" he said, his voice tight.

"Just one. I visited Annie Baxter's shrine the other day. The family created a special area for her, and I found lots of mementos inside. Did you ever see it?"

"Years ago. It was nicely done."

"I found something unusual. It was placed at the head of the shrine underneath the cross. A pen."

"A pen? Okay."

"It was a new-looking pen with your father's law firm inscribed on it."

"That's odd."

"I thought so. Do you know if your father ever visited the site?"

"No, but anyone could have put it there."

Matt wasn't defensive. "True. But visitors generally placed personal stuff. You weren't there recently, were you?"

"I told you I was there years ago. What are you suggesting?"

"Nothing. I'm trying to understand who and why someone would have stuck a pen in the ground." I stopped before making an accusation.

"Well, I don't like your inference. My father might have been unfaithful to my mother over the years, but he's no killer. I'm not defending him. I hate the guy, okay? But you're not going to connect him with her murder." He stopped. "I have to get back to work. I hope you clear Luca's name," he said and disconnected.

FOURTEEN

I drove to Fort Totten arriving at 10:00 A.M. The parking lot outside the fort was almost full, and I found a spot near the exit. It was summer, and like for many New Yorkers, being outside in bright sunshine, with a cool breeze and birds chirping everywhere, was precious.

Several cars lined up at the guard house, and I waited until they checked in before approaching the sentry. After the last car passed, the guard spotted me approaching and nodded.

"Can I help you?" Friendly enough. The guard, a young black male, followed my approach.

"I hope so." I pointed beyond him. "I used to hang out here as a teenager. Is it still open to the public?"

He turned and peered inside, then at me. "Sure is, but there's been a few changes over the years. We still have an Army Reserve presence, but most of the fort became a public park run by the city. The visitors' center's been refurbished and has a museum with exhibits. You might find that interesting."

I might, but not today. "What about cars? I noticed they stop before entering."

He pointed at the parking facility outside the fort. "Unless drivers have a sticker, they're required to park in the lot. It's still a base."

I nodded. "Makes sense. I'm a private investigator. Mind if I ask you a few questions?"

He narrowed his eyes. "Dealing with the fort?"

"An old case. Shouldn't take long."

He squinted at an oncoming car. "You might wanna move a little closer, otherwise you could get clipped."

I hustled over. "Thanks. Like I said, it has to do with an old case: a missing person. Twenty-five-years to be exact."

The guard screwed up his mouth. "You're kidding? Sir, that's like ancient. Heck, I've only been here a few years, so there's not much I can offer."

I smiled. "You must have been a toddler at the time."

He returned it. "I'm twenty-seven, so yeah. The name's Kirk."

"Hi, Kirk. I'm Hank. Like you said, there's been changes over the years, but as I recall, the guardhouse is still the same. Do you know if the army had CCTV monitoring back then?"

"I'm sure they did, but if you're asking about the tapes, I'd be surprised if they kept them."

"I figured as much," I said. "This is a long shot, but is there any way to find out who was on guard duty back then? The police originally assumed the guy in question disappeared from the Whitestone Bridge area, but recently, I discovered he vanished from here."

"Hold on a second." A white Camry pulled up. Kirk checked the sticker on the front windshield, then waved the driver through. Back to me, he said, "I really can't answer that either. But I'll ask around. You have a card?"

I plucked one from my shirt pocket and handed it to him.

"Tell you what, I'm off in a few hours, I'll check then." He placed my card on a small table.

"Oh, one more thing," I said. "There was an incident last night around 4:00 A.M. Do you think I can talk to the sentry on duty?"

He scrutinized me. "What happened last night?"

I pulled the hair back on my crown. "I didn't see it coming, but I'd like to find the bastard who did it."

He squeezed his nose. "That sucks. I guess I'll eliminate P.I. work after I get discharged. Okay, let me think. Cindy Moran was on that shift. I'll check with her."

I thanked Kirk and was about to leave when he asked, "What if the person you're looking for vanished on purpose? Could be he was running from the law."

I hadn't mentioned Annie Baxter's murder, but what if Kirk's loose theory was true? "Interesting. Maybe you should consider private investigation."

Heading to my car, I noticed the driver of a black SUV entering the parking lot, slowly moving like he was searching for something or someone. I crouched down between two vehicles as he made a semi-circle, his eyes scanning about. The passenger window was open, and as he passed me, I struggled to see the driver. That was when I noticed him wearing a Mets ball cap.

FIFTEEN

The tall man with thinning gray hair went by Lee. His constituents called him Mr. Jensen, his girlfriends, sexy, and his wife muttered, "jerk." She had put up with his dalliances over the years and swore he'd done unethical things as well. But she relied on him financially and knew he'd screw her over if she demanded a divorce.

Now, the Teflon man fidgeted in his seat. The unexpected call the other day threw him off and spoiled his golf game. Today was no better. Way over his ten handicap. Hell, he'd never played so badly.

For years, he'd been able to eliminate thoughts of his past deeds, lock them up, and throw away the key. Now, twenty-five years later, this P.I. Reed was looking for the key to unlock part of the past. And opening one door would certainly lead Reed to finding others. Looking back, his big mistake was burying the problem in plain sight.

Jensen adjusted his seat, leaned back, and closed his eyes. He'd been sitting for the last hour in his BMW, overlooking the Hilton Head Country Club. To calm his nerves, he turned on the radio and searched for a New Age station. The soothing sounds emanating from the speaker freed him temporarily.

He didn't know Hank Reed, only that Reed hung out with the Whitestone boys, mostly on weekends, when his godfather brought him to his home in Whitestone. Bobby Larkin, the desk sergeant at the 109th Precinct, had to be retired by now. Was he helping Reed? Not that it mattered. Larkin had no idea who was involved that night. If he had, he may never have had a chance to retire.

Jensen squirmed, forcing himself to admit he was getting worked up over nothing. Or something. Someone broke into Reed's office, and it wasn't *his* people.

He turned up the volume, but the voice in his head returned. The mid-day sun shined through the windshield, and he slipped on his Fendi sunglasses. Golfers strolled by, chatting about their game, something he should be doing.

His anger toward Reed erupted, and he ripped his scorecard into pieces, tossing them on the passenger seat. He opened the glove compartment, removed the recently purchased burner, and punched in a number.

"Who's this?" the receiver grunted after the fourth ring.

Jensen wiped his forehead and gritted his teeth. "Who else were you expecting on your burner? Now we can talk openly."

"Oh, right. You sound upset."

The guy's an idiot.

"Upset! We have a powder keg ready to explode and you're wondering if I'm upset. What the hell are you doing about the investigation?"

"Still looking. I didn't call because I have nothing to report," he defended. "I told you last time I'd get back when I have information. Reed is still nosing around."

"Of course he is, you idiot! Where the hell is he looking? And who's he talking to?"

The caller, Jensen's flunky, Jimmy Savage, rattled off a few names and places. "That's it, so far. Remember, Reed is investigating cold.

He started with the Whitestone Bridge, like any good P.I., and then went to Fort Totten."

"Why the hell would Reed go to Fort Totten? Everything in the report pointed to the Whitestone Bridge. I'm telling you, he's onto something. What was he doing there?"

"Where?"

"The fucking fort."

"Oh, right. Just shooting the shit with the security guard."

Jensen punched off the radio. "And you didn't think that raised a red flag. Are you stupid or something? Why the hell do you think Reed was there? He wasn't chatting it up. He was asking questions."

"Come on, nobody knows Luca wound up there."

The man slapped his head. Imbecile. "Why do you think Reed went to the guard house? It sure as hell wasn't to shoot the breeze. He's *investigating*."

"So what?" Savage said. "Do you really think that guard was on duty twenty-five-years ago? Get real. And as far as the Army keeping records, there's nothing to report. I told you at the time, it was easy in, easy out."

Jensen glanced in the rearview mirror and touched his mustache. It needed coloring. "Just the same, why would he show up unless someone tipped him off? Find out *who* that someone was and fast."

"Okay, settle down. You're too worked up. Why don't you go out and play a round of golf?" His laugh had a nervous edge.

Jensen shot a look at his torn scorecard and swore to himself.

"So, are we good?"

"No, we're not good. Keep following Reed. And make sure your other cop friend, Snip, or whatever his name, is doing the same."

"Kip."

"Whatever. I want you to call me every time Reed goes some-place that could be problematic for us. This thing needs to die."

"Thing or person?"

A deep breath. "When the time comes…you're the one tailing him, it'll be your call."

"Don't think for a moment I'm doing this alone. You're gonna help. I have a lot on the line, and sure as hell don't wanna spend my retirement in orange."

The boss snorted. "You mean spending your retirement away from the house I helped pay for."

"Okay, don't get funny."

"Just keep working," Jensen demanded and disconnected. He took a breath. What he needed was a drink and a few hours of distraction. His personal cell chirped, and he glanced at the number. He wasn't in the mood to talk to an unknown caller and waited to see if the person left a voicemail.

A fellow golfer strolled by and waved. He returned it listlessly then heard a ping that a voice message was waiting. He listened.

"Say, Uncle, it's been a while."

SIXTEEN

I drove back to Fillmore's hoping to find Conor, but he wasn't behind the bar; Finn was. The place was empty, which suited me fine.

"Say, Finn."

He smiled but didn't appear to recognize me. We'd only met a few times back in the day.

"Conor's friend, Hank Reed. From our teens."

Still no recognition.

"Bobby Larkin's godson."

"Oh, of course."

We shook hands.

"Are you visiting Bobby?" he asked. "Haven't seen him in a while."

"Me either, so I decided to spend a few days at his house. I thought I'd stop by and say hi to Conor. Is he around?"

Finn's eyes glazed over. He'd apparently been dipping into the liquor inventory.

"He mentioned something about running errands. Not sure

when he'll be back. It's a quiet time anyway. I'll tell him you stopped by. How about a drink before you go?"

It wasn't yet noon, but I asked for a Peroni.

He poured a draft, his hand slightly unsteady.

"Did Conor mention I'm investigating Luca Falcone's disappearance?" I said casually.

Finn's brow creased. "Don't believe so. It's been —"

"Twenty-five years," I finished.

"Right. A long time ago. Are you on the force, Hank?"

"Used to be. I'm a private investigator. Luca's sister, Lisa, received information exonerating him from the murder. As for his disappearance…" I shrugged. "I need to get in touch with the Whitestone boys and whoever the police interviewed that night, including you and Conor."

Finn averted his eyes. "Not much to add. I was working the bar and Conor was downstairs."

"The basement?"

"Right. He was too young to serve drinks, so I kept him locked up in the cellar." He chucked softly. "Where we store the beer and booze."

"Until closing?"

He nodded. "Back then, we closed up together. At the time, he lived with me and didn't own a car."

"He does now, I assume."

"Oh, yeah. A Chevy Trailblazer. He loves it."

I bet.

I studied Finn then sipped my beer. "From what I learned, the murdered woman's friend was here at the bar that night. Seems she'd been waiting for her, but her friend never showed up. Later, she left with a guy and wound up at the crime scene. Terrible finding her friend like that."

Another nod. "Horrible experience. I don't really recall seeing the friend since we had a full house. The cops arrived before we closed, and we gave them a statement. Conor and I had alibis, of course, so they asked more about the friend and the guy she was with here. Conor remembers better than I do."

"Conor?"

"That's what he told the police, anyway."

I took another sip. "But you said Conor was locked in the basement. How would he have known about the friend up here?"

Finn squeezed his eyes. "I don't recall. Maybe I told the police."

"No, it's in the report. Conor claimed he recognized the friend."

Finn looked around, then he grabbed a rag and absently began wiping down the bar. "Conor must have come upstairs for something, maybe with a keg of beer. Is it important at this point, Hank?"

The truth is.

I gulped my beer. "Nah, probably an oversight."

"Yeah, that's it." He stopped wiping, tossed the rag aside, then rubbed his hands on his pants.

"By the way, who's your attorney?" I asked.

His eyes flared. "I need a lawyer?"

I laughed. "No, I mean for civil stuff. Wills, things like that?"

He eyed me like I was crazy. "Gee, Hank, I haven't used one in years." He scratched his receding hairline. "In the past, I used Lee Jensen for my will. You need one? A will, I mean?"

"Nah, just work stuff. Jensen any good?"

Finn shrugged. "I suppose. It wasn't very complicated. Everything goes to Conor. But Lee doesn't practice anymore. He's retired."

"Oh, too bad. Come to think about it, my godfather told me Jensen used to hand out ballpoint pens to his clients. Very cool with a silver ring. He ever give you one?"

He shrugged. "Gee, I really don't remember."

I nodded, then checked my Fitbit. "I better get going. Lots to investigate. Good seeing you again, Finn." I put down a ten, but he brushed it back. "On the house."

As I reached for the door, Finn called out, "Tell Bobby to stop by once in a while."

When I hit the street, I spied a black Chevy Trailblazer heading my way. As the driver saw me, he rolled up the window, then glanced at the bar door. It was Conor, wearing a Mets ballcap. He nodded, then continued down the street.

Conor was on to me, which meant I'd have to corner him somewhere. I was sure it wouldn't be at Fillmore's.

Francis Lewis Park was up the road, and I pulled into a spot facing the river and walked toward it. Seagulls were scavenging for food, and I was hunting for a killer.

My phone chirped. It was Tara. I hoped she wasn't calling about tailing Jesse. She sounded upbeat, so I assumed our meeting put her at ease. She gave me the phone numbers of the remaining White-stone boys: Kyle, Alex, and her husband, Jesse.

"I told Jesse you'd be calling. He was excited." Tara paused. "I think he means it, Hank. He knows if Luca were still around, I'd be married to him. Still, he and Luca were great friends, and Jesse said he was the lucky one."

Jesse's sentiments didn't sound like he was having an affair. Then again, if he was sleeping with Lisa...

I thanked her and disconnected. At noon, I assumed everyone was at work but called Kyle anyway. After a few rings, I got his voice-mail message: "I'm in the fields and will get back to you after 5:00 P.M."

The fields?

I snickered and decided the others were probably not available until tonight.

That afternoon, I returned to my office and scooped up my mail, thumbed through it, and tossed all but one in the trash basket.

A wedding invitation from a former client made me smile. It was a tough case that turned out successful. I was sure my buddy, Senior Detective JR Greco from NYPD was also invited. He'd given me the gig; the client was his cousin.

A light tap at my front door broke my concentration. Given my recent threat, I tossed the letter aside, drew my Glock from my waistband holster, and walked to the window. I peered out, but the street was empty. Probably just my imagination.

I opened the door and found a manila envelope at my feet. Without a stamp, return name, address, or postmark, I scooped up the light envelope and laid it on my desk. What to do. After a few moments, I sliced open one end, then turned it upside down, my eyes following a flat point 9mm bullet landing at my feet. Inside the envelope a note read: YOU WON'T SEE THE NEXT BULLET!

SEVENTEEN

At first, Jensen thought the caller had the wrong number. He had a nephew, but the kid had been in a Mexican prison for years and not expected to be released for another five.

"Danny?" His eyebrows arched.

"How many nephews do you have? It's me. I need your help and fast," he said out of breath.

Hell of a greeting. Worse, the man hoped he'd never hear from Danny again in his lifetime. Especially now.

"Where are you?" Silly question.

"On the run. You have a trip coming. I know you don't like flying but—"

"Hold on a second. You're out of prison? I thought—"

"I escaped and am lying low in Tijuana. You need to bring me a new passport."

This wasn't happening. "This is too much to grasp, Danny. I can't just fly down and pick you up. I'll have a passport made up and send it." He stopped. "That won't work. Besides, I don't have a recent photo of you." He paused, scratched his head. "You're asking too much. Can't you sneak across the border like everyone else?"

THE BRIDGE TO MURDER

"Not funny, Uncle. You gotta do this. I can't spend another night in that fucking hell hole. I'm texting a recent photo. Tell me when you get it."

How the hell did his convicted nephew get a phone or his number?

"I'm on the run, so you gotta move it!"

"Danny, please, I can't come. There's gotta be another way."

"I'm listening."

Of course, there wasn't another way. He was sure none of his lackeys would help, not with his mercurial nephew.

"I don't have much time," he said, not waiting for an excuse.

Jensen was thinking, plotting like he always had.

"Uncle!"

"I'm thinking. You caught me at a bad time. I'm not in New York."

"I don't give a shit where you are. I need you now—or else."

'Or else' was not something Jensen wanted to hear. Danny could create more problems than Hank Reed. "Your aunt isn't going to let me take off unexpectedly."

Danny chuckled. "Not with your history. And don't tell her I called. This is between you and me. Holy shit, I can't believe I broke out. These motherfuckers are nuts."

Jensen opened his text message feature and gasped. "The fuck happened to you?"

"Now you know why I gotta get out of that god-forsaken place."

"Okay, hold tight. I'll figure a way. I'll call this number tomorrow."

"No later."

They disconnected. Jensen thought a long moment, trying to stay positive. After contemplating his next step, he realized Danny's situation might be a blessing in disguise.

95

EIGHTEEN

I don't like threats, and if the bullet at my doorstep was Conor's doing, he got my attention. My hands shook as I punched in Fillmore's number. When Finn picked up, I demanded to speak to Conor.

"Now."

"Hank, he's not here. Do you want his cell number?"

"He's not returning my calls. You tell him, if he doesn't get back to me ASAP, I'm going to the police. He knows what it's about," I said and disconnected before Finn could protest. I sucked in a much-needed breath. The bastard.

Ten minutes later my phone rang. He finally got the message, only it wasn't Conor.

"Hi, Hank, this is Kirk from Fort Totten. I was able to get the information you asked about. You know, the guy on duty that night years ago, and last night."

I tried calming down and sat in my chair. "That's great."

Kirk began with Army procedure, and—maybe he wanted to impress me.

"Kirk, the name please."

"Oh, right. Nick Collins. He's retired from the Army and works as a security guard for a contract company in New Jersey. I have his number, but he doesn't know I'm giving it to you, so please keep this between us."

"Promise. And Cindy Moran, the guard on duty last night?"

"Right. She found nothing out of the ordinary. Sorry."

Except my head getting slammed.

"I'm texting over Nick's number. Tell me when you receive it."

It arrived a minute later. "Got it, thanks. Can I send you a bottle of something? What do you drink?"

"I don't," he said. "I'm glad I was able to help. But…"

"Yes?"

"Maybe you can call me when you resolve the case."

If I resolve it.

Lee Jensen had no relationship with his son, Matt, who, over the years, watched his father fall deeper and deeper into the dark side. His daughter hated him for giving up her child.

Now, his nephew and murderer, Danny Caruso, had escaped from a Mexican prison. How was that possible? Worse, he wanted help getting over the border. Ironic, twenty-five years ago, Jensen helped his nephew cross the border in the other direction. He'd hoped to rid himself of Danny Caruso forever. Finding a safe spot in Cancun, Mexico, Jensen figured his nephew would settle down, get married and have kids.

Fat chance. Danny was a bad seed and wound up killing a pole dancer. Couldn't he have just screwed her and gone on to the next one?

Waiting for his flight, Jensen attempted to overcome his aversion to flying. No such luck. Memories of his father taking the family on their first vacation made him cringe. The flight from JFK to Miami International was two-and-a-half hours, but it became hell for Jensen. While his sister raved about the cloud formations, the views of Miami, and the art deco buildings that lined Miami Beach, Jensen reached for an air sickness bag. On the way home, he begged for an aisle seat.

Today was no different, but Jensen hoped he was prepared. He slipped into an aisle seat, snapped on his seat belt, and took a breath, all before the flight attendant gave orders. He was too busy obsessing over his motion sickness to appreciate the thirty-something strawberry blonde knockout in the middle seat. A quick smile before fastening on his black sleeping mask and waiting for the Xanax to kick in, Jensen prayed he wouldn't need the barf bag on the flight from Atlanta to San Diego.

From there, he'd rent a car and drive to a hotel, check in, and hopefully, a package would be waiting for him. He'd then place a call to his nephew to find out where he was hiding.

A tap on his shoulder jolted Jensen's already tense body. He whipped off his face mask and blinked. It was the knockout smiling.

"Sorry, I need to pass."

Jensen squeezed in his legs. He wasn't about to stand for her or anyone. He pulled down his mask and waited anxiously for her to return.

When she did, Jensen continued formulating his plan, suddenly forgetting he was thirty-thousand feet above sea level. The Xanax had finally kicked in. He knew his paranoia about Reed finding the truth and the predictable consequences ... he didn't want to go there. He needed Danny to handle the problem before it got out of hand.

Bottom line: Hank Reed had to go.

When the flight attendant announced their arrival, Jensen was grateful he hadn't needed the barf bag. Touching ground, he whipped off his facemask, smiled at the strawberry blonde, unfastened his seat belt, and waited for the plane to come to a full stop.

Nick Collins answered with a southern drawl.

"Hi, Nick, my name is Hank Reed. I'm a private investigator working on a cold case murder/disappearance just outside Fort Totten. I discovered you were on guard duty the night in question."

"Who did you say you were?"

"Hank Reed. You can Google me if you'd like."

"I guess it's okay. Did you say Fort Totten? That was eons ago."

"Twenty-five to be exact. I realize I'm calling out of the blue, but your recollection could prove vital to my case."

Collins snickered. "You really expect me to remember that far back? Hell, I have a problem remembering yesterday."

"Me too," I said, humoring him. "But anything you recall might help."

"Well, off the top of my head, I don't remember that period. I mean, if something happened inside or directly outside the fort, I would have reported it. I don't recall reporting much over the years. Sorry." He paused. "You said you were a private investigator."

"Correct."

"How did you get my name and number? I retired from the army years ago."

Lie number one. "I checked with the army, and they believe based on the heinous crime, you might be helpful. Unfortunately, their records were sketchy, so all they had was your name. I found your number on my own."

I heard him breathing. "Yeah, typical Army bullshit, handing out information. Okay, give me the details."

"On July 6, 1996, it was a Saturday, a murder was committed

under the Whitestone Bridge. A teen was accused of killing a woman. That same night, the accused teen vanished, and, through recent discovery, it turns out he wound up outside Fort Totten around four in the morning. It's unknown whether he entered the fort, but that's where I'm hoping you'll come in."

Collins snorted. "You said a Saturday. Do you know how many guys got into drunken brawls on weekends, especially Saturday nights?"

"I can imagine, but this was different. According to the witness, the person in question was alone and not drunk. Apparently, he was waiting for someone. The witness left before anyone showed up, so we don't know whether the teen met someone and, if he did, what happened next. Based on his disappearance, it's likely he didn't go voluntarily."

"Hold on a second, it's noisy in here. Damn loudspeaker." A moment later, he returned. "It's possible, but *if* he was waiting for someone, there might not have been an altercation, in which case, the kid hopped in the car outside the fort and took off."

Not the version I wanted to hear, so I pressed. "True, but we believe the driver in question might have had bad intentions, and the teen attempted to escape. It's also possible the driver chased him *into* the fort and nabbed him."

"Unlikely. The driver would have had to stop at the guard gate and show a pass. You can't just drive through. That's what the guard is for." He stopped. "Unless, of course, the driver had a pass."

I grimaced.

"That's why we have sentries guarding forts. So unwelcome visitors can't charge through. If that's what you're suggesting, and the driver attempted to drive past me, he would have been arrested soon after. And if that were the case, I would have remembered. The Army would have a record of the incident, and if there was an arrest, it would have been kept in a permanent file. You might consider going back and asking if there was an incident report that night, but, as I said, I would have remembered."

"Thanks, I will," I said, defeated.

A loudspeaker blasted in the background. "I'm being called. I'm sorry I can't be more helpful. I hope you find what you're looking for."

NINETEEN

Lee Jensen gripped the steering wheel as he stopped to show his passport. He hadn't done anything wrong, but the thought of him returning with Danny created stress. The guard verified the credentials and smiled.

"Welcome to Mexico."

Right. Crossing the border, Jensen headed south on I-5 toward Tijuana, a half-hour drive. He'd heard about striped donkeys, strip joints, and prostitutes roaming around, not to mention tequila. But Jensen didn't have time for fun. His mission was to grab his nephew and drive straight back over the border.

Later, after flying to JFK, he'd drop Danny off at a cheap motel in Queens until the job was done. Then he'd find a safe place for the kid, hopefully one permanent and far away from civilization. He didn't trust his sister's son. Not after killing Annie Baxter, and then another woman in Mexico. Jensen realized killing Reed would put Danny Boy in the serial killer category. He'd make sure it would be his nephew's last kill.

Despite the air on max, Jensen's forehead beaded with perspiration. He wanted to turn around, go home, and play a round of golf, but he was too far into the plan. As much as Danny needed him, he also needed his nephew. A symbiosis of the worst kind.

They agreed to meet at *Gasolinera de la 10,* just south of the downtown area. When he arrived, Jensen parked in the back and called Danny on his burner.

Jensen fumed. Why the hell wasn't he picking up? He was about to disconnect when Danny answered.

"Sorry about that, Uncle. I was taking a piss."

Great. "I'm in the back. Look for a white Nissan Rogue. Hurry up."

"Okay, I'm gonna buy a taco first. I haven't eaten all day. Want one?"

Crazy bastard. He'd probably puke after taking a bite. "No. Just hurry up." Jensen kept staring at the gas station door and waited for what felt like hours until Danny swaggered out, munching a taco. What happened to his nephew's angst?

Danny saw the car and waved. Jensen didn't return it. He kept the engine running.

Hurry, Hurry, Hurry.

The door opened and he was greeted with a cheesy smirk. Jensen thought he'd prepared for his nephew's new look, but when he saw him, his jaw dropped. Deep scars traveling north and south on his face looked far worse than the photo.

Danny slid in, took a final bite, and tossed the paper to the ground.

Jensen rolled his eyes. Still a pig.

He threw his arms around his uncle, who pulled back from the stench for not taking a shower in God knows how long.

"You haven't changed, Uncle. Okay, maybe a little older." Danny searched his uncle's face. "So good to be home."

They weren't home. They had to cross the border first, but why spoil the moment for the kid. As for Danny's face, it was obvious Mexican prisoners didn't like gringos.

"My passport?"

Jensen pointed to the glove compartment. "Best I could do in a day."

Danny looked at his photo and swore. "I'll never find a woman looking like this." He turned to Jensen, "Know a good plastic surgeon?"

TWENTY

Nick Collins had a good point. If Luca was waiting for someone, there probably wouldn't have been an altercation. But who and why? Luca was heading to Fort Totten for a reason in the middle of the night, during his birthday party, no less. None of the Whitestone boys knew Luca was meeting up with anyone.

Unless one of them did.

I was still in my office when my cell vibrated showing an unknown caller. I dismissed it. The same persistent number appeared minutes later. Damn, telemarketers. When the caller followed up a third time, I bristled at the phone. "Goddammit, who is this?"

"Oh, hi. This is Monsignor Valencia."

Definitely not a telemarketer unless Heaven was selling something.

Monsignor. "Oh, hello, Monsignor. Sorry about that. You have no idea how many scam calls I get." I just lied to a priest. "Did you mean to call this number? You called three times but didn't leave a message."

"Yes, yes, I called your number, but I didn't want to leave one.

Sorry for the annoyance. It has to do with Father Alex Weber. I assumed you called him. Well, you must have."

"Sorry, did you say *Father* Alex Weber? I didn't know Alex was a priest."

"Yes, he's been a priest for years. I guess you knew him before he took his vows. Again, I'm sorry for the intrusion, but it's important I reach someone who knows him. And since your number was the last one left in his voicemail…"

"Yes, I'm waiting for his call. Is he okay? You sound concerned."

A long sigh. "You said you didn't know Alex was a priest, so you must be a childhood friend. Sorry, what's your name? You left it on his phone, but I was so worried, I drew a blank."

"Hank Reed." Now I was getting concerned. "We lost touch over the years, but something's come up, and I need to speak with him."

"That's why I'm calling. Alex is missing."

"Missing?" I stood and peered out the office window.

"I'm worried sick. That's why I called." The Monsignor continued, repeating himself nervously, finishing with, "This is so unlike him."

Visions of a disappearing Luca returned. "Is it proper to call him Alex? That's how I knew him."

"Yes, of course, you're his friend."

"When did you realize Alex went missing?" I asked.

"A few days ago. He left a note saying he was visiting friends from the old neighborhood, a reunion, and promised to return before Sunday morning mass. That was yesterday."

"A reunion? Did he mention where the reunion was being held? I'm asking because as far as I know, there is no reunion, at least not in Whitestone, where he grew up."

"That's strange. His note mentions Whitestone."

I turned away from the window and dropped in my seat. "It doesn't make sense," I said.

The monsignor thought for a moment. "Mr. Reed, I hope I'm

THE BRIDGE TO MURDER

not intruding, but you said you called Alex for a reason. May I ask what it was about?"

"Of course, and please call me Hank. I'm investigating the disappearance of a mutual friend who went missing twenty-five years ago. It's a long story, but our friend was accused of murder the same night. Recently, his family received an anonymous letter suggesting he wasn't responsible for the murder. I was hoping Alex might remember something that skipped his mind back then. It was just a chance—"

"Murder? Missing person? Sounds ominous. Alex was there that night?"

"Not at the crime scene. The guys were celebrating our friend's eighteenth birthday under the Whitestone Bridge. I'm both a friend and private investigator, so I have a personal interest in the case as well."

The Monsignor said, "Would Alex know why you called?"

"If he picked up my message, yes. But he never got back to me. It might just be a coincidence, him missing and my call."

When the monsignor didn't reply, I said, "I'm sure there's an explanation—"

"Father Alex has been in my parish for six years. This has never happened. In any event, he wouldn't have left a note; he'd come directly to me if he wanted time off. That's what worries me."

"Maybe he was in a hurry," I added, attempting to relieve his anxiety.

"Well, he did leave in the middle of the night and took one of the cars. The old one. At least he left the more reliable one for us."

And then it hit me. "Monsignor, how do you know I called?"

"What?"

"I called Alex on *his* phone. Did Alex leave his phone behind?"

"That's exactly what happened. Another reason for my concern. Who leaves their cell phone behind? Well, maybe folks my age. I'm a senior citizen." He laughed quietly.

I began taking notes. "Did you call the local police?"

He hesitated. "In light of his note, I decided to wait another day. Maybe I should contact them now."

If the monsignor called the locals, they'd rush over and disturb the premises. "Hold off," I said. "If there was foul play or his car broke down, the police would have notified you by now. I assume Alex had identification on him."

"I guess, but then again, he left his phone—"

"Tell you what. I'll make a trip and check Alex's room. If there's no reasonable explanation, I'll suggest you call the police."

"Okay, Hank, how soon can you get here?

Father Alex Weber served St. Williams' Catholic church, a small Tannersville parish in the Poconos, about two-and-a-half hours from my office. I arrived shortly before one that afternoon and peered through the windshield at the two-story brick rectory.

The monsignor must have heard my car tires crushing gravel because the door flew open, and a short, rotund man around sixty-five hustled toward me out of breath.

I emerged from the car and smiled. "Hello, Monsignor."

"Welcome to St. Williams, Hank."

He shook my hand with exuberance. He was dressed in dark trousers and a black shirt, complete with his white clerical collar. An anxious look crossed his face.

I inhaled the brisk country air and gazed around at the dense forest adjacent to the rectory.

"Nice place you have," I said, taking in a lungful of Pocono's finest.

He looked around quickly. "Yes, it's our little paradise."

We studied each other for a few moments. With a drawn face and a slight eyelid twitch, the monsignor was clearly nervous.

"Thanks for coming. Let's talk inside. I made coffee, and we have a few noshes if you're hungry."

Both sounded good. I trailed him to a comfortable living area with modest furniture, the walls adorned with religious paintings, all replicas, I assumed. Da Vinci's *Last Supper* had to be a replicate, or St. Williams was a rich parish.

"It's just the two of us today," he said, continuing to another room. "Father McCarron is meeting a few parishioners. He's aware of Father Alex's disappearance."

We wound up in the dining room with a formal wooden table and four straight-backed chairs. The scent of freshly brewed coffee wafted through the room.

"Please, have a seat." He nodded absently to a chair, then poured our coffees, his hand trembling slightly. "Milk, sugar?"

"Neither, thanks."

"Like me."

"So, just the three of you reside here? Including Father Alex?"

He offered a plate of cherry Danishes. "Mrs. Haviken, our housekeeper during the week, takes very good care of us and bakes wonderful pastries, all fattening, of course." He smiled. "My expanding waistline is proof of her excellent talent."

He realized he hadn't answered my question. "Yes, just us priests. Mrs. Haviken lives with her husband nearby." He shook his head. "She's distraught over Alex. He's been like a son to her. She and Henry never had children, and she took to him instantly. Alex feels the same about her. Anyway, you might get to meet her later. She's running a few errands."

He stopped. "Sorry for talking so much. I'm nervous. Nothing like this has ever happened before." He took a seat across from me, took a breath, and feigned a smile.

I wanted to assure the monsignor that Alex was fine, but I had no idea whether he was dead or alive and dared not infer the former.

"We'll find him," I said. "There has to be an explanation."

He removed a folded paper from his pants pocket. "This is the note he left on top of his desk. It's self-explanatory. Reunion, and then return for Sunday mass."

He nudged the plate of Danishes my way. I scooped up one, took a bite, and read the note. I peered up. The monsignor's face was pale and tired-looking, and I suspected he hadn't slept much since Alex's disappearance.

"What do you think?" he asked, nodding at the note.

I took a healthy bite of the pastry, then washed it down with strong coffee. "Kudos to Mrs. Haviken."

"I'll tell her." He paused. "What about the note, Hank?"

Right, the note.

There was no doubt the note was written in a rush. I had no idea what Alex was thinking at the time, but considering he took off in the middle of the night, he didn't have time for prose. I peered up.

"To be honest, I haven't seen Alex in twenty-five years, so I can't offer any theories. As you said, his disappearance seems highly unusual. Checking his room might provide a better sense of who he is now. In the meantime, what can you tell me about him?"

Monsignor Valencia, who had been clutching his coffee mug, sat back and smiled wistfully. He spoke like a proud parent. "Alex is a wonderful priest and friend. Father McCarron is as well." He hastened to add, "But you're interested in Alex. He arrived about six years ago, I think I already told you and was exactly what we needed at the time. Father Russell had just retired. Alex came from a larger parish in Jersey City. He had previously contacted me wondering if there was an opening. When I asked why he was interested in our parish, he said he'd visited the area several times as a child and was enamored with the beauty of the surroundings, the mountains, and the peacefulness of the Poconos."

He paused. "When Father Russell retired, I thought of Alex immediately and requested permission. He's been a great source of comfort to the community, both spiritually and as a wonderful

THE BRIDGE TO MURDER

human being." He chuckled softly. "God provided us the best environment. It's rural and quiet. After all, this is the Poconos."

"I'm sold."

"And Alex has me. Not to pat myself on the back, but I'm a good leader."

"Maybe I should have considered the priesthood."

"You're Catholic, Hank?"

"I was baptized and confirmed, but I guess you'd consider me lapsed."

"I won't hold that against you," he said with a thin smile. "It sounds like you found your calling as a private investigator."

He continued, "Alex's predecessor didn't have a sense of humor, which was fine; he helped the community. But when Alex arrived, the parishioners took to him immediately. He's funny, compassionate, and a mensch." He paused. "It's Yiddish for a person of integrity and honor."

"I'm familiar with the term," I said in a friendly tone. "I'm from New York."

"Yes, of course. That's Alex." He paused, gazed at his coffee cup, and took a breath. "That's why I'm concerned something serious happened to him. Am I getting ahead of myself?"

Without adding more stress, I said, "You said Alex left his phone behind."

"Yes, I found it in his room."

I gave the Danish a longing glance but held off. "And he took one of the cars?"

"Right. We don't own our cars, but three are available thanks to the congregation. Alex took the oldest, a 2010 Honda Civic. It had just been serviced for brakes. He usually drives the Camry, which is relatively new." He stopped as though he had an epiphany. "I pray there wasn't a problem with the car."

If Alex took the oldest vehicle, he probably wasn't planning on traveling far, or he'd need one more reliable.

"The police would have notified you by now if the car was in an accident," I encouraged.

"I suppose. None of this makes sense." He absently tore off a piece of Danish and tossed half in his mouth, chewing slowly, followed by a sip of coffee.

"How about we start with Alex's bedroom? You never know what we might find."

The monsignor dropped the pastry on his plate and rose. "Good idea."

He hurried toward the stairs, me in tow. When we reached the second level, I noticed three rooms. The monsignor headed to the far end, stopping in front of a door. He stared at the doorknob for a moment before turning it.

"Alex never locks it," he said and flipped on the light switch. "Take as much time as you need."

The monsignor stepped out of the way to allow me to pass. The sparse uncarpeted room and furniture appeared old and were likely inherited from a prior priest. A twin bed sat at the far end near a window. I ambled over and peered out. A lush garden burst with sunflowers, painted daisies, and chrysanthemums. They probably provided Alex with peace and calmness.

"That's Alex's garden. Beautiful, no? He spends hours nurturing the plants like they were his children. I never had the patience myself, but Alex told me if he hadn't become a priest, he might have gone into horticulture."

"I can see that." I sensed Alex would have gone into any field that soothed the soul. Inside the room stood a twenty-seven-inch TV perched on a rustic stand and a wall full of books squeezed together on two shelves. On the other side, a small desk angled toward the window, and I suspected Alex watched over his garden in between whatever he did on his laptop, which was now sitting on top and closed.

"As you can see, the room is simple but adequate. Alex never complained about space." He sighed. "Alex never complained about anything." He pointed at the bookshelves. "He's a voracious reader."

Alex was also a neat freak. The room was immaculate, and his bed was made up as though he hadn't slept in it. Which made sense if he left in the middle of the night.

"Is this how you found the room? It looks like it hasn't been touched in a while."

Remaining at the doorway, he nodded. "Alex is very neat. Not that he ever has visitors. That's forbidden."

Neat and quiet, unlike his home life, I thought and snapped on a pair of latex gloves.

I sat at the desk and opened his laptop. The screensaver showed a young woman smiling in front of the church. I'd ask about her later. The computer was password protected, which was no surprise. Most people kept secrets, even small ones.

"Looks serious," the monsignor said, nodding at my hands. He remained in the doorway, and I wondered whether he thought Alex might suddenly barge in on us.

"A habit, I'm afraid. It's normal procedure." I didn't want to suggest the room might be a potential crime scene, though surveying around, I doubted it.

The clothes closet was next. Alex's religious and street garb were pressed and organized. I counted a half-dozen empty hangers.

"It appears Alex took enough clothes for a while."

The monsignor narrowed his eyes. "His note suggested otherwise." He shook his head, looked around the room, and pointed. "What about in there?"

I opened the dresser drawer. My hands searched around. Underwear, socks, and other apparel you'd expect to find. Nothing out of the ordinary. I hoped I hadn't wasted my time coming here.

I stood and shrugged. "Nothing unusual." I glanced around at the bare walls. Not a single photograph of my friend's past. Maybe

Alex wanted to leave Whitestone behind. I suddenly felt sorry for him, remembering his upbringing.

I searched the bookshelves and wondered what Father Alex, the priest, read these days. We were comic book kids: the *Spectre*, *Starman*, and anything published by Marvel. I brushed through one shelf, then the other. I didn't know what I was looking for, but as they say, 'I'll know it when I see it.'

And then I saw it. Hidden between hard covers was a soft-cover book. I tugged on it gently as it appeared to be fragile from use. *Coming to Terms with Yourself,* by Walter Simon, an author I wasn't familiar with. The cover showed a man in his fifties, with salt and pepper hair, staring into space.

The first page was personal. "To Alex, glad you are finding your way." The dedication page read: 'To Lost Souls, May You Find Happiness,' and was published in 1997, a year after Luca went missing. I gingerly flipped through it and stopped midway at a dogeared page. God knows how often Alex reread these passages. A yellow highlighter had slid over several paragraphs.

I could feel the monsignor's eyes on me, and my gaze shifted to him.

"Find anything?"

I held up the book. "Are you familiar with this one?"

He slipped on his glasses. "It was popular in the nineties. As I recall, the story is about redemption. The author is a local psychologist."

"Would you mind if I snapped a few photos? Some pages appear to have some significance to Alex."

He shrugged. "Sure. Are you looking for anything specific?"

I stared at the title. "Like I said, I haven't seen Alex in many years, so I have no recent history of him. I don't even know what he looks like."

The monsignor edged into the room. "I can help with that when we return downstairs." He took a cursory look around. "There has to be an explanation, Hank."

I shrugged. "And there was never a hint Alex was in a hurry to leave? Maybe out of fear?"

"Fear?" The monsignor's head jerked. "Alex never feared anything. I remember a few years back while we were hiking in the woods, a black bear appeared on our path. I grabbed his arm and told him we'd better retreat. Alex ditched my hand and told me to go back, that he would scare off the bear."

"Did he?"

"I wouldn't leave without him, so I watched. He began making crazy noises, waving his arms. He had a whistle around his neck and began blowing like crazy. At one point, Alex removed a knife from his pocket, which surprised me because I didn't know he owned one. He claimed it was a souvenir and would never use it on any person or animal."

"So, what happened?"

"With the bear?" The monsignor smiled. "It ran off, and we headed back to the trailhead. I asked if he had ever encountered a bear before. He said no, but it was fun." He paused. "Maybe for Alex, it was fun."

As a teenager, Alex never showed signs of bravery. And I never saw him with a knife, though there'd been rumors he slept with one under his pillow. Luca said Alex was afraid of his father and hoped he'd never have to use it.

The monsignor interrupted my thoughts. "I keep thinking about the note and reunion. Alex clearly lied to me. In the years he's been here, I never once denied him anything important. I pray there's a good explanation for his actions."

I asked about the cell phone. "Where did you find it?"

"Oh, right." He pointed at the desk drawer. "It was inside. Alex hadn't come down for breakfast that morning, so I checked up on him. That's when I found the note. It was addressed to me." He frowned. "After reading it, I naturally became upset and called him. It continued ringing, and I got increasingly anxious. Before his voicemail kicked in, I heard a muffled sound coming from inside the drawer. When I opened it, the phone was still ringing. At that point, I assumed he would come back for it." He sighed.

Alex was either in a rush and forgot his phone or didn't want anyone tracking him with the phone's GPS feature. I opened the desk drawer and removed a black pen and yellow pad, like the one he used to write the note. I blinked at a vintage wooden Optimo cigar box. My godfather owned one of these. He'd enjoy a cigar in his younger days on the force, and though he stopped smoking, he kept the box as a memento. Inside, I found his Army dog tags and photos of former girlfriends. Okay, I peeked that day.

I placed the box on the desk. It was light, so I assumed there wasn't much inside.

"I never smoked and wondered what people used them for afterward," the monsignor said looking over my shoulder.

He had mentioned Alex's knife when confronted by a bear, and when I opened the box, I assumed the one inside was the same one.

"So that's where Alex stored it. It was with him the day we saw the bear."

As I placed it in my hand and turned it over, I realized it wasn't Alex's knife. Not with the initials L.F.—Luca Falcone, engraved on it.

TWENTY-ONE

Crossing back over the border was anything but relaxing. Jensen briefed his nephew to let him do the talking unless the guard specifically spoke to him, in which case, keep it short.

Jensen provided Danny with an 'I Love New York' ballcap and told him to lean back and pretend he was asleep. All he needed was for his nephew to rant about Mexico's fucking prison system.

They made it across without an incident. Danny was fast asleep and wasn't bothered by the border guard. Jensen dreaded the flight from San Diego to New York and was too uptight to fall asleep. He also worried some passengers would stare at his nephew's scars. Danny's reputation for violence had only gotten worse in prison.

Once they arrived at JFK, Jensen relaxed. Danny slouched in the rental car and glanced out the window, watching jets circle above. "Good to be home, Uncle Lee. Can't wait to start a new life."

Right, new. Jensen would appease Danny until he didn't need him anymore.

"Danny, it's important no one knows you're back yet, not even your mother."

"The fuck you talking about?" His expression turned angry, accentuating his scars. "Why the hell not?"

God, those scars were scary. He touched the kid's callused knuckles. "Only temporarily, son." He took a breath. "We have a problem that has to be dealt with, or you might be doing time in the States."

"You're not making sense. I haven't been here—don't tell me."

Jensen nodded. He opened with Hank Reed's investigation. "He needs to be dealt with. Your return was divine intervention, happenstance, serendipitous." He continued pouring it on. "Danny, Boy, I need you."

Danny scowled and tossed the I Love New York cap in the back seat. He folded his arms, and Jensen was concerned his nephew would do something to the car. Or to him. Up ahead, he took the exit and found a McDonald's, where he parked and killed the engine.

"I'm not fucking hungry. I'm pissed."

Help me Golden Arches. "Let's settle down and I'll discuss the plan."

"Plan! I'm gonna kill the bastard."

That was what Jensen wanted to hear, only with less fury. "Relax, Danny. We can't go half-cocked. It would most certainly go badly, and then…" Jensen waited until Danny unfolded his arms. "Listen to me, this can be done, but I need you to calm down and be rational. We'll get through this, I promise. Then you can surprise your mom. I'll find a place for you with a garden, hell maybe on the water. And a job." He touched his nephew's stiff shoulders. "What do you say?"

He waited a click, watching Danny with uncertainty.

He rubbed a facial scar. "Tell me about your plan."

TWENTY-TWO

The pit of my stomach tightened as I dropped the knife back into the box. Luca would never have given away his most precious possession. Not even to Alex. Yet, here it was, sitting in Father Alex Weber's cigar box.

What bothered me was the knife found at the crime scene and locked up as evidence wasn't Luca's. Would it have mattered considering Luca's blood was found on the murder weapon? Maybe not, but the fact that Alex hadn't produced it to the investigators led me to believe Alex was hiding something.

I felt the monsignor's gaze on me and had to make a quick decision. There was no way I would leave without the knife and told him it was vital to my investigation.

He eyed the knife. "Do you think it would help find Alex?"

I hated lying to a priest, but I needed that knife.

"Absolutely."

"Then, by all means, take it."

I wanted to rush out the door, but the monsignor offered coffee and another of Mrs. Haviken's tasty Danish. How could I resist? He also had additional information, so I sat down and waited for him to return with the goodies.

"Be right back," he said after pouring me a cup.

I stared at the cup. I needed to find Alex and demand an explanation.

The monsignor returned with Alex's cell phone and turned it on. No password required. He smiled at the home screen photo and handed it to me. "This was taken last year nearby at the Lower Gorge Falls. A beautiful place."

I studied the photo of my friend who was now in his early forties. He and the monsignor were dressed in plain clothes, just two guys hiking. Like me, Alex had changed over the years. His hair was still brown, though his hairline had begun to recede. There was one thing missing: his glasses.

"He wore thick, coke bottle glasses when I knew him," I said. "The change looks great."

"I must admit," the monsignor said, "it changed Alex's appearance. Soon after he arrived, I asked if he'd like to try contact lenses. He was thrilled. Don't you think it makes him look more youthful?"

"Very." I held the phone up. "Who took the picture?"

"Let's see. Oh, right, a parishioner joined us. A lovely young woman. She and Alex are great friends."

The woman on Alex's computer screensaver?

I removed my pen, but needed a sheet of paper, and asked the monsignor for one. When he left, I began searching for text messages, phone calls, and finally, his contact list.

When the monsignor returned, I said, "The phone calls and text messages should help provide a road map to whom Alex was in touch with before he disappeared."

"Besides you, Hank."

I looked up and smiled. "Right. That helped get me here." I jotted down recent voice messages, which were limited to mine and

Lisa's. There was a local 570-area code, maybe a parishioner. Another from area code 631—Long Island—intrigued me.

The monsignor watched with interest. After I finished, I asked him for the make, model, and plate number of the car Alex was driving.

He anticipated my request and slipped me another sheet of paper.

"Please find him, Hank."

Soon after leaving the rectory, I speed-dialed Tara. The call went to voicemail, and I framed my message, "We need to talk. Important."

Entering I-80, my cell buzzed. It was Bobby wondering if I'd been getting in trouble again. I told him about my trip, the monsignor, and Alex's disappearance.

"Alex is a priest?" He snorted. "You can't be serious. He's the son of an atheist!" He paused. "Actually, it makes perfect sense. He sent his father a fuck you message. And now he's missing twenty-five years after Luca. What the hell, Hank?"

"I know, it's crazy." I mentioned the note Alex wrote and the supposed reunion. "I didn't discover foul play, and the note appeared legitimate. I hate to admit it, Bobby, but Alex probably went AWOL, and it can't be a coincidence he disappeared soon after I called about the investigation."

I paused. "There weren't any traces of his teenage years in his room. No photos on his desk or walls. You'd think he'd have a few fond memories with his Whitestone friends. Nothing. Except...and I hope you're sitting down: I found Luca's knife in Alex's room. Hidden in a cigar box."

"What do you mean, Luca's knife? It's with the —"

"Cold case files? Nope, I have it in my possession, initials and all. Alex has some explaining to do."

"This is very strange, Hank—"

The sound of a call coming in interrupted the conversation. It was Tara. "Bobby, I have to take this. Call you later."

When I switched calls, Tara sounded like she was in a rush. "Hank, your message sounded serious. Does it have to do with Jesse and Lisa?"

"No, something else. I just left a local church in the Poconos where Alex has been living as a priest. I found Luca's knife in his bedroom. Were you aware that Alex is a priest?"

"What? No. And what was he doing with Luca's knife? I hope you asked him."

"I would, except he's missing."

"Missing?"

"Afraid so."

"That's crazy, but I'd like to know how Alex wound up with Luca's knife." She kept ranting about Luca never parting with it and Alex hadn't come forward.

"Tara. I'm as confused as you are, but until I find Alex, we won't know."

That slowed her down. "Yes, of course. You said he's missing."

I tapped on my brakes as the traffic slowed due to police emergency lights ahead. "According to Alex's monsignor, he disappeared in the middle of the night. I'm guessing it had to do with him finding out about my investigation. He claimed he was attending a childhood reunion."

"What reunion?"

"Exactly. I think Alex is running from his past. Maybe Luca's knife has something to do with it."

"Could he have stolen it?" She stopped. "Wait a second. If Alex has Luca's knife, whose knife was found at the crime scene?"

The rest of the day was shot, so before heading back to my office, I called Lisa. School was about to be let out, and I drove toward Flushing High School. She answered on the first ring.

"Your ears must have been burning. I was just thinking about you. We haven't spoken in a while. I'm finishing up, then heading to my mother's house."

"You're not going home?"

"Not today. Mom can use the company. Chuck is fine with it. Give me about ten minutes, and I'll call when I get in the car."

School traffic was always heavy, so I parked a block away and waited. Ten minutes later, I noticed Lisa's white Camry exiting left, away from her mother's house. I let her pass before making a U-turn, then followed her to Northern Boulevard, where she made a right toward Manhattan.

My cell chirped. "Back again. Any news on the investigation?"

Three car lengths behind her, I updated her on my adventures, including the head incident.

"Oh my god, that's terrible. Did you call the police?"

"Not yet," I said, knowing I wouldn't. "I need time to sort things out. I'm expecting calls, so maybe after that." I rattled off more nonsense.

"Okay, if you think that's best," she said with a sigh. "I hoped your investigation wouldn't be dangerous—"

"I'd love to see you," I said. "How about we meet? It's easier to talk in person, and I can be at your mother's house in less than a half hour."

"No, no, not today," she said too quickly. Her car swayed slightly. "How about tomorrow?"

I suppressed a snicker. "Sure, tomorrow's good. Until then." I disconnected and tailed her as she entered the Van Wyck Expressway, then shot across into the HOV lane.

A slew of cars blocked me from entering, and I struggled to keep sight of her. "Come on, dammit." After the last slow-moving vehicle passed, I slid in and picked up speed.

Where are you going?

Lisa was moving quickly, and I struggled to keep up. Fifteen minutes later, jets from JFK Airport flew overhead and distracted me. She was now beyond sight and when I saw a sign for Rockaway Blvd, I signaled. Waste of time.

Swinging around to the western highway entrance, I spotted the Hilton Garden Inn, and a white Camry entering the parking lot. I swung right into the lot, watching for the driver to park and emerge.

When Lisa did, my stomach heaved, and not only for Tara.

Tara's intuition was right: Lisa and Jesse were lovers. I wanted to leave, forget what I'd envisioned, but there was no way to report back to Tara without witnessing the rendezvous. Without hesitation, I parked and hustled between cars to get a better look. My cell camera was ready to shoot, but then Lisa turned my way and smiled. I froze.

Only she wasn't smiling at me. She walked toward Jesse, two cars between us. God, I could inhale her perfume. Or was it my imagination? But then she stopped, and I observed them closing in, his back toward me, followed by indecipherable mumbling and a quick kiss.

Their voices began to fade, and I peered over a vehicle. If I wanted results, I needed to shoot a few frames and dashed between two cars until I was even with them. But the angle was off, and I had only moments before they ducked inside. Lisa took one last look around, perhaps feeling paranoid or guilty.

One more car length away and I peeled off multiple shots. As they entered the hotel, I trudged back to my car, dropped into my seat, and viewed the photos. I felt terribly sad and wished Tara hadn't given me the assignment. I wanted my feelings toward Lisa to remain as they were years ago, but that was no longer possible. The photos were clear, mostly side-shots, but there was something off. Not with the frame. It was Lisa's companion. I remembered Jesse years ago; he didn't have dark hair. His face was round, not like the guy she was with. Lisa wasn't with Jesse.

People change over the years, and after twenty-five, nothing should surprise me. But seeing Lisa and Matt together threw me off. Upset and disappointed, I wondered if Lisa and I were married, would I find her here with Matt or another guy? But I wasn't here for suppositions; I could allay Tara's fears.

You're safe, Tara. At least with Lisa.

The drive to Bobby's place, where I'd spend the night, was filled with disappointment. Thoughts of *them* together didn't help. I tried rationalizing that Lisa wasn't mine, but after seeing her again, I couldn't help imagining she was. Some psychological explanation was required.

I was still obsessing over Lisa and realized I was exceeding the speed limit. I signaled and entered the middle lane. I needed a distraction and called Kyle, hoping he'd be back from the *fields*.

He answered immediately. "Hank, it's been ages." His excitement made me feel a little better.

I said, "Too long. Your message said you were in the fields. We haven't been in touch in years, so I'm at a loss."

He chuckled. "Oh, that. I'm a farmer. Been on Martha's Vineyard for years."

As I recalled, Kyle was the most studious of the group. He told me he returned to farming years after his father realized land values on Long Island were worth more than crops. It must have been in Kyle's blood.

"You mean cows and stuff?" I asked.

He laughed. "Not quite. My wife and I grow organic fruits and vegetables, unlike my father who farmed potatoes. It's a comfortable place, just over 70 acres near West Tisbury. Been here about fifteen years. I can't imagine doing anything else," he enthused.

I was happy for Kyle. He sounded upbeat, and the way he spoke, apparently found his calling.

"Lisa said you'd be in touch, and I'm glad we finally connected. I've been thinking about that night and told the cops everything I knew. That whole incident became a blur, and I hadn't seriously thought about it until she called. Don't get me wrong, I think of Luca all the time..."

"You moved on," I said, not accusatory. "I mean, that's a good thing. Sounds like life is good."

"Very, and I owe it to Sarah, who's put up with me for twenty years. Funny how we met. She was a flight attendant, and I was heading to Boston. We got to talking and had so much in common, particularly planting vegetables. She lived in Quincy, and I asked her out. The rest is history." He stopped. "Don't get me wrong, White-stone was great. I miss the times growing up, but emotionally, I needed to move on."

"I totally get it. We can never go back," I said, with a bit of sadness.

Kyle said, "Did you know Luca and I planted vegetables in my parents' backyard every spring? He loved it. Said he wanted to save enough money to go to agricultural school. Heck, we could have been partners. Tara loved the idea." He paused. "They were great together. I was surprised she married Jesse. Nice guy, but the alcohol..."

I went back to discussing planting. "My godfather, Bobby, told me Luca loved to plant roses, that he'd get excited every spring."

"That, too," Kyle agreed. "Gardening was a side of Luca most people didn't know about." He fell silent, and I could hear a long sigh. "Sorry, I'm getting nostalgic."

I was enjoying our chat, but after exiting the Van Wyck Expressway, I didn't think Kyle could add to my investigation, and was about to end the call, when he said, "Lisa's call got me thinking about that night. I'm not sure if it's worth discussing. It's just a gut feeling."

My ears perked. "Gut feelings are good."

"Please don't take this as an accusation or indictment," he said, his voice hesitating. "But the following day—actually, that day, I started talking to the guys, trying to piece together what happened. We were stunned and afraid for Luca, considering the murder occurred the same night. We thought he might have been killed by the same guy who killed Annie Baxter. But they never found his body.

"At some point that night, Luca left the group, but none of us knew when or why. We started discussing it, like investigators, Matt, Jesse, and me. Alex refused to engage in our theories."

Light rain hit my windshield and I turned on the wipers.

Kyle continued. "He withdrew immediately and left for college without saying a word. He and Luca were as close as the rest of us. Through the grapevine, I heard he'd become a priest. I thought, good for him. He deserved a peaceful and spiritual life."

I mentioned my visit to the parish and Alex's disappearance.

"No way. Just like that? Do you think your investigation set him off into a dark place?"

"Perhaps," I said, not committing.

"Looking back, I recall Matt, Jesse, and I were at the park entrance waiting for Luca and Alex. Luca showed up with a bottle of Vodka and looked tired, not his usual energetic self. And it was his birthday party. Alex showed up a half-hour later, nervous and very quiet. Okay, he was always quiet, but that night, he was extremely pensive like he was holding up the world. That was before the murder and Luca's disappearance," Kyle emphasized. "I had previously offered to pick him up at his house, like I did the others, except Luca. He lived only a few blocks from the park. But Alex wanted to walk and arrived with a six-pack of Bud, looking pale and sweaty. At the time, I chalked it up to the walk."

I suggested, "It could have been he'd been arguing with his father. Alex's home life was in tatters. His parents were constantly fighting."

"Maybe," Kyle said, not convinced. "They were *always* bickering."

"Still—"

"I told you Alex wanted to walk to the park. Except Alex was afraid of the dark. Always had been, even as a kid. He blamed it on not seeing well at night. Which might be true. Then how come he decided to walk to the park *that* night, which was almost a half mile away?"

I didn't have an answer. "Did you ask him?"

"Sure. He said he had a lot on his mind but wouldn't elaborate. I remember him nursing a beer, which was unusual. He could drink a six-pack in no time."

"Maybe he drank the rest after you guys conked out."

"You'd think, except there were five remaining cans in the wrapper the next morning. I'm telling you, Hank, Alex didn't fall asleep. He had to have seen Luca leave. How come he didn't follow him? Or wake us up?" He let a few moments pass. "I think Alex knows something."

My wipers began fighting the heavy rain, and I pulled into a strip mall and parked. I closed my eyes. *Alex, what's going on?*

Kyle continued. "The cops woke us up and scared the shit out of us. I thought we were going to be arrested for, I don't know, having liquor or disorderly conduct."

I asked, "I know this is going back in time, but the police reports claimed you all had similar statements. How come you didn't mention Alex's strange behavior?"

I waited for an answer, but it was slow in coming.

"Hank, you have to understand, there was a lot of confusion at the time, and…to be honest, I didn't want to get anyone in trouble with just an observation. It was bad enough that Luca went missing."

"And now? What do you think of Alex's disappearance?" I said, peering out at Angelo's Pizzeria.

"Maybe I should have said something back then, but I'm not going to beat myself up for not mentioning it. As for Alex, I can't read his mind, but he definitely knows something."

Kyle sighed. "That period was very difficult. I lost a good friend, lost touch with the others, and headed for college. I'd like answers like everyone else, and I think Alex is the key."

I threw Kyle a curve ball and mentioned Luca's knife I found in Alex's cigar box. "What do you make of it?"

"No way would Luca have parted with it. I'm telling you, Hank, you need to find Alex. He might be the only person who can vindicate Luca."

TWENTY-THREE

Jensen finalized instructions with his nephew and begged him not to deviate. He knew Danny's temper, so he impressed upon him that any mistake would be costly, meaning arrest and conviction.

He wasn't about to stick around and babysit. He had others to handle Danny, and the further he was from exposure meant the road wouldn't lead back to him. He also had to deal with his wife, who, despite their non-existent marriage, became argumentative when he returned from a trip. A sore spot that never healed. Especially now that he was retired. A prior client commitment was beyond believable. No question: her husband was meeting a woman.

Jensen grew increasingly anxious that Danny would blow the hit on Hank Reed—

"This is a shit hole," Danny said, interrupting his thoughts. "It's almost as bad as my Mexican prison cell. All I see is a warehouse across the street. Christ, what a sight."

Jensen needed to keep Danny happy. "Don't worry, you'll have your own place with a new car and cash to keep you going until I find you a good job. What's important is to concentrate on the plan. The sooner you eliminate Reed, the sooner you can be driving a… hell, whatever you want." Damn, he was getting as nutty as his nephew.

Danny touched his cheeks. "And plastic surgery."

"That, too." He nodded quickly.

Big scary smirk.

"I'm counting on you, Danny. I have two guys watching out in case you run into trouble. Retired cops who have been on my payroll for years."

Danny eyed him. "Cops?"

"They're clean, don't worry."

Danny laughed. "Clean? You mean dirty."

This conversation was giving Jensen a headache. "You know what I mean. They helped rescue you the last time, so no worries."

Danny dropped to the floor and started pushups. "It helps me think. Too bad they don't have a gym in this place. I guess you can't throw in a membership somewhere."

Jensen scratched his head. Nerves. He wanted to leave and never see his crazy nephew again.

"Okay," Jensen said, getting dizzy watching Danny. "You have the plan, phone numbers, all burners, so you can talk freely to me and the others. And remember, until Reed is dead, you can't call your mother. I know you miss her cooking."

Danny jumped up and stretched. "Mom's ravioli is to die for. Nobody makes Italian like her."

"Which means the sooner you get rid of Reed, the sooner you can eat all the Italian food you want." Jensen peered out the slimy window. It gave him the creeps. He'd have to take a shower once he checked into his four-star hotel. He dared not tell Danny which one.

"There's a McDonald's a few blocks away. They serve breakfast, lunch, and dinner. Just keep your cap on and wear the clothes we bought before. Oh, and you'll need a car, so one will be available in the morning."

"Okay," he said, then gave Jensen an inquisitive look. "You want me to take care of Reed first. You never said nothing about the witness who saw us that night. What about him?"

TWENTY-FOUR

Bobby was on the computer when I arrived. He looked calm, not like the last time when he kept screaming at the monitor.

"I thought I heard the door open." He looked over his shoulder. "That must have been one hell of a drive to the Poconos. You look like crap."

"Thanks, I'll tell you about it over a beer." I walked into the kitchen and grabbed a Bud. Bobby was a Bud guy. "Want one?" I called out.

"Always."

We sat in the living room, me on the sofa holding Alex's cigar box and Bobby on his favorite chair. He nodded at the box. "I'm listening," he said, sipping his beer.

Mine was a gulp. "I told you Alex is missing. Out of the blue according to his monsignor. He left a note, but it was bullshit."

"I hope you didn't use that language with the monsignor." He winked. "Cursing is a venial sin."

"Not in so many words. He's worried, of course, as I am, only for different reasons. Alex disappeared on purpose, I'm sure of it."

"Go on."

I held up the box then placed it back on my lap and opened it, removing the knife. Bobby narrowed his look. "Hank, are you going to keep me in suspense or what?"

"It's Luca's knife."

His forehead creased. "I don't think so. Luca's knife is locked up with the cold case file."

I held his gaze. "That's what I thought." I handed my godfather the knife. "Look for yourself."

He studied it, initials and all. After a beat, he said, "I don't understand. Then whose knife is in the file?"

I shrugged. "It's anyone's guess, but it's not Luca's. The knife in your hand is clean. I'm not saying it was never tainted. It seems the detectives assumed the knife at the crime scene was Luca's and never searched further. Hell, if they had shown Tara the knife they recovered, she would have told them it wasn't Luca's. Mind you, Luca had some explaining to do, but it now sheds light that Alex held it for a reason."

"And now *he's* missing," Bobby added.

I leaned back and mentioned Kyle's theory. "Alex acted strange, hardly drank, and was awake but didn't notice Luca missing. And afterward, refused to discuss the murder or Luca's disappearance. What's Alex holding back?"

Bobby inspected the knife again, his fingers sliding over the initials.

"Luca had it the day of the party," I said. "That's when he carved his initials inside the heart behind the bench outside Fort Totten. Sometime between Luca's returning from the fort until he went missing, Alex obtained it."

"Hank, are you suggesting foul play?"

"With Alex, no. There weren't any signs of an abduction. I believe he left on his own."

Bobby handed back the knife, and I placed it in the box. "I want you to hold on to it for a while. I don't trust my office or house anymore."

He nodded.

Darkness had set in, and I looked out at the park, its lights illuminating and capturing a peaceful image. But then, my brain teased with another one: Matt and Lisa.

"On a lighter note," I said turning to Bobby. "Kyle's a farmer on Martha's Vineyard, been married over twenty years. He said Luca would have loved farming, and they could have been partners."

Bobby smiled wistfully. "Good for him. According to Luca, Kyle was the most focused in the group."

I mentioned how Kyle met his wife. "As I recall, you dated a flight attendant years ago. Carla or someone. You never told me what happened. You guys seemed serious. At least, that's what my father told me."

My loquacious godfather was suddenly lost for words.

"Don't tell me you don't remember. She was very attractive. You talked about her all the time."

Bobby cleared his throat. "Carlota."

"That's it. What ever happened?"

He held back a moment and rubbed his moist eyes. "She died."

"Oh, I'm sorry, I didn't know. She was young and—"

"A car accident in Lisbon. I don't want to talk about it, okay?"

"Sure, I understand."

Bobby stood and trudged into the kitchen. I obviously hit a nerve despite their relationship being years ago.

———

Around nine, Bobby bid me good night, which even for him, was early. I sat at his desk with another Bud and studied the information from Alex's phone. I Googled the FINDPERSON site for the 570-area code in Tannersville. A woman named Emily Swift popped up. There'd been several calls back and forth days before Alex vanished.

I assumed she was a parishioner and held off calling. The second number, a 631-area code, was the same as mine on Long Island. To my surprise, it belonged to Jesse O'Neil, Tara's husband.

They lived in Smithtown, so it made sense. What struck me was Tara never told me Jesse and Alex had kept in touch. And judging from four calls within the last week, I'd say, they definitely reconnected at some point.

I texted Tara and asked if she could talk.

She shot back immediately and texted:

> Perfect, all alone.

When she answered, I said, "Did you know Jesse and Alex had been in contact recently? There were several calls made between them, the last, the night Alex disappeared."

She hesitated. "Gee, Hank, Jesse hasn't brought up Alex's name in years. I'd be surprised. It's not like they were that close anyway. Are you sure you have the right number?"

I recited it.

"That's Jesse's, all right. You said the last call was made the night Alex disappeared. I'm shocked. Honestly, I had no idea. They were friends, but Alex was closer to Luca than Jesse." She paused. "Jesse wasn't as close to the guys on account of his drinking." She sighed. "I guess I should have realized…sorry, I didn't mean that."

Maybe she did, but I wasn't about to judge her. "From his phone log, Alex initiated the call. After that, it went back and forth. When do you expect him home?"

"Not for a while. He's at a pharma conference in Estes Park, Colorado."

"When did he leave?" I asked like an interrogator.

"Yesterday. You're scaring me."

"I need to get in touch with him. There may be a connection between him and Alex's disappearance."

When Tara didn't respond, I said, "It's important, Tara. If I can't reach him, or if he calls you instead, get back to me. And, please, don't mention Alex."

"Okay. What about the other thing, Hank? Have you made any progress?"

"Just recently. Jesse and Lisa aren't having an affair."

———

Colorado was on Mountain Standard time, two hours earlier than New York. When I texted Jesse, it was 7:30 P.M. his time.

> We need to talk.

A few minutes later...

> Busy right now. Later.

> When later???

> Don't know. Very busy!

Unlike a phone call, where one can detect an inflection or tone in a person's voice, a text was tone-deaf, so I couldn't get a read on Jesse. How busy was *very*? Tara told me he was drinking less. Maybe he was irritable from *not* drinking. Or maybe he was just avoiding me.

I texted Tara.

> Says he's busy. Where is he staying?

> Lake Estes Hotel and Conference Center.

She added a phone number.

I called the hotel and asked to be transferred to Jesse O'Neil's room. It eventually kicked into voicemail, but I didn't leave a message. At least I knew Jesse hadn't lied about his location.

Waiting for him to call back, I fell asleep on the sofa and slept through the night. At seven the next morning, I checked my phone. No Jesse. Screw him, it was 5:00 A.M. his time, so I called and left a terse message: "I know what's going on. Call me."

It was too early to stop by Fillmore's and confront Conor, so I headed to the park. Early morning joggers and dog walkers were already active. I headed to the river, where black-eyed Susans, dahlias, and lavender shared the park.

My eyes swept the shoreline, stopping at a lone fisherman casting a line about twenty feet from me. He didn't appear to be a serious fisherman, just a guy in blue jeans, a gray sweatshirt, and a plain black ballcap, relaxing like he hadn't a care in the world. Lucky him. While waiting for a tug on his line, he glanced my way and nodded. I nodded back.

He brought in his line that had accumulated seaweed, which he picked from the hook before baiting and casting it again. He looked over and shrugged as though there was always a next time.

I approached and followed his gaze, which remained on the line, waiting for the next pull.

His bucket was empty, but I asked, "Any luck?"

He kept looking at the line. "Nah, I don't expect much. I'd be lucky to pull in a gizzard shad, but you can't eat those, so whatever I'm lucky to get, I'll toss back." He turned to me. "You fish?"

"Only as a kid. My father owned a Boston Whaler on Long Island. He'd take me on the sound, and we'd fish all day. I never really got into it. You certainly look peaceful. You fish a lot?"

He pulled the line in lightly and nodded. "Now that I'm semi-retired, I come here more often. I used to fish all the time as a teenager." He nodded at the concrete base wall holding up the bridge about two hundred feet away. "Can't fish over there on account of the fence and gate. A security thing after 9/11. A shame. I used to fish on the other side."

I peered over. "The Malba side? Makes sense, it's quieter. Not as many kids horsing around." I paused and smiled. "I'm afraid I was one of those kids back in the day."

His look was warm and friendly. "That's what teens did back then. That, and hang out at the park. Some of my friends would make out with their girlfriends behind the bridge. They still call it that?"

"Making out? Sure." He didn't mention he had. "I used to make out there too, back in the nineties," I said, remembering Lisa and me messing around.

"Then you must be from around here, son."

"Hank. I grew up in Eastpoint, but my godfather, Bobby Larkin, lives down the block. I'd stay with him in the summer."

"I know Bobby. Nice guy. My name's Charlie by the way. I grew up in Whitestone, a few blocks from your godfather, only we had a different circle of friends. I was into sports, and Bobby was into girls." He chuckled softly.

"Still is," I said, and we shared a laugh.

"Whitestone was a great place to live. Nothing ever happened here."

That was what Bobby said until it did.

I asked, "Were you around in the mid-nineties when a young woman was murdered on the backside of the bridge near the park?"

Charlie nodded with a sigh. "A tragedy. I say a prayer for that woman every day. And for her killer. They never caught the guy, I understand. People assume he's dead."

"They accused the wrong person," I said defensively. "His name was Luca Falcone, and he was my friend. He'd never hurt anyone. I'm convinced he was set up."

Charlie jerked his line. "Oh, I hadn't heard that. If you're right, do you know if the police are actively involved anymore?"

"They're not, but I am."

Charlie turned to me. "Are you a police officer?"

"Used to be. I'm a private investigator. Luca's family asked for my help finding the real killer. It certainly would be a great relief to them if I do."

"I wish you the best, Hank. Especially since it's personal." He pulled on the line and shrugged.

My eyes drifted to the Malba side of the bridge.

"You weren't fishing here that night, were you, Charlie?"

He jerked the line a little hard. "Me, no, I wasn't," he said quickly. He then checked his watch. "Guess I better get going." He reeled in the line.

He gathered his gear and looked nervous, unlike when I arrived, and my heart quickened. "Maybe you know someone who was here that night. Maybe not fishing."

He looked away. "I really must go."

I picked up his fishing chair and held it out for him. Our eyes met, but he quickly averted his.

"Charlie, if you know something, please tell me. The family is begging for closure. Luca's mother is up in age and frail. She needs to know the truth," I pressed.

He took a long breath, placed the mesh chair back on the sand, and sat. He stared at the river. "I wasn't here. I don't fish at night."

I examined his face. "But you *know* someone who was here that night." Not a question.

Charlie winced. His body language begged me to stop questioning him.

Kneeling in front of the old man, I said, "Whatever you know might help my investigation. Please."

Charlie closed his eyes and mumbled as though in prayer, then reopened them slowly.

"My brother was there."

TWENTY-FIVE

Jensen jerked his head. "What witness?"

Danny waited a beat. "He was hiding in the bushes about thirty feet away. I couldn't get a good look, but he must have figured I saw him and took off. He probably saw you too."

Jensen slumped on the bed, his ass hitting the springs. "Christ, how come you didn't mention it at the time?"

"Seriously? We had to get the hell out of there."

Jensen scratched his head. "I don't know, Danny. The witness would have come forward at the time. I think maybe you thought you saw someone—"

"I know what I saw." He spit. "He might have been with that group partying by the bridge. It wasn't Luca. He was there, but...you know the story. If the witness knows about Reed's investigation, he might find the balls to come forward. That means he's gotta be taken care of."

Jensen took a breath and shifted his butt off the springs. "If there was a witness, he would have gone to the cops. The only eyewitnesses reported seeing someone resembling Luca walking to Fort Totten. The detectives never pursued it." He shook his head. "I'm not wasting time going after a ghost. If he suddenly decides to blab, we'll deal with him. Right now, it's Reed we want and only Reed. Got it?"

Danny mumbled.

Jensen stood and massaged his ass. "If this so-called witness knows about Reed's investigation, he might contact him. Again, that's not likely, or Reed would have done something about it already."

"Like what?"

Jensen hated all the questions. "Look, if this witness suddenly shows up at the precinct, the cops are gonna be pissed off that he hadn't come sooner and figure he's just blowing smoke up their asses. We need to stay focused on Reed."

He touched his nephew's shoulder. "Let it go, Danny." He glanced around. "The sooner you're finished, the sooner you're out of here."

"Whatever."

Jensen thought about Reed's recent interviews. According to his fixer, Jimmy Savage, he went to Fort Totten. And Fillmore's. What would Reed hope to gain going there? The bartender and his son had air-tight alibis. And, as for the fort, there's nothing to find.

Jensen scratched his head. Something shifted in his brain. Someone was doing crazy shit to Reed, like breaking into his office. Maybe it was the witness afraid Reed would continue investigating and find him. If he thought Reed would be intimidated by the witness's shenanigans, fat chance.

Jensen peered over at Danny whose eyes narrowed on him. He was one terrifying bastard. To humor him, and only if he promised not to do anything rash until after he finished Reed, he would tell him who he *thought* the witness was. But by then, Savage and his partner would have other plans for Danny Caruso.

TWENTY-SIX

Lisa's name popped up on my cell. She'd have to wait. I glanced back at Charlie, his head slumped in his hands.

"Your brother? Fishing here at the bridge?"

He nodded. "He was alone."

The report hadn't mentioned detectives interviewing a fisherman or anyone other than Luca's friends near the bridge. "What's his name?"

"It was Ralphie. He passed away a month ago." Charlie tightened his watery eyes.

The name Ralphie never showed up anywhere in the file, and I asked, "What's your last name, Charlie?"

"McGowan."

Ralphie McGowan didn't ring a bell. "What did Ralphie see that night?"

He wiped a tear, then another. "The teenagers."

I waited for him to continue. "It was fairly dark, and my brother was about a hundred feet away from them."

I looked beyond where Luca and his friends had been partying. "The Malba side," I said.

He glanced at the bridge and nodded. "Ralphie told me they were having a great time celebrating something special. He didn't want to get too close but noticed there were five of them, all boys. They were whooping it up, drinking, singing, just having fun. Sounded like a birthday party, which I later found out in the papers was for the missing boy."

"Luca," I added.

He nodded. "My brother was like me. He didn't care if he caught anything. He just enjoyed the serenity of being outdoors near the water. But as the party continued, the noise got to him, and he thought about packing it up. Still, he waited, and not long after, the boys grew quieter and conked out. He guessed it was around midnight."

He took a breath. "Soon after, one of the boys headed toward the wooded area." He pointed to the crime scene. "He figured the kid had to relieve himself. But then he heard voices, and Ralphie figured they were arguing."

"They?"

"Not the group of friends. They were sleeping. Someone else. Ralphie was reluctant to get involved, but when the other boys didn't stir, he slipped past them toward the confrontation. He wanted to get close, not too close, and stopped when he noticed one of them holding a knife."

Charlie paused a long moment. "The kid without the knife put his hands up in self-defense, and the other one jabbed him in one hand. Not hard, maybe just to frighten him."

My eyes shifted to the crime scene area. "Then what happened?"

Charlie shook his head. "Sounds crazy, but the aggressor handed the knife to the other teen like he wanted the kid to cut him back. Instead, he tossed it in the bushes and took off." Charlie shrugged. "What can I say?"

I peered out at the river. That made no sense. Two teens, one *not* a Whitestone boy. And then it dawned on me. Blood brothers. Each of the Whitestone boys had drawn blood the prior summer. A common ritual among teens. Conor wanted to join the group but was repeatedly shunned. Had Conor nicked Luca, begging him to become a blood brother?

I blinked as a boat sped by, a passenger waving at the shore. I wasn't friendly enough to wave back.

"Was your brother able to describe the two guys?"

He thought for a moment. "Both were white, one taller than the other, but he wasn't close enough to see their faces. Ralphie did say the one originally holding the knife was sort of chubby.

"Chubby?" None of the Whitestone boys were chubby back then, but Conor was. His father never cooked, so they resorted to fast food. I envisioned Conor picking a fight with Luca for not letting him join their group. Which meant he knew they were having a party and wasn't invited. That would have pissed him off.

Charlie stared out at the river. I didn't know if he was relieved to reveal what he'd learned from his brother or just exhausted.

"I'm guessing Ralphie didn't want to intervene. Otherwise, there might have been a different outcome."

He turned to me. "It happened so quick, Ralphie didn't have to," he defended.

Right. "So, what did your brother do after that? Go back to fishing?" I asked sarcastically.

Charlie put up a hand. "Hank, it wasn't like that. The aggressor ran out of the park, so my brother decided to follow the other teen to make sure he was okay. But he first had to run back and hide his fishing gear."

"And this all happened around midnight. Was your brother sure of the time?"

Charlie needed a moment. "Thereabouts. He wasn't concentrating on the time, only that the boy was okay."

I pedaled back and nodded. "Fair enough."

"My brother followed him to the park."

I creased my forehead. "If it was Luca, he was already in the park."

"Sorry, not Francis Lewis Park, the Little Bay Park near Fort Totten."

Both eyewitnesses in the file recalled a teen heading toward Fort Totten but hadn't mentioned anyone tailing him.

"At that point, the boy—should I call him Luca?"

"That was his name."

He nodded. "Once Luca reached the park, he continued to the fort. It was dark, and he tried getting his bearings. Ralphie had the same problem, but there was enough light for him to follow Luca."

"Did they reach the fort?" I asked, pushing the story faster.

"Close enough. Luca appeared nervous and kept moving around until he found a bench and sat. My brother said it was as if...Luca picked a certain bench." Charlie shrugged.

The bench with the heart inscribed.

I asked if his brother noticed Luca checking the back of the bench.

"The back? Ralphie didn't say. But he did notice Luca looking around like he was expecting someone."

The jarring sound of a horn blasted, and my eyes shot to a tugboat pushing a barge.

"Those horns spoil the serenity of the place," Charlie said.

"I agree," I said, and we shared a nervous laugh.

"You said Luca might have been expecting company. Did anyone show up?"

Charlie nodded nervously. "Ralphie remembered car headlights driving in from the street outside the park." He stopped, took a breath. "Hank, this is the first I'm telling anyone what Ralphie saw that night."

"I understand. Please, go on."

"Luca leaped off the bench and freaked out. He began pacing like he might have to run. The car spooked my brother. Not waiting around, Ralphie high-tailed it back to the Whitestone Bridge, grabbed his fishing gear, and ran home."

I shook my head in disgust. "And that was the end of the story for Ralphie until he told you recently? Why the hell didn't your brother go to the police? The guy who confronted Luca was probably Annie Baxter's killer. He could have, at a minimum, told the cops what he'd seen. The real killer is probably still out there somewhere. Who knows if he killed again?" I pointed at Charlie's chest. "That's on your brother."

Charlie looked down, then struggled to face me. "Hank, it's not like he didn't care: Ralphie was a felon and afraid to get involved."

"That's bullshit!" My head swirled, and I wished his brother was standing in front of me.

Charlie put up a hand as a peace gesture. "Let me explain. Ralphie was caught for armed robbery when he was a teenager and paid for his crime. He swore he'd never get involved with the police, no matter how small."

"Murder isn't small."

"You know what I mean. Ralphie wanted to help. He called the precinct the following day. Two times, from different pay phones, but was afraid to leave his name."

"That was him?"

Charlie nodded. "It's what he told me, and I believed him. I don't know if the police ever followed up."

"Apparently they didn't."

"Oh." He waited a few moments. "Maybe it's not too late. I sent a letter to the family a few weeks ago. I attempted to right a wrong."

I flinched. "That was you?"

He nodded rapidly. "It was Ralphie's last wish. He begged me to get in touch with them. I wanted to, so help me, I did. I prayed to do the right thing, whether it might hurt them after all these years, I didn't know." He paused. "I told you I pray for the victim and her family daily. And for Luca. I sent a letter to his sister. I didn't know if she still lived there, but figured someone in the family would receive it." He stopped. "I tried, Hank."

Charlie's expression asked for forgiveness, but I wasn't ready. "You're about twenty-five years too late." I glared. "What about you, Charlie, what's your excuse for not going to the police instead of sending an anonymous letter? Are you a felon, too?"

He attempted a soft smile. "I'm a priest. My brother confessed to me on his deathbed a month ago. After giving Ralphie the Last Rites, I had to make a decision whether to contact the family. I knew it would cloud Ralphie's past, and I wanted to protect him. He was a good person despite the trouble he'd gotten into. We all have flaws, Hank, and maybe sending a short letter without explaining the full story, was mine."

I eased up on Father Charlie McGowan and nodded. He told me he believed today's meeting was divine intervention and was grateful we met.

He wiped his forehead. "If you want, I'll go to the authorities and tell Ralphie's story." He pressed his lips.

I thought about his suggestion. "Right now, I want you to write down everything you told me. We'll go from there."

"Yes, of course. And, Hank, for the record, my brother didn't think Luca was responsible for the woman's murder. I know it's too late, but…"

We were drained, but I was anxious to get on with the investigation and dug in my pocket for a business card. "When you finish writing our conversation, please give me a call."

He peered at the card and nodded. "I promise."

"Do you have one?" I asked innocently.

"A business card?" He smiled softly. "No, but you can reach me at Saint Mel's unless I'm out here fishing. It soothes the soul."

Father Charlie left, and I remained sitting and peering out at the East River, thinking about our conversation. I was now convinced Luca wasn't meeting a friend that night.

I attempted to connect Annie Baxter's murder investigation by the 109th precinct with Luca disappearing in the 111th. Why hadn't the detectives followed up, at a minimum, made contact with their neighboring precinct? Was there a disconnect between precincts? Or worse?

I returned to Bobby's house and found him sitting on the sofa playing with his iPad. When he saw me, he drew a wide smile.

"Hank, my boy, you left early. I was up at seven and checked in on you. I was hoping you weren't on another mission."

"As a matter of fact." I stopped. "Do you remember Father Charlie McGowan from St. Mel's?"

He put aside his iPad and nodded. "Sure, but I didn't realize you attended mass. Or, was it confession?" He chuckled. "Seriously, why the question?"

"Hold on." I hurried into the kitchen, poured a cup of coffee. When I returned, he grinned and asked, "I'm guessing you met him somewhere. Was it some kind of divine intervention?"

"That's what he said." I mentioned the unexpected meeting and my godfather's expression changed from amusement to serious. He put up a hand. "Hank, slow down already. My mind doesn't compute that quickly anymore."

"Sorry, I'm excited." I brought it down a notch and waited for his reaction.

"Damn, Luca was innocent. I mean, I knew it all along, but this…this is big news. And Father Charlie will attest to his brother's account that night?"

I nodded. "He said he would. He remembers you from your youth. Said you were in different social circles."

Bobby smiled. "Oh, yeah. We were a bit rowdy. Charlie's a good guy. You said he's still at St. Mel's?"

"Unless he's out fishing. He's semi-retired."

"I knew his brother, Ralphie. Got himself into trouble hanging out with a bad crowd. I remember when he got arrested, he didn't resist arrest, did his time, and returned home to his parents. I lost track after that."

"He pretty much kept to himself, never married. His life revolved around fishing. That's why he didn't want to get involved that night. In some way, I get it."

Bobby thought otherwise and scowled. "As far as I'm concerned, he had an obligation to come forward." He shook his head. "I can use a cup of Java. I'll offer you another if you promise to slow down the conversation."

I laughed. "Promise." I handed Bobby my white mug with black lettering that read 'Old and Sexy.' "I think this was meant for you old man."

He grabbed it. "Smart ass."

He returned with our coffees. "What are you going to do?"

Bobby was probably testing me. He knew I was beginning to have doubts about the original investigation. I took a sip, then another. "Not sure. But I wanna follow up before I take it to the locals."

Bobby nodded. "I understand. Look, if you're concerned about cops not doing their job, well, the detectives on the original case are long retired."

I nodded. "Just the same, a confession by a deceased probably won't mean much. Especially given the time factor. And who knows if or when they'd reopen it?"

Bobby mulled over my comments, laid his cup on a table, and sighed. "I'm with you either way, Hank, you know that. I want you to catch the bastard for both of us."

My cell pinged.

"The police located Father Alex's car!" Monsignor Valencia was pumped, and I had to hold back the phone.

"Where?"

"Newark Airport of all places. He didn't leave a note and, so far, the police haven't figured out where he was going. The keys were left under the driver's seat."

Still excited, he continued. "Hank, I don't know if that's good news or bad, but at least I know he wasn't in an accident."

Newark was an international airport in New Jersey. "Does Alex have a passport?"

"A passport? You think he might have left the country?"

I shrugged. "I'm trying to eliminate possibilities."

"Oh." He thought for a moment. "A few years ago, Alex and I were invited to Rome, so, yes, we have passports. You don't think—"

"I don't recall seeing one in his room. Can you check? If it's there, we can eliminate an international destination."

"Yes, of course. Hold on."

His breathing became labored, and I assumed he was climbing to the second floor. "I'm entering his room now," he called, out of breath. "I remember Alex keeping important papers in a small portable travel case under his bed. I'm surprised you didn't see it when you were here."

"I don't remember seeing it."

"The box is gone." He muttered something like he was getting too old to kneel. "Not good," he said. "Oh, Alex, what is going on with you?"

"Monsignor, is there a place the priests keep valuables? A safe perhaps. Maybe—"

"Yes, yes, of course. Mrs. Haviken had an old safe in her house and donated it to the church. It's in the study closet. Not that we needed one," he continued. "She was very kind, and...sorry, I'm nervous again."

"Take your time, Monsignor."

A few minutes later, I heard him mumbling numbers and assumed they were those of the safe. "I should have paid attention when she gave us the combination." Then, "Ah, good, that's it."

A moment later, he called out, "Found it, Hank. He didn't leave the country!"

That was good news, but Alex was still missing. I thanked the monsignor and was about to end the call when I recalled Emily Swift's name from Alex's phone log and mentioned her.

"Emily? She's a parishioner and a close friend of Father Alex. You'd think they've known each other forever. Not in a romantic way, of course. Why do you ask?"

I told him about Alex's phone log. "Apparently, they'd been in contact within days of his disappearance. I don't know whether the exchange of calls was relevant to Alex's disappearance, but I think it would be helpful to talk to her. I hesitate to call without your permission or advice, considering the sensitivity and trust between a priest and parishioner."

"Yes, of course. I understand completely and thank you for respecting protocol. How about I call Emily and ask if she has concerns about discussing Alex with you? Quite honestly, given the gravity of the situation, I think she'd be open to it. One of us will get back to you."

According to Tara, Jesse left for Colorado, and I wondered whether Alex did as well. A coincidence? I tried Jesse again and left another message. I wanted him to know I wouldn't stop calling until he returned mine.

While waiting for Jesse, an incoming call crossed my screen, the same 570-area code number Alex had in his log: Emily Swift.

She introduced herself and said she had told Monsignor Valencia she'd be open to discussing Alex with me. To a limit.

"I'm not sure I can help, but I'll do my best to answer your questions," she said, her tone friendly. "For the record, I honestly don't know where Alex is, and, like the monsignor, I'm terribly worried about him."

She referred to him as Alex, not Father Alex. "And please, call me Emily."

"Thank you, and I go by Hank." I took her into my confidence to an extent.

"When a mutual friend called Alex about my investigation, it might have sent him into a dark place. I'm interested in his state of mind when you last spoke with him. Can you tell me what the conversation was about?"

Emily's voice faltered as she began. She'd known Alex for several years and was quick to point out she was studying for her doctorate in psychology and that Alex was *not* a client.

"That said, I have boundaries as a friend and must weigh those with what you ask me. I hope you understand that while I'm able to talk freely, my input may not be all-inclusive."

"Fair enough."

"And one other thing. What we discuss today mustn't be shared with anyone, including Monsignor Valencia."

"I understand," I said.

After a moment, she started. "Alex has had a history of depression but held it together through prayer. He told me he became a priest to help others but also to help himself. I mention this because the last few times we spoke, Alex wasn't himself. My take was it had to do with your call. We never discussed Luca's disappearance, and Alex admitted that since that night, his life has changed forever." She paused. "Actually, he said, it began before that night."

Before that night?

That threw me off.

"After your call, Alex freaked out. He said it was starting over

153

again: the guilt, the nightmares, and begged me to meet him." She stopped, drew in a long sigh.

"We met at a popular trailhead here in the Poconos. Alex loves hiking and says it calms him. When I arrived, he looked terrible, and was perspiring profusely. He looked like he'd aged overnight, and I was frightened he might have a heart attack. He thanked me for coming, and we started walking immediately. I waited until he was ready to confide in me, which was about ten minutes later."

I asked, "You mentioned guilt. What sort of guilt?"

She delayed her answer. "He wouldn't say, and I didn't press. I know when to hold off asking too much at once, so I waited until he was ready. But the little he admitted had to do with events leading up to that night."

"The night of Luca's party," I confirmed.

"And before that night, yes. If you ask me, whatever Alex felt guilty of, he's been holding it in all this time."

Emily mentioned 'before that night' again, and I asked if she would elaborate.

"Alex wouldn't discuss it."

I waited for Emily to continue. "I'd be guessing, but it's possible Alex witnessed the murder. That would certainly haunt him, especially if he didn't go to the authorities. My guess, again, is that Alex wouldn't have gone to the police for a reason. I have no idea what the reason might have been. Does that make sense, Hank?"

I thought a moment. What concerned me was Alex's reason for not coming forward, if, in fact, he knew something. Given that, I could never accept Alex knowing that Luca's life was on the line and ignored it. I said, "Luca was the only person of interest, and from there, he became the only suspect. He and Alex were close friends. I'm having difficulty accepting Alex's refusal to help him under any circumstance. Sorry, Emily, but that's how I see it."

Emily hesitated. "Not to play devil's advocate, but what if Alex saw Luca kill the woman, would you expect him to come forward?"

I remained silent. *What if?*

"Sorry if I threw in a wrench, but—"

"No, there have been many theories bantered about. Just not that one. At least, among us friends."

Did Emily know something she couldn't repeat? She was both a parishioner and Alex's friend. Emily claimed she wasn't Alex's therapist, and I wondered how close their relationship was.

"You said Alex loves to hike, that it calms him. Did he ever mention his favorite hiking trail?"

"Favorite? He has many here in the Poconos."

"In another state, perhaps."

She thought a moment. "Alex told me he once took a trip to the Colorado Rockies. He said the beauty of the mountains made him feel whole, if only temporarily. He felt at ease and wished he could spend more time in the area. In fact, Alex told me that one day he might retire there."

The Jesse–Alex connection became clearer: they were meeting in the Rockies. I got tired of waiting for Jesse and called The Estes Park Hotel and Conference Center, where he was staying. I asked to be transferred to Alex Weber's room, but no one under that name was registered. I then asked about the conference Jesse O'Neil was attending.

There wasn't one. Frustrated, I texted Jesse my own lie. At least he wasn't a priest.

A breakthrough on Luca's disappearance.

Jesse called back twenty minutes later and out of breath.

"Hank, I know you're pissed, but it's been crazy here—"

"There is no conference! Put Alex on the phone."

155

"Alex? What are you talking about? I'm—"

"Christ, Jesse, I know Alex flew out to meet you." Another lie.

"Believe me, Hank, I don't know where he is."

"You said you don't know where Alex is. Why didn't you say, I assumed he was at his parish church? You know he's a priest."

He remained silent

"His monsignor is worried about him. I know he's been holding back on Luca's disappearance. My call set him off and I need to know why. I haven't spoken to you in twenty-five years, but we were friends. Do you want to find the truth about Luca's disappearance? Put Alex on the phone. Now."

"I can't."

"Can't or won't. Which is it, Jesse?"

"Let me explain. Alex took me by surprise when he called a few days ago out of the blue. He said he needed my help. Why me? I'm a broken-down drunk. I hadn't seen him since we left Whitestone, but he sounded desperate. Truthfully, I had no idea what he was concerned about, but he said he was flying to the Rocky Mountains."

"And just like that, you flew to Denver to talk. Come on, Jesse. That's a stretch."

"I know how it sounds, Hank, and I wasn't going to, but I was afraid he might hurt himself." He paused. "The truth is Alex and I had a special relationship back when we were kids. Nobody knew it. We'd spend hours talking about our screwed-up families. We were embarrassed but found comfort in each other. Maybe that's why he called me. So, yes, I flew out. I know what desperation feels like. I lied to Tara about the conference. That's the truth."

"So where is he?"

Jesse hesitated. "I'm not exactly sure. After we met at my hotel, Alex wanted to hike the Deer Mountain trail. He said he was familiar with it and found it peaceful and comforting. He looked terrible and was a nervous wreck. He felt guilty lying to his monsignor, and that alone concerned him.

"He appeared distracted, so I started making small talk telling him he looked the same, maybe a little older, and glad he got rid of his glasses. It wasn't until we reached the trailhead that he opened up."

"What's so special about those mountains?" I asked. "Other than finding them peaceful and comforting?"

"That was the first thing I asked him. He claimed he'd visited the Rockies years ago on a retreat. He felt safe there, so when we reached the trailhead, he started spilling his guts, telling me stuff I hadn't known. Hell, none of us had. After a few hours, he thanked me for being a good friend and for meeting him. He said he felt the weight of these years beginning to melt away, and that if anything ever happened to him, I should tell you what he told me."

"Happened to him! Please don't tell me you left him alone. You did, didn't you?"

I heard a hard swallow. "He appeared okay when I left him. He said he wanted to stay longer, so I gave him space. Maybe I should—"

"Get back up there, and don't hang up until you find him."

"I would except my phone is running out of juice. I'll call you when I find him, I swear," he promised and disconnected.

Bobby had gone out for a walk, so I had the place to myself. I trudged to the kitchen and poured a glass of water, downed it, then poured another. I prayed Jesse was fit to climb the trail again and quickly. I Googled Deer Mountain trail, which was popular among visitors, so maybe there were too many people on the trail for Alex to do anything rash. The summit stood at 10,000 feet; the climb was around three miles one way.

My guess was Alex had already reached the summit. What would he do next, sit on a boulder and pray? Or?

I called Jesse and he sounded out of breath.

"Does Alex have a burner phone?"

"Burner? I don't know. He has a phone."

"He left his back at the rectory, so give me the number he called you on? Can you do it without stopping?"

"Shit, Hank, I'm not thirty anymore. Hold on."

He repeated the number twice and I entered it into my phone. "Okay, where are you?"

"How the fuck do I know? I passed where I left him, that's all I can tell you. There's an overlook I remember seeing."

"Don't stop."

"Hank, just in case something goes wrong, Alex told me he saw Conor running just below the crime scene. He thinks Conor killed the woman. He wouldn't elaborate, but I don't believe that's the only thing Alex has been holding back."

Jesse disconnected again leaving me unsettled. I was right and wrong, but I needed Alex to elaborate, and called him. I wasn't surprised when he didn't answer, so I called Emily.

"Alex is probably using a burner phone, but maybe if he sees your number come in, he'll pick up. I desperately need to talk to him. I'm texting his number. You're my only chance of reaching him at this point. And please call me either way."

I couldn't remember how many times I paced back and forth on Bobby's living room black and white rug, waiting. Then Emily called, sounding desperate.

"Alex answered the phone! He thanked me for calling and told me he loved me and was grateful for our talks. I begged him to return to the hotel so we could continue our wonderful chats. I told him I needed him and asked him not to do anything impulsive." Then she cried. "Hank, Alex wouldn't say anything. I'm so frightened."

I stood frozen and swallowed hard. "Is there anything you can tell Alex that might make him change his mind about what I'm afraid he'll do?"

"I really don't know, but I'll try again," she said, and disconnected.

I called Jesse.

"You're killing me. I'm almost at the summit. There are hikers all over the place, but I don't see Alex."

"If you find him, use force if necessary. We want him back alive."

"I can hardly breathe."

I disconnected and called the monsignor. "We know where Alex is. Our friend is climbing the trail to get him down."

"Climbing?"

"Alex is on a hiking trail in the Rocky Mountains. Apparently, he wanted to go back and pray." I couldn't think of another explanation.

"I don't understand—"

I did but wouldn't elaborate. "I know, it's strange, especially him not telling you where he was going. My hope is he'll reach the summit, look around, say a few prayers, and return."

"I need to talk to him, Hank."

"We can't get through." *God, I'm going to hell!*

My cell buzzed. "I have to take this."

"Hank, I'm at the summit, but I still don't see him. I've looked everywhere." His breathing sounded worse, and I hoped Jesse wouldn't succumb to a heart attack. Ten thousand feet above sea level can be brutal on an aging body.

"Hold on."

The monsignor had previously texted a photo of Alex. I gazed at the forty-five-year-old, who was in jeans and a T-shirt, obviously not dressed for mass. "I'm sending you a photo. Ask around, see if anyone has seen him." This was getting crazier by the minute.

"I told you my phone is running out of juice. Okay, hold on, I hear the ping."

A moment later. "Okay, good picture. I'll ask around. I gotta hang up before I'm completely out of power."

"Call me as soon as you see him," I said, but Jesse had already disconnected.

Back to the monsignor, I asked, "Do you have a particular saint you pray to?"

He thought for a moment. "Saint Cajetan for good luck." He murmured in prayer.

Come on Saint Cajetan!

TWENTY-SEVEN

Waiting for Jesse, I headed back to my office. Mail had probably piled up and after the break-in, I wondered if I was in store for more threats.

Arriving, the exterior looked safe. Out of the corner of my eye, I noticed the roofer tenant emerging from his pick-up truck. He appeared in his early thirties with a heavy brown beard that was dotted with roof debris. His AC/DC T-shirt was caked with God knows what.

He glanced my way, waved, and walked over. "You the P.I.?"

"Right. Hank Reed."

"I'm Mickey. Sorry I didn't get back, but I've been busy as hell. Everyone's got leaks. Don't get me wrong, it's great for business. Anyway, I wish I could help, but I didn't notice anyone near your office the day you asked about." He paused. "I did see someone the day before though. Some guy got out of his SUV and peeked inside your office window." He pointed. "I didn't think much of it at the time. I figured he was a client."

"The day before," I said. "Do you recall the time?"

As Mickey rubbed his beard, roof shingle particles descended to the ground. "Pretty early. I generally leave around seven, go for breakfast, and head to my first customer." He thought for a moment. "Yeah, around seven. Like I said, I didn't think much of it at the time. Maybe I should have because when the guy saw me, he froze, like he was caught. But then he casually drifted back to his vehicle as though it was no big deal." Mickey stopped. "Sorry, the way I'm explaining it, the more I should have had my antenna up. I'm not a morning person, so—"

"That's okay. Can you describe him? And the car? You said it was an SUV?"

"That I do remember."

Bobby called me, his voice filled with excitement. "My guy came through and found prints on the pen. I guess you were right—"

"Conor Mulcahy," I said without hesitation. I was in my office and shifted the phone to my other ear. "I knew it. And just now, my neighbor saw a guy resembling Conor peeking through my office window the morning before it was trashed. I'm guessing he was preparing for something sinister. I don't doubt the bump on my skull was his doing as well. And now this. No wonder he's avoiding me."

Bobby waited a bit. "You're saying Conor murdered Annie Baxter then Luca? Gee, Hank, I just don't see it."

I mentioned Jesse meeting Alex in the Rockies. "Alex saw him running below the crime scene. What does that tell you?"

TWENTY-EIGHT

Saint Cajetan came through, only not as I had wished, especially when Jesse called in a panic.

"I found Alex sitting alone on a rock and crying. He was dazed and confused. I told him he should return to the church, and after some persuasion, he agreed. We got about a quarter way down the trail when he stumbled on a rock and hit his head on a boulder. Hank, he's bleeding badly, and I can't wake him up. A hiker loaned me his cell phone to call emergency. I pray they get here soon. I'll call when we reach the hospital," he rushed and disconnected.

I took a breath, then called the monsignor. He didn't take it well.

"Pray for him, Hank."

TWENTY-NINE

Bobby's insistence that Conor was more likely a witness than the killer didn't convince me, and until I confronted him, I'd still hold him as a suspect.

I asked my godfather to park at Fillmore's the next morning and wait for Conor to arrive, then call me. Like a good soldier, Bobby showed up at nine and yawned into the phone.

"Conor hasn't arrived yet. "Just Finn."

"You sound tired. I guess you had a rough night. Who was the lucky woman?"

"Sally. She makes a great Hungarian Goulash."

"Who's Sally? Never mind."

"You sound jealous, Hank. Sorry that none of my friends have unmarried daughters."

"Very funny. I'm leaving my house and should be there in an hour. Don't fall asleep." I chuckled.

"Okay, but l need a bathroom break. I can go inside, have a drink, and do my business."

I'd forgotten about my godfather's prostate problem. "A drink at nine in the morning? Okay, go ahead. Maybe chat it up with Finn."

We disconnected.

Thirty minutes later, my car crawled through backed-up lanes onto the Cross Island Parkway heading west toward Whitestone. I checked the car's clock. I was running late, and Bobby hadn't called, which meant Conor hadn't shown up. I tapped the steering wheel and speed-dialed my godfather.

It went to voicemail. "Are you okay?" I asked like a concerned parent. "Call me when you get this message."

Bobby called a few minutes later. "Sorry, I never interrupt a good pee. What's up?"

Seriously? "Did Conor show up?"

"Nope, it's just me and Finn."

"There's heavy traffic on the parkway, so I'm delayed. I'll be there in thirty minutes."

When I arrived, Conor's SUV was sitting in the lot. I rushed inside and found Bobby kibbitzing with Finn, but no sign of Conor.

"Hey," I said greeting them both. I gave Bobby a 'what gives' sign, and he shrugged.

"Say, Hank, how's the investigation going?"

Like father like son. "Where's Conor?"

Finn surveyed the bar. "He's not here at the moment."

No kidding. "His vehicle is outside. I told you I needed to speak to him."

"Oh, right. He said something about going for a walk. He probably headed to the park. The boy's had a lot on his mind lately, so I don't mind stepping in. I get bored at home." A thin smile crossed his face. "If you don't mind me asking, is there something going on I should know about?"

My eyes locked on his. "Conor knows what happened the night of Annie's murder, and I need to know what he's holding back."

Finn's confused expression might have been due to the glass of scotch in his hand. Or maybe he was hard of hearing.

"Say again?"

I glared. "You heard me."

He stepped back. "Hank, I hope you're not suggesting Conor had anything to do with the murder." He searched the empty bar and when he looked at me, his expression turned grave. "We haven't spoken about that night—"

"Until I showed up."

He downed his drink, searched the empty glass. "Conor's a good kid and has never been in trouble. He watches out for me, especially since his mother died. He'd never harm anyone. I don't know why you'd even suggest it." He turned to my godfather. "I'm right, Bobby, tell him."

I side-glanced my godfather who remained silent. Finn suddenly removed a dish towel from below the bar and began wiping down the top, not looking up.

"Why has he been following me around? A witness saw your son at my office the day before it was trashed. What's up with that? And the pen he planted at Annie Baxter's shrine. It was from Lee Jensen's law firm. Was he trying to throw me off course, suggesting Jensen had something to do with her murder?" I narrowed my look. "Should I mention he probably slammed my head at Fort Totten?"

Finn stopped wiping; his eyes widened. He turned to me, his expression grave. "Hank, I—"

"I'm not leaving without answers."

Finn's face paled, his attention shifting to Bobby. "I need another drink," he muttered and stepped unevenly to pour a straight scotch, his hand trembling. He turned to me. "Want something?"

"Only answers," I demanded.

Bobby said, "This is serious, Finn."

The old man took a gulp, poured another, before turning to us. "You have to understand, Conor is all I have. After his mother died…Look, Hank, I don't know much about that night. It's true, Conor left the basement at some point. I didn't know it at the time.

He wanted to see what the Whitestone boys were up to. He knew about Luca's party and was upset the guys refused to make him a member." Finn paused and took a breath. "I guess he wanted to know what he was missing out on."

He peered inside his empty glass and spoke softly. "Conor was angry, hurt, and felt like an outcast. He helped me at the bar since he was a teenager. He didn't have a girlfriend. Outside of me, he had no one. And I'm his father, Hank. What could I offer besides the bar?"

He met my gaze. Finn was emotional and wiped an eye. But then his expression turned to fear, and he searched the front door as though someone might barge in on us.

"Hank, Conor didn't kill that girl, and he certainly had nothing to do with Luca's disappearance. But he witnessed…something, and it scared him. He wouldn't tell me for fear if I knew I'd be at risk. He was frightened and believed if he came forward, he'd be killed."

I grabbed the bar top and leaned in. "By whom? Conor must have recognized the guy." I turned to Bobby whose expression turned dark and pointed to Finn's glass. "I'll have whatever you're drinking."

"Hank?"

I closed my eyes and nodded. Finn didn't ask what I was drinking, and I didn't much care what he poured. He set the glass in front of me, thought a moment. "Like I said, Conor refused to tell me who he thought killed the woman.

"And then he found out you were investigating based on an anonymous letter Lisa received. Maybe it was a hoax, but his fears returned."

I glared. "What did wrecking my office have anything to do with it?"

Finn put up a hand. "Okay, that was foolish," he finally admitted. "Conor realized it was stupid. And honestly, Hank, I had no idea he hit you over the head. I don't understand his actions. Conor would never hurt anyone."

Bobby said, "Tell me why Conor left Jensen's business pen at the shrine? Does he suspect him?"

Finn wiped his mouth and nodded.

I said, "Here's the way I see it. Conor left the bar through the basement door and took off for the bridge. Beyond the park, near the bushes, he witnessed a murder and saw Lee Jensen. Is that close?"

He shook his head.

"Dammit, what then?"

"Conor didn't witness the murder. Like I said, he was interested in seeing what the guys were up to. He didn't want to get too close, so he crossed the park and looked through the bushes. Conor heard two guys arguing near the crime scene. One was Luca, the other, Conor had seen before but didn't know the guy. His shirt was covered with blood."

"Son of a bitch!"

Bobby jumped off his stool and rushed toward Finn, fists clenched. I grabbed him before he did something foolish. "Fighting won't get us anywhere."

"Luca was like a son to me," he shouted. "And your fucking son didn't come forward. What kind of person does that?"

"I'm sorry for Luca and his family," he cried, raising his hands. "And you, Bobby. But maybe it's not too late."

"It is for Luca," Bobby spit. "All these years—" He stopped, scrambled for the door.

"Bobby," Finn called. "I'm sorry."

I pointed a finger. "If Conor doesn't call within an hour, the police are getting involved." I started for the door.

"He was here!"

My head jerked around. "Who?"

Finn was about to pour another drink, and I lunged for him, knocking the glass out of his hand. "I need you sober. Who was here?"

Finn shot a look at the door. "Last night. We were serving drinks when this guy pops in and sits on the end stool." He pointed with his chin. "He was maybe mid to late forties, a little disheveled looking. He had scars across his face, and a bunch of tattoos like he might have been in prison. He had a crazed look, like he was ready for trouble. I thought I might have to call the cops."

He stopped. "But I held off and asked cordially for his order. He wasn't interested in me serving him and pointed at Conor. Said he wanted him to pour a drink." Finn paused. "Conor's a better bartender than I am, and normally it won't matter. But that guy gave me the creeps, and I wondered why he wanted my son to serve him. I called over to Conor and said the guy wanted him to make his drink.

"Conor approached with a smile, but then fear crossed his face like he'd seen a ghost. The guy sneered like he knew Conor recognized him." Finn took a breath. "I can't get this part out of my head. The guy said something, and I could tell by his facial expression that he didn't stop by for a drink. Whatever he told Conor, it made my son's body stiffen. When I approached, the guy turned to me, his expression full of rage. I stepped back and watched him get up and leave. I took one look at Conor and knew he was in trouble. The fear in his eyes was unlike anything I'd ever seen."

Finn stopped and I let him compose himself. "Conor hasn't been the same since. He told me he couldn't sleep last night. Today, he came in for a bit and…I have no idea where he went." He stopped. "Just by the conversation, Conor swears the guy who showed up was the killer."

I studied Finn's dark expression. Something didn't add up. Why after all these years would the killer suddenly appear? If he'd known Conor witnessed the crime back then, why wait until now? I paused. "What I don't get is why Conor thinks Jensen is involved."

Finn averted his eyes. "Conor watched the guy and Luca arguing. He was going to call the cops but then Luca took off. He then heard a voice call out nearby. He knew that voice: It belonged to Lee Jensen."

The basement door slammed shut, and I pointed a finger at Finn. "Conor's been here all this time."

Finn stiffened. "He's scared, Hank."

An engine fired up, and I jerked my thumb toward the door. "You tell Conor that if he doesn't call me, scared might be the least of his problems."

THIRTY

Danny Caruso shook his head. The piece of shit red Nissan Juke he sat in, or, rather, squeezed in, caused his nuts to grind against each other. And what was with all those lights in the front? Christ, he'd hoped his uncle would have swung for something sporty.

He hadn't driven in decades, but, hey, it was like riding a bike. Easy peasy. And he had a legitimate license under the name of Carey Burke, whoever the hell he was.

Across from the bar, Danny had a perfect view of the parking lot. He twisted in his seat as he surveyed Fillmore's and waited for the bartender to arrive, though after last night, he wondered if the guy would show up at all. Maybe he should have listened to his uncle about holding off introducing himself.

He sneered. Nah, he wanted to see Conor's face when he told him he knew he witnessed the killing. His uncle told him to wait until he finished Reed, but hey, he deserved a little fun after all these years in the slammer.

Danny leaned back and touched his crotch. He wanted to get laid, but the good uncle told him to wait until the job was done. The big tease. He said a hooker would be waiting for him at the motel, but first, he needed to get rid of any blood on him. It wouldn't look cool if the babe saw him post stabbing.

He licked his lips and waited.

"Hold on," he said to himself. "A black SUV just pulled up, and the almost dead bartender got out." Danny liked to talk to himself. It began when the Mexican guards isolated him from the regular population.

Right, regular. "He's running for the door. I must have scared the shit out of him last night." Danny would give the bartender about ten minutes to settle in. He rubbed his hands. The first customer would pee himself when he walked in and saw Conor boy cut up like a rabbit. Hell, he'd need a drink.

Danny checked the car clock and was about to go in when another vehicle pulled into the lot, and some old guy stepped out.

"*Maricon*, it must be his old man." Danny talked to himself in Spanish too. Especially the swear words he'd learned over the years. He rubbed one of his facial scars, the largest of three he got as a welcoming gift while protecting himself from some *pendejo*. That El Hongo prison in Tecate, Mexico, was one crazy joint. They hated gringos, especially the ones that killed their women.

"What to do, Danny boy?" He rubbed his now shaved head. "Kill them both? Oh, well."

Danny sat up and glanced to his right. Another old geezer stepped out of his car and crossed the street to the bar. There's a parking lot, asshole. Dumb shit. Must be a customer, but who drinks at nine-thirty in the morning?

He glanced at the photo of Reed his uncle gave him. Couldn't be him. The guy was too old. He touched his pocket where he held the Kershaw Launch 11 switchblade. Three people? That could get messy.

His uncle gave him a contact guy, some retired cop named Jimmy Savage, in case he needed help. What a crazy name. He picked up his cell and called Savage.

"The bartender showed up, but he has company. Two old guys. Want me to waste them too? I mean, it's no big deal. Just say the word."

Savage couldn't contain himself. "Are you fucking crazy? Your uncle gave you strict orders to go after Reed first. You shouldn't even be there. He'd never approve what you're suggesting. I can't believe you'd consider a bloodbath."

"Hold on, Savage. Another car pulled up. Booze must be on sale today." He looked at the headshot again. Oh, yeah, it was the man himself: Hank Reed. "Make that a four kill."

"Do not go inside until I get back to you," he demanded. "I need to call your uncle. You hear me, Danny?"

"Yeah, sure." He fidgeted, deciding whether to screw Savage and finish the job. He held off, waiting for his uncle's lackey to get back to him. He didn't like the way the guy talked down to him, and that might not bode well for the Savage man.

Savage called back in less than five minutes. "Your uncle wants you to get the hell out of there and make sure nobody sees you. You'll have a chance with Reed soon enough. You have his address. Got that, Danny?"

"Sure, Mr. Savage. I hear you." He disconnected and folded his arms. After being told what to do for years, neither his uncle nor Jimmy the creep Savage was about to tell him what not to do. Nobody would.

THIRTY-ONE

L isa must have sensed my avoidance and texted me.

> Just finished classes. Have time to meet?

I sighed heavily. *Not the Hilton.*

> Where?

> Moms house now.

> Sure. Half-hour?

> Perfect!

Lisa sat on the brick stoop, a wide smile crossing her face that reminded me of when Bobby dropped me off on summer weekends. He'd pick me up from Eastpoint on a Friday night and drive me home Sunday. I loved those weekends with the Whitestone boys, and particularly with Lisa.

My heart fluttered until I thought of Lisa and Matt.

"Perfect timing." She rose and kissed my cheek. "Like the old days."

I breathed in her perfume. It was the same sweet scent she wore at the Hilton Inn parking lot. "I remember," I forced out.

Lisa sighed. "We better go inside before the neighbors start talking."

Wrong guy.

"I hope my mother remembers you after all these years," she said, holding the door. "Like I told you, she's having difficulty recalling things these days."

I remembered the living room. Except for photos of Luca plastered across one wall, nothing much had changed. Same comfortable furniture.

"Mom, Hank is here," she called out.

Mrs. Falcone walked in from the kitchen, bringing a warm and sweet aroma of onion, basil, and garlic. Must be marinara sauce. I guessed I was invited for dinner.

"Hank, is that really you? You've grown." With effort, she walked over and gave me a hug. "You look great." She turned to Lisa. "Doesn't he, Lisa?"

"Very handsome." Lisa winked at me.

Her mother whispered, "You were my only choice."

I smiled. "Thanks, Mrs. Falcone."

She held up a hand. "That was years ago. Call me Marie."

"Marie."

"You're staying for dinner."

Not a question.

"Of course. I missed your pasta."

"Good. Lisa said you were in the neighborhood. Are you visiting Bobby?" She cast a wistful glance.

Lisa hadn't told her.

"I am. It's been a while."

She sighed. "Me too." Peering over my shoulders at the wall, she stared at photos of Luca, and I was sure her eyes rested on the one with Luca and Bobby.

"We'll talk more at dinner," she said.

I waited until Marie left. "Your mom looks and sounds good. You'd never know she was failing."

"You got her at a good time. After Luca…Anyway, she took her meds at lunchtime. I checked. How about a glass of wine?"

I needed a drink and nodded.

"Red or white?"

I didn't care, but said red.

"Not a problem. You're walking distance to Bobby's." She laughed softly.

As Lisa strolled into the kitchen, I surveyed the adorned wall. Luca was everywhere. Alone, with Lisa, family, and friends. And one of us, standing near the bridge smiling. It was the Christmas before he disappeared. At the time, Luca didn't have a care in the world. He was happy to be in love with Tara, who took the photo.

"Good times, huh, Hank?"

I turned. Lisa held two glasses of red.

"I remember when this picture was taken," I said pointing.

She handed me a glass. "To the good old days."

We toasted with Chianti, a good choice.

"Remember this one?" Lisa pointed to one of us. We were standing in front of her mother's black Grand Prix at the Jones Beach parking lot, holding hands.

I was afraid the past would catch up and needed to get off the memory merry-go-round.

I looked at the staircase to the second floor. "I'd like to check Luca's bedroom after dinner."

Lisa frowned as though I'd taken away her temporary happiness. Touché.

Marie had prepared lasagna, my favorite. Over dinner, she asked about my life, wife, kids, and all the rest a casual conversation might include. Life without a wife or kids. I left out the divorce for no apparent reason. I included my stint with the Suffolk County Police Department and Chief of Police of Eastpoint but left out my current gig as a private investigator.

Marie struggled with her life post Luca, as though the incident occurred recently. Fortunately, Lisa stepped in and brought the conversation to herself and Chuck and their children. She left out the Matt part.

Afterward, we took our wine glasses to the living room, where I settled on the sofa, and Lisa slipped in beside me, maybe a little too close. Marie sat across on a leather chair. She smiled and sighed. "If only…" A sigh. "I remember Luca telling me once he wanted to be a police officer. He was about ten."

"We all wanted to be cops back then. Or firemen," I added.

"Mom, Hank's a private investigator."

Marie gave her a blank look. She turned to me. "Oh."

I side-glanced Lisa hoping she wouldn't continue, but she did. "I asked Hank to investigate a few things. Old stuff. Just to put an end…"

Marie's eyes squeezed shut, and when she opened them, they blazed. "Luca is dead, Lisa. He's not coming back."

"But, Mom, you believe in your heart that Luca will return one day. You told me that. Hank just wants to—"

"Stop, Lisa. I'm too old to go on hoping. You know that. The pills, the memory loss. If Luca ever returned, I probably wouldn't recognize him. My own son." Her eyes softened as she turned to me. "Hank. I'm begging you, let it go."

I turned to Lisa, praying she wouldn't bring up the anonymous letter. She stared at me, and I shook my head once. She nodded.

With effort, Marie pulled herself off the chair and trudged over to me. She lowered her frail body and kissed my cheek.

"It's been wonderful seeing you, Hank. I hope you'll stop by again. I'm tired and going to bed."

When she left, I turned to Lisa. "That went well."

"She needs to know. This is for her, as well. Our last shot. She's not getting any younger. Luca needs to be exonerated, even if we never find him." She lifted her drink off the table and finished it, then eased back and closed her eyes.

"Now would be a good time to see Luca's bedroom."

His room was exactly as I remembered it. "Nothing's changed."

"After the investigators finished, Mom put everything back as it was." She walked to the closet and opened it. "His shirts and pants are still on hangers. It got too creepy for me, so I stay away from this room. I'll meet you downstairs."

I was glad to be left alone. Aside from my disappointment in Lisa, I wanted to visit my friend's room by myself and reflect on our past.

I remember this room, friend. The jokes, the secrets, sharing love stories. It was where Luca told me about his mobster father's murder when he was fifteen and became the man of the house.

I navigated the room, the floor creaking as I recalled. The closet included a few baseball bats and trophies. His clothes were neatly folded in drawers. I noticed a stain on the white rug and smiled to myself. Sorry, Mrs. Falcone, that was me spilling a Coke.

I checked his bookshelf. The same softcover books, mostly crime novels.

Talk to me, Luca.

One book spine stood out from the rest, and I removed it. A romance novel titled *Our Summer.* I chuckled to myself and opened the first page. Tara had bought it for him and inscribed something sweet.

She wrote that life was ready to add to their love. I stopped. Tara was pregnant, but she claimed Luca wasn't aware when he disappeared. What if he was? Was he ready to become a father?

I placed the book back on the shelf, wondering if his disappearance had anything to do with her pregnancy. Closing the bedroom door, realizing it would be the last time I entered Luca's room, hit me with a sense of loss. I hoped for a miracle but reality set in, and I knew my friend was gone forever.

Back in the living room, Lisa was gulping another glass of wine looking defeated.

"Anything?" she asked.

"Only memories. I'm heading to Bobby's. We'll talk soon."

She got up and spilled her drink. "Shit." She reached clumsily for my hand. "I wish things had turned out differently between us."

Her breath smelling of Chianti turned me off. Or was it the situation with Matt?

"We were young," I said, my hand slipping away, and let myself out.

Back at Bobby's, I called Tara and mentioned the book I'd found in Luca's bedroom.

"Oh, God, I remember. It was called *Our Summer.* I loved that book and thought of Luca immediately. I wrote something special inside. Did you read it?"

"I did," I said. "It was very sweet. You guys were in love and—"

"I thought I was pregnant," she said with a sigh. "I was nervous and afraid Luca would be upset and reject me. I thought the novel would show how much I loved him. The note was cryptic, so I don't know if you picked up on it. Luca hadn't, at least he never asked if I was pregnant. Fortunately, I wasn't pregnant. Not then."

She stopped, took a breath. "But as you probably know, I did get pregnant. I took a pregnancy test the day of Luca's party and almost passed out. I had to tell my parents, but I wanted Luca to be the first to know and tried sneaking out my bedroom window."

She stopped for a moment. "My father caught me, and I blurted it out. He went crazy. I mean, he was livid. I'd never seen him so angry. He blamed Luca, of course, and not his little girl."

I walked to the living room window and pulled back the sheer curtains. Next door, a black sedan sat parked, its engine off. I couldn't tell if anyone was inside because the driver's window was tinted. The car didn't belong to Bobby's neighbor.

"So, Luca didn't know you were pregnant when he disappeared that night. That must have been a heavy burden on you. Being pregnant and losing your love at the same time."

"I cried for days." Tara paused, followed by a sniffle. "God, Hank, I loved him so much. I love Jesse but in a different way. They say your first love…" She stopped. "Our child has grown now. I often wonder what it would have been like…"

I turned back from the window. "I'm sorry I brought up the book," I said. "I was hoping to find something helpful. Being back in his room stirred fond memories. I miss him, too."

Another sniffle.

"I didn't mean to pry and thanks for clarifying. Obviously, his disappearance had nothing to do with your pregnancy."

"He never knew."

I asked, "When was the last time you saw Luca?"

"That I remember because I used to think about it all the time. Still do sometimes. It was the day before he disappeared. We went to Fort Totten and roamed the tunnels, like we had so often before. Luca loved talking about the fort's history dating back to the Civil War. It was as if I had a private guide. I loved that about him. At one point, we walked to the back of the fort and made out under a tree."

She stopped.

"Tara?"

"Sorry. As I'm reminiscing, I picture us there. I used to think about that scene for months afterward. It provided solace, yet it was sad." She sighed heavily.

"If you don't want to discuss it—"

"No, no, I'm fine. I remember at one point, Luca seemed to be studying the sea wall, and said it would be cool to escape into Little

Neck Bay and swim to Douglaston. I thought he was nuts. I mean, have you seen that stretch of water? Don't get me wrong, Luca was a strong swimmer, but that's a heck of a swim."

I blinked. "He actually said that?"

"Well, maybe not in so many words. Is it important?"

Was it? Was Luca scouting a possible escape route?

"Hank?"

"Sorry, it's probably nothing. A good story, though. So, then Luca took you home?"

Tara thought a moment. "We left the fort and sat outside on a bench. I bought him a birthday present and kept it in my bag. I told him I was disappointed I wouldn't see him the next evening and handed it to him. It was a Pearl Jam CD, I think called *Vitalogy*."

"Good choice," I added.

"Luca thought so. Anyway, it was getting late, and we started back to my place. Almost immediately, Luca became pensive, and I assumed he was thinking about his party. When we arrived at my house, he told me he loved me and that no matter what, I would always be his girl. He would say sweet things, but he looked sad. God, Hank, I was a kid back then and never saw it coming."

Luca obviously had plenty on his mind, especially if he was planning an escape route.

I peeked outside. That damn car was still there. I couldn't get a read on the plate, but the orange and black lettering told me it was New York State.

"Tara, I have to run." I disconnected and dashed out the front door. The car's engine was now on, so the driver must have sensed me coming and screeched out of the spot. He shot to the corner not braking for the stop sign and missing an oncoming car by a few feet. By the time I reached the corner, the vehicle was several blocks away.

My fists were clenched, and I crossed the street, entered the park, and followed the path to the river. I searched for a quiet spot. When I found one, I perched on a boulder and peered out at the river. Unlike me, it was calm.

I stood and stretched. This little nugget of Whitestone had always provided a sense of peace. That was before the investigation. When this mess was over, I'd return and enjoy my little spot in the sun.

THIRTY-TWO

Lee Jensen returned to Hilton Head. The mission hadn't gone as planned, not with Danny out of control. He needed to be far away from the problem and would put pressure on Savage to rein in his nephew, only he wasn't holding his breath. Danny Caruso wasn't listening to anyone.

He sat in his car outside Elsa's on the Water, a waterfront restaurant on Hilton Head Island known for its prime-cut steaks and romantic views of the harbor. He'd been planning to meet his new lover, and since his wife was out of town and he didn't cook, Elsa's would provide a perfect evening.

The parking lot was near empty since the restaurant didn't open until five, so he had time to think. But time turned short as his cell buzzed. He frowned as he checked the incoming number. Jensen never knew what to expect when Jimmy Savage called.

"I'm outside Bobby Larkin's house," he said in a rush. "Reed's inside on the phone with your daughter." As he continued, the excitement in his voice was evident. And annoying.

Jensen sat up, adjusted his seat. "What the hell are you talking about, outside his house? Can't Reed see you?"

"That's the best part," Savage said. "He doesn't know I'm here. I'm in my car with a parabolic microphone, and my windows are heavily tinted."

Jensen thought for a moment. "I heard of those things. That's where the mic picks up voices. Okay, talk to me, but slow down. You sounded like you were auctioning off your house."

"Sorry. Reed's on the phone with Tara asking about Luca's disappearance. I can't hear her response, but Reed's repeating a lot and it sounds like she and Luca spent part of the day before his party at Fort Totten. Hang on, I'm getting more." He paused. "So cool, I can use this surveillance contraption like the CIA."

Jensen snorted. "You got lucky, pal. Are you going to follow him everywhere?"

Savage answered with less enthusiasm, "Why not?"

"Just blowing smoke up your ass. I'm fine with your surveillance work. I'm not surprised he's calling people from the past. He wouldn't be a decent P.I. if he didn't. As far as Tara, I'm not concerned. She doesn't know anything about the murder or Luca's disappearance. And during the police interview, I did most of the talking."

"Hold on. He's asking about a knife he found in another guy's cigar box. Someone named Alex. Shit, he claims it was Luca's knife. Sounds like he's connecting the dots. I thought you said the knife at the scene was Luca's."

Jensen stiffened. "That's what I thought. That means the one they found at the scene belonged to my nephew. Strange, Danny's DNA wasn't on it, only Luca's and the woman's." He tried processing this latest revelation. "At this point, it doesn't matter whose knife it was. The detectives were satisfied with Luca's prints on the one they found at the scene."

"Maybe, but Reed isn't going to stop with the knife. He's interviewing everyone, including the bartender and his old man. Reed already stopped by the bar. Trust me, he wasn't going for a drink.

The bartender might have clammed up years ago, but what if he decides to talk now and identifies Danny? That would be disastrous for you as well."

Jensen shifted in his seat. "Why me? I didn't kill the woman. And after twenty-five years, it's his word over mine. Would the cops believe a respected lawyer and councilman or some guy who finally had the balls to come forward?"

"Just the same, what if Danny gets cornered? He knows things that would implicate you. Keep that in mind."

Jensen remained silent. He wished things had turned out differently. He really liked Luca despite getting his daughter pregnant. But being in the wrong place...

Savage cried, "I gotta get out of here. Reed's ending the call."

Jensen blinked out of his thoughts. "Then I suggest you hurry up."

"I hear movement like he's heading somewhere. Maybe the front door. Shit, this equipment is clumsy. I hope I don't break anything."

"Hurry, dammit."

"Reed's at the front door looking my way. He must sense something going on and is dashing toward the car."

Jensen heard rubber crushing the pavement. When Savage remained silent, Jensen yelled, "Did he see you?"

"I don't know, but he's running toward the car. Shit, there's a damn stop sign in front of me."

"Forget the stop sign. Just keep going!" Jensen shook his head, disconnected, and checked the time: another half-hour before his date arrived. He needed time to relax, but his fist pounded on the steering wheel. Fucking Reed.

THIRTY-THREE

C onor was running scared. After keeping his secret tight for twenty-five years, reality returned. No longer was he safe, not after being confronted last night. The killer knew him, where he worked, and surely, where Conor lived. That meant I was running against time. I needed to find Conor and fast.

Hints he left directing me toward Jensen now made sense, and I would focus entirely on him. The problem was the former councilman lived in another state, which meant he was the puppeteer.

Matt and Tara hadn't spoken to their father in years, but I needed Jensen to know I was on to him and called Tara.

She picked up on the second ring.

"Sorry about shortening our conversation before. Something pressing came up."

"That's okay. I realize you have a lot on your plate."

She should only know.

Tara had heard from Jesse and thanked him for being there for Alex, who was now in an induced coma. He felt the need to stay a few days and she agreed.

"I want you to call your father," I said, not conveying Jensen's involvement the night of the murder. "I know you haven't spoken in a while, but you need to mention my investigation, though, by now, I'm sure he's aware of it. Tell him I asked about the statement you gave to the detectives. I'm assuming they came to your house. Do you remember what you told them?"

"Gee, Hank, that was so long ago, and I was in a fog. I remember them asking me about my relationship with Luca, if I knew about his knife, stuff like that. Thank God my father was with me."

"Why is that?"

"Because he knew the detectives and answered most of the questions for me."

"Helpful," I said.

"Very. But outside of that, I don't remember much. Does that help?"

"It does. I want you to tell your father I'm getting close to finding the real killer."

"Are you? That's great news. But why do you want me to tell him? Am I missing something?"

I took a breath. "You need to trust me on this. I realize your relationship is strained, but it could help exonerate Luca."

She didn't hesitate. "Anything for Luca."

Tara called back an hour later. "I called my father like you asked," she said, her voice subdued. "I mentioned your investigation and brought up the interview and the knife. He grew increasingly upset and started ranting, claiming you were stirring up trouble on a cold case and that you were attempting to break up our family. Hank, he wasn't making sense. I'm beginning to think my father is hiding something."

She sniffled into the phone. "He told me he loved Luca and wished circumstances were different. I wonder if he meant it."

I smiled into the phone. *Thank you, Tara.* "I know he's your father, so the last thing I want is to cause additional problems. But I need to seek the truth, no matter where it leads me, or the outcome, and I'm asking you again, to trust me."

"I'll try."

"What I'm about to tell you is vital to my investigation, and you have the right to know."

THIRTY-FOUR

Back home, Jimmy Savage wasted no time complaining to Jensen. "Kip just called. It's been almost twenty-four hours, and he has no idea where your nephew is. It's like he vanished."

"Vanished? Where the hell could he have gone?"

"Beats me. Kip drove by Reed's place, and all was quiet. He didn't know where to go next, so I suggested your sister's house. I know you told Danny to hold off until the job was done, but he's disregarding everything you told him."

"Is Kip there now?"

"Yeah, there's nothing going on, but he noticed your sister went out for about an hour and returned with bags of groceries. Quite a few for one person, so I'm guessing Danny called her."

"Shit. I told him—"

"What do you want Kip to do?"

Jensen breathed heavily at the bathroom mirror. He was losing more hair. "Have him sit tight another hour or two, then tell him to leave for the night. Fucking Danny, he's been a problem his entire life."

"Since birth?"

"Hell, almost. When Danny was a kid, my sister complained about his behavior. Said he'd pick up stray cats and dogs and bring them home, only to swing them by their tails and heave them."

"Damn!"

"He constantly got into trouble in school and was kicked out of every one." Jensen paused. "You'd think my sister and brother-in-law would have sought help, but they blamed his condition on hyper-activity."

"There were drugs for that," Savage said.

"No shit. I suggested a few. I looked up his condition: Something like an attachment disorder. It's…hell, I gave her the name of a good shrink. But they hid their head in the sand." He paused. "I liked Danny, took him to Yankee games, that sort of thing. He liked me, too, and was always respectful. But he hated his father. His old man was never around, and when he was, couldn't find anything good to say about the kid."

"Yeah, well I think the *kid* is out of control. Now we have to deal with him."

Jensen waited a beat. "I think Danny killed his father."

When Savage didn't answer, Jensen continued. "It was closed out as an accident. My brother-in-law fell off the roof fixing a gutter. He was agile, and the ladder was supposedly balanced on the ground. Danny was the only one home at the time. After the fall, he never called for help and claimed he was inside playing video games."

"Maybe you should have told me before we started," Savage said, annoyed. "Look, it's getting dark, and Kip told me before he had to pee. He said he'd give it another half-hour before taking off for a gas station."

Jensen sighed. "Whatever."

"So, if Danny shows up, what do you want Kip to do? Join them for dinner?"

"Funny. If he sees my nephew before he leaves for the night, tell him to call me. Otherwise, I'll contact Danny myself. If he doesn't answer his phone, I'll call my sister."

"Talk about the devil. Kip's on the other line. I'll call you back."

"I just got off the phone with Jensen. Are you still outside Danny's mother's place? He said if you spot Danny, call him. You got that?"

When Kip didn't reply, he said, "Are you there?"

"Stabbed," he breathed.

"Who's stabbed? Did something happen to Danny?"

"He stabbed…"

"Oh, Christ, stay with me, Kip. I'm calling for help." Savage punched 911 and told the dispatcher what he'd heard. "He's a retired cop!"

Back to Kip. "I called it in. Hang in there, buddy. Kip. Kip!"

Savage lived forty miles away on Long Island, too far to help his friend, and called Jensen.

"Your nephew just stabbed Kip. Why the hell would he do that? You gotta stop him, Lee. He's out of control!"

Jensen stuttered, "Are you sure it was Danny? Kip wasn't on our hit list. He must have spooked him. Look, I can't get involved right now, you know that. You'll have to take care of it. How would it look if I knew what he'd done? And Jimmy, stop him at any cost."

At any cost. Easy for him to say. The fact was, he had no idea where the psychopath went after he attacked Kip. Maybe to Reed's place. He checked the time. It was after 7:00 P.M. Maybe he should let Danny finish the job and then stop him. Or alert Reed and have him ready for Danny. But if he called Reed, how would that look? Unless he did it anonymously. A real dilemma.

After considerable thought, Savage decided to stay put. After all, Danny Caruso wasn't his problem. Not yet.

Lee Jensen was exhausted. He must have paced across his dark blue and teal bedroom area rug a hundred times, but he couldn't stop thinking about his problem. He entered the bathroom and peered at the mirror. Big mistake. He looked haggard and needed to cover his gray mustache. He'd never find a woman looking like this.

Thank God his wife was out playing mahjong. She'd only ask questions about his appearance. He wished he was back in his hotel room with the minibar. Heck, he was too tired to walk downstairs to his own bar.

He sat on the bed, phone in hand. He hesitated to call his sister. What would he ask her? Has your psycho son shown up with bloody clothes? His gut told him to wait, but he called anyway. Only his sister, Jane, didn't answer; Danny did.

"Hey Uncle, how's it going?"

He was serious. "I gave you strict orders not to visit your mother until after the job was done. And why in hell did you stab the guy sitting in his car? He was one of us and a retired detective. The cops will be all over the place looking for his killer. You better get your ass out of there."

"I didn't know who he was. He spooked me. I thought—"

"He was watching out for you!"

"Okay, okay, I'm sorry. I wanted to see my mother. And I was hungry. Mom was so excited to see me after all these years. I made up some bullshit about being taken by a mind-control group and wound up in South America. She bought it. She's great, my mom."

Jensen squeezed his eyeballs. This can't be happening.

"You there?"

Jensen wished he weren't. "There's too much going on, so you have to hold off a while—"

"You mean Reed?"

"Of course, I mean Reed. Let this blow over. He'll probably

realize the murder has something to do with his investigation, and he'll be on the lookout for trouble."

Danny said quietly. "Okay, I'll give it another day or two."

"Good."

"I'm just getting used to being back with Mom. Wanna say hello?"

Hell no. "Another time. Look, Danny, if you want to stay out of prison, you have to be smart about taking chances. Know what I mean? Otherwise, you'll be back where you don't want to go. *¿Entiende?*"

"Hey, Uncle, your pronunciation isn't bad. It's *¿Entiendes?*

"Okay, I'll be careful. Anyway, Mom's calling. She bought cannoli. You know how I love them. You sure you don't want to join us?"

Jensen was numb. What a nightmare. He disconnected, fell back on the bed, and stared at the ceiling.

Danny was stuffed and curious about the past. He gave his mother a hug and told her he needed a walk.

"You be careful, son. There's a maniac killing people. I don't want to lose you again."

He smiled. "Don't worry, I can take care of myself. Oh, and if the police stop by, don't tell them I was here."

"Okay. Don't stay out too long."

He shot out the back door, jumped over a neighbor's fence, sneaked through their yard, and entered the street a few blocks from Annie Baxter's crime scene. Just like the old days. He surveyed the street then hustled to the park, his eyes peering up at the majestic Whitestone Bridge. He missed it.

In his deluded thoughts, Danny Caruso was dying to go back to the spot. Okay, dying wasn't the right word, but he was curious to see the site after all these years. His mother had mentioned a shrine where that poor girl, Annie Baxter, had been murdered. In fact, she'd gone a few times to pay her respects.

Before entering the park, Danny walked over to where the pay phone booth stood twenty-five years ago. It was gone. He took a breath. Good thing it was there when he called his uncle after killing the woman.

He entered the park, dodged a few people milling around. It changed very little since he was here last. He worked through the bramble to the crime scene. He didn't need directions. How could he forget where the kill took place?

Arriving, he used the cell's flashlight and waved it about, stopping at mementos, cards, and other stuff you'd find at a shrine. He snickered. Maybe he should have bought a card saying he was sorry.

Sorry he wasn't. He reminded himself it wasn't his fault: Annie Baxter taunted him. She agreed to go into the park and find a secluded spot to hang out. To Danny, that meant she wanted sex. Instead, she told him she didn't do *that* on the first date, if in fact, it was a date.

He tried getting friendly, but she pushed him away. "I don't have sex with someone I don't know very well. And it appears I made a mistake coming here with you. I wouldn't have sex with you no matter how long I knew you." She laughed in his face and turned to leave.

Bad decision. Don't diss Danny Caruso.

The sound of sirens approaching jerked him into reality. He blinked rapidly and realized he had a few more jobs on his agenda.

THIRTY-FIVE

The cell phone buzzing jolted me, and I scrambled for it, blinking at the number. Lisa.

"There's been another murder in Whitestone! Not far from my mother's house," she cried. "A retired cop. They found him slumped over the steering wheel."

I rubbed my eyes.

"Murder?"

"Sorry, Hank, I didn't realize what time it was."

"It's okay, I needed to get up." I headed to the kitchen and poured a glass of water.

"Hank, are you there?"

"You said a retired cop. Do they have a name yet?"

"No. It's all over the media. I'm driving to my mother's house."

"Hold on." I hustled to Bobby's bedroom and knocked.

"Enter."

He was safe and probably alone. "Come out when you're dressed."

To Lisa, "I'm at Bobby's. I'm surprised I didn't hear the commotion."

"It's terrible. I already called in for a substitute teacher."

"Okay, call me when you get there."

As I disconnected, Bobby appeared in flannel PJs.

I suppressed a laugh and pointed. "It's summer, old man."

He looked down and shrugged. "My lady friends like them. What's up?"

While Bobby was on the phone with a police contact, I left to meet Lisa. She was sitting on the stoop, looking pale and nervous. I suppose the murder brought her back in time.

She stood and gave me a hug, her body trembling. "This is crazy, Hank. Whitestone is relatively safe."

I held her. "It's okay, we'll find out what happened. Bobby's making calls, so hopefully we'll learn who the victim was and a possible motive."

She nodded. "It happened down the street," she said, pointing. The normally quiet block was anything but. Though the murder occurred last night, police cars still blocked the area.

"Who found him?"

"A neighbor walking her dog noticed a car parked close to her house. She didn't recognize it and looked inside. That's when she spotted his bloody neck and called the police.

As we approached, Lisa stopped and grabbed my hand. "There's something about this street."

I looked down at her hand. "Like what? It's a typical Whitestone block. I'm sure you've walked here over the years."

"It's not that." She dropped her hand and pointed at a house across from the car in question. "I know who lives there."

"The Cape Cod with a steep shingled roof?" I asked following her hand.

She nodded. "Lee Jensen's sister."

My eyes drifted to the crime scene across from her house. "Interesting. That would make her Matt and Tara's aunt."

She nodded.

"What do you know about her?"

Lisa shrugged. "Not much. Nice lady. Lives alone after her husband died years ago."

I looked back at Jensen's sister's house. Most families have at least one child and I wondered whether she had any. I asked Lisa.

After a moment, she said, "They had a son, but I don't know what happened to him. There'd been rumors he died years ago. I think his name was Danny. As a kid, he was a handful. He'd get kicked out of one school, then another. I lost track after that. He was slightly older than Luca, so they never hung out together, thank God."

I nodded absently. "What if he's not dead? You said it was rumored he died. Was there ever a funeral?"

"Gee, Hank, I don't know. What's the sudden interest in Jensen's nephew?"

I waited a beat. "I think Lee Jensen was involved in Annie Baxter's murder. Not that he killed her, but a witness heard him call out to someone that night near the murder scene. What if the guy was Danny?"

"Lee Jensen?" she said a little too loud.

I shot a glance around again. "A witness saw someone dash from the crime scene heading out of the park. That's when he noticed he was running toward Jensen."

A confused expression crossed her face. "Who's the witness?"

"I'm not ready to say. I need to question…the witness further."

She said nothing.

Lisa's romantic relationship with Jensen's son, Matt, hindered my trust in her, and I dared not mention Conor as the witness. "Jensen knows about my investigation, and the witness is afraid if the word got out, the killer might…Look, I know it's hard to take in right now but trust me, I think the source is credible."

"Why didn't he or she go to the police back then? If what you're suggesting is true, how come Jensen and his…nephew let your witness live? God, I can't believe I'm saying this."

"No, you're right. I don't have an answer. Tara mentioned my investigation to her father, and he didn't take it well. Maybe he's afraid I'll go directly after him."

Her face turned grave. "What are you going to do? Confront him? He'll deny everything."

I said, "I need your help."

"Anything."

I swallowed hard. "I need to know if Matt ever suspected his old man. I know they had a falling out years ago; at least, that's what I gleaned from a conversation I had with him. Can you find out what that was about?"

She raised a brow. "Why are you asking me?"

When I didn't answer, she scowled. "What do you think is going on between me and Matt?" Her voice turned cold and accusatory as though *I* was the bad guy.

"Look, it wasn't intentional, but while investigating, I spotted you and Matt at the Hilton Inn."

Her eyes widened. "Not intentional? You bastard. What I do is none of your business. You and I were a couple years ago. You have no right to follow me. Damn you, Hank." She stopped, shook her head. "Are you going to tell my husband?"

I stepped back. "Don't be ridiculous. I have no reason to tell him or anyone. Your secret is my secret. Do you love him?" I heard myself ask.

"So that's it? You're jealous? I can't believe this. I should fire you."

Actually, I wasn't getting paid, but I got her drift.

"I'm not jealous of Matt or anyone else. I'm only interested in finding the truth, and I'm going to do that. Your life doesn't belong to me, and I hope we can remain friends."

She huffed and took off.

Bobby was on the phone, and judging from his conversation, it was about the recent murder. He put up a finger, so I left for the living room.

He walked in a few minutes later and settled on the sofa next to me. "The murder victim is Arnie Lefkowitz, but he went by Kip. He'd been stabbed multiple times in the neck sometime in the early evening."

"Did you know him?"

A nod. "Oh, yeah. He was a retired detective from my precinct." He paused, his eyes on mine. "I don't like talking badly about the dead, but I didn't much care for the guy. There was something sneaky about him."

Bobby shrugged. "You know the sense you get when something's not right? It was just a feeling I got over the years. He partnered with another detective. I didn't care for either and sensed they were into stuff. Like I said, it was more a gut feeling. Anyway, Kip had a clean record and retired years ago. He lived in Wantagh."

"That's Long Island. What do you think he was doing here?"

Another shrug. "I asked my contact the same question. All Kip had on him was his license and a few bucks."

"Maybe he was doing some P.I. work."

"Maybe."

I mentioned the victim's car parked across the street from Lee Jensen's sister's house.

"Coincidence?"

Bobby met my gaze. "Jane Caruso? I know her. Nice lady. She's been living alone since her husband died after falling off a ladder. Strange accident." He studied me for a moment. "I'll look into it. I'm not crazy about coincidences."

THIRTY-SIX

W hile waiting for Bobby's update on the cop's murder, and Monsignor Valencia on Alex's fall on the hiking trail, I drove back to my office. By six, I was famished and strolled over to the Irish Embassy Pub nearby. I asked for a table in the back like some mob figure worried about taking a hit.

Rita, the hostess, was a thirty-something redhead from Dublin. All smiles.

"Do you need a menu today, Hank, or have you memorized our complete fare by now?" Her infectious brogue came through.

I smiled. "I'm a creature of habit, Rita, so I'll have the glazed salmon with a Peroni. You can bring the beer first."

While waiting, my cell buzzed. I don't normally answer in restaurants, but the number was unfamiliar, and I was curious.

"Is this Hank Reed?" asked an unfriendly voice.

I sat upright. "Depends. Who's asking?"

"Let me offer some friendly advice. You're wasting your time going back twenty-five years. You're gonna come up empty-handed and feel like a loser. What's past is past, so why not drop what you're doing and save your client money? Like I said, it's just friendly advice."

"You'll have to be more specific," I said, scanning the entrance. "I'm working on several cases. You obviously know I'm a P.I., so which client are you referring to?"

"Smart ass. You know the case. Old and dead."

Draw out the voice, Hank.

"Oh, you mean Annie Baxter."

There was a pause. "And the missing kid."

"That kid had a name, asshole." I raised my voice then regretted it, as it drew stares from other patrons.

When he didn't respond, I lowered my voice. "Let me give *you* some advice. You're not my client, so unless I'm told to stop, I'm not going anywhere. Tell that to your boss, Lee Jensen."

His silence bought me time. "I know he was involved, and you can tell the former councilman I'm getting close to having him arrested."

"Fuck you."

"Nice talk."

An uncomfortable silence hung over us until the caller said, "Look, Reed, I'm trying to save your life. There are some bad people out to get you."

"People like Jensen? I know, I got his warning the other day. You oughta learn to be a little patient."

"The hell are you talking about?" He stopped. "You're bullshitting, right?"

I removed the souvenir bullet from my pocket. "I'm looking at the flat point 9mm you dropped off at my office."

He hesitated. "Just be careful, Reed. Go back to your dinner. I hear the salmon is to die for." He laughed and hung up.

I leaped out of my seat and charged for the door. Outside, I scanned the lightly lit street, and I expected a car to be hightailing it out of there. Where the hell was, he?

Inside, I lowered my head. The patrons stared at me as I returned to my table. My stomach churned, and I was glad I hadn't begun eating.

My beer had been waiting for me, and I took a much-needed slug. I'd obviously hit a nerve. When Rita returned with my food, she must have noticed my expression.

"Something wrong, Hank?"

"I just realized I have an appointment. Can you wrap it up for me?"

Outside, I surveyed the street until reaching my office. Inside, I locked the door, wheeled my desk chair away from the window, and closed the curtains. I realized I'd been holding my breath and forced out a lungful of air.

———

The following morning, my phone jolted me out of my office chair, where I'd been attempting to sleep.

"Hank, good news," Bobby said. "Finn called a few minutes ago. Conor wants to talk. He'll meet you at the bar around nine. He's been in panic mode ever since Annie Baxter's killer showed up at the bar."

I rubbed my eyes. "Why didn't Conor call me himself?"

"I don't know, but Finn assured me he'd be there."

My lower back was stiff, and I wish I'd had Bobby's easy chair last night. "Okay, go to Fillmore's and wait for me. I'll be there in an hour. And Bobby, be careful. I'm sure the killer is searching for Conor."

"Got it."

The usual morning traffic along the Northern State Parkway set me back at least a half hour. I speed-dialed Bobby and got his voicemail.

"Are you there yet?" I said, leaving a message.

Trapped in a sea of cars, I swore I'd have to move closer to the city. I called Fillmore's and Finn answered.

"Has Conor showed up yet?"

"No, and I'm getting worried. I called him a couple of times, but it goes directly to voicemail. How about you try, Hank?"

"I did, but he wasn't picking up." I put on my signal to enter another lane. "Come on, dammit!"

Twenty minutes later, as I approached the Cross Island Parkway, Conor called.

"I'm scared, Hank. The killer told me not to go to the police. He said he wants to meet and clear things up."

"Listen to me, Conor; he does *not* want to clear things up. I believe his name is Danny Caruso, and he's Lee Jensen's nephew. He wants to finish what he started twenty-five years ago. Where are you?"

"Home."

"Not good. Get out of there immediately. Caruso must know where you live. Get in your car and drive to the Fort Totten Park parking lot. I'll be there in about thirty minutes. And Conor, I know you've been doing weird stuff to get my attention, but for the record, I know you didn't kill Annie Baxter."

When I arrived at the parking lot, there were a dozen cars, but Conor's SUV wasn't one of them. I circled the lot twice hoping I'd missed it, but Conor was missing in action.

I called. "I'm here and you're not," I said, my tone harsh. "Where are you?"

I took an end spot, got out and found a bench strategically placed in front of the parking lot. All I needed was for Conor to show up.

I began to panic and called again, leaving another message. My stomach tightened. Maybe I should have considered meeting him at Fillmore's. I called the bar.

"Conor was supposed to meet me at Fort Totten Park. Has he called you?"

Finn sounded like he'd been drinking, and with a slur, said he hadn't.

"What about Bobby? Has he showed up?"

"Not yet."

"Give me Conor's address."

Two cars sat in Conor's modest ranch driveway, one belonging to my godfather. I jumped out and ran for the front door. I pounded and rang the bell simultaneously. When no one answered, I tried the doorknob, but it was locked.

It was eerily quiet, and I circled around back, looking inside the kitchen window. A cell phone lay on the table. I called Conor and the phone came alive.

The back door was unlocked, and as I stepped inside, the sound of "Rest in Peace" by Extreme greeted me. I hustled toward the music, and that's where I found Conor and Bobby.

THIRTY-SEVEN

Lee Jensen sat in his car outside the country club. He needed privacy from his wife. He envisioned the retired detective's neck, sliced by Danny's blade across from his sister's house. Sick bastard. And now, the kid confronted the bartender and scared the hell out of him. He needed Savage to stop his nephew.

Jimmy Savage picked up on the first ring. He must have anticipated Jensen's demands and quickly shot him down.

"I'm not a killer. Besides, I'm afraid of him. Look what he did to Kip."

"Christ, Jimmy, he doesn't know what you look like. Kip just happened to spook him. Look, he's got to be stopped before he gets caught. He'll incriminate both of us. You have to fix this before it's too late."

When Savage didn't answer, Jensen quipped, "And don't tell me you never killed anyone. Did you suddenly forget about Luca?"

A deep sigh. "Where's Danny now?"

The coppery scent of blood nauseated me, but I had to make a quick decision: Conor or Bobby. Conor lay face-up, eyes closed, a bloody mess. His T-shirt was drenched in blood, and he was barely breathing. My godfather was curled up nearby, moaning, but I couldn't tell how bad he was until I turned him over. He was conscious, and through the slits of his eyes, recognized me.

"Hank," he breathed and attempted a smile. He tried to move, but I kept him in place. Like Conor, his shirt was bloody but not drenched. "Did Jensen do this?"

"Jensen? No. Young guy with scars." His lids fluttered.

I punched 911 and identified myself as a retired police officer. "I need responders for two stabbed victims in critical condition."

I crossed the room to Conor. "It's Hank, can you hear me?" When he didn't respond, I lifted his shirt. His chest and stomach were perforated. I ran into the bathroom and opened his linen closet.

"Stay with me, guys," I called out, not expecting an answer. I grabbed every towel I could find and ran back to Conor. I applied a towel to staunch the blood, but the towel was soaked almost immediately.

I looked at his hands, and I could tell Conor had put up a fight. Defensive wounds looked like he'd been fending off a long-blade knife. I placed another towel on his chest.

"Hang in there, Conor. Help is on its way." Back to Bobby, I pressed a towel against his chest and held his limp body in my arms.

"We'll get through this, old man. I swear." My heart pounded so quickly I could hardly breathe. If anything happened to my godfather, I'd never forgive myself. I kept reassuring him he'd make it, but I didn't know. I only knew help was nearby as the screaming sirens became louder and louder. I kissed my godfather's forehead and unlocked the front door. This was personal.

THIRTY-EIGHT

Conor's house flooded with first responders, cops, and CSI personnel. After identifying myself and my relationship to the two men down, I stood in a corner and waited until both Bobby and Conor were placed in ambulances.

The detectives from the 109th knew Bobby and assured me they'd find the perpetrator. I assumed now, after twenty-five years of silence, the investigation would finally crack open. For me, that meant bringing down Lee Jensen.

With blood saturated on my shirt, I sped home to take a shower and change. I needed to be more vigilant, and as I drove back to Huntington, I peered through the rearview mirror. If Danny Caruso, Jensen's supposed dead nephew, was, in fact, alive and responsible for the recent attacks, he wouldn't stop until he came after me.

As I entered my complex, my cell buzzed, and I prayed it wasn't someone informing me that Bobby and Conor hadn't made it.

I was relieved to hear Father Charlie's voice.

"Hank, is this a good time to call?"

Crazy question, but I told him it was.

"Since we met, I've been thinking about my brother's confession.

I now realize I left out a few details. After Ralphie told me what he witnessed that night, I jotted it down, almost word for word, in case I needed it one day."

"Yes?"

"I read it over several times and realized I'd missed something when we spoke. I told you Ralphie was an ex-con and didn't want to get involved with the police."

"Yes," I said quickly. "And?"

"They were there, Hank. The police."

I shook my head quickly. "At the bridge, I know."

"No, no. The park."

"Fort Totten?"

"Yes. That's why my brother high-tailed it out of there. He didn't want to get involved."

I paused. "Are you sure about this?"

"Positive. I can't believe I left that out. Most definitely. He saw a patrol car's roof lights swirling in the night."

Luca was alive when the cops arrived.

"Hank?"

"Sorry. Just absorbing this. Do you know what precinct serves Fort Totten?"

"Fort Totten? I believe it's the 111th."

"Not the 109th?"

"No, because a parishioner lives…well anyway, it's the 111th. Do you think someone from that precinct might be able to help you?"

"Maybe."

The 109th oversaw the murder investigation, not the 111th. What if the squad car was from the 111th? What was it doing there early that morning? A routine stop? Maybe? But Luca apparently was waiting for someone. The police?

I shivered at the thought that Luca was apprehended by the police and then disappeared. The question was which precinct showed up?

THIRTY-NINE

"It's done," Danny gushed with morbid excitement. "The fucker was bleeding like a pig when I left, but he put up a good fight." He stopped. "But there was a situation."

He was on the Whitestone Expressway toward the city. Up ahead, Danny noticed a rest area outside LaGuardia Airport and pulled in. He needed to change his clothes and ditch the bloody ones. Uncle Lee's orders.

"What do you mean, a situation?" Savage said, his harsh tone demanding. "It's either done or it's not. Did you kill Reed?"

When Danny didn't answer, Savage said in frustration, "God-dammit, Danny, who? Not the bartender, I hope. You were told to hold off until you got to Reed."

"It got complicated. Some old guy wound up at the bartender's house. How did I know? He started banging on the door. I figured the neighbors would hear, so I opened and...I didn't have a choice. He forced my hand."

"You killed them both? What about—"

"The bartender, yeah, but the old guy, I'm not sure. Possibly.

THE BRIDGE TO MURDER

Look, what was I supposed to do, invite him in for tea? Anyway, it's done. Tell my uncle I'm heading back to the motel to get laid. Have him send someone over in an hour. I want her blond, beautiful, and with big tits. Tomorrow, I'll deal with Reed."

Savage said with effort, "*You* call your uncle."

I checked my front door. All good. Inside the same and I grabbed a Peroni from the fridge, finishing in two gulps.

After showering, I slouched into my usual living room chair and waited for my breathing to return to normal. I'd notified Finn about the attack, and he was inconsolable. Poor Finn. I then called Flushing Hospital and asked about my godfather's and Conor's condition. When the information wasn't forthcoming, I took out the card Detective Joe Enrico from the 109th handed me at the crime scene and called him.

"I'm at the hospital now. Bobby's in surgery. He lost a lot of blood, but his wounds are superficial. No arteries affected, thank God. It looks promising."

"And Conor Mulcahy?" I asked, almost anticipating.

"Not good, Hank. Unlike Bobby, the attacker punctured major blood vessels. The perp must have been one angry son of a bitch. He took it out on Conor like he was on speed." He paused. "It's a good thing for Conor that Bobby walked in on him and threw the guy off. I'm certain he would have continued attacking him. Thanks for giving me the heads up on your investigation. I'll keep you up to date."

I hung up, shaken. I was afraid to close my eyes and sat up in my chair waiting for something to happen. I finally dozed off wondering about the squad car driving up to Fort Totten. It made little sense. If the 109th investigated the murder and needed help, they would have called the neighboring precinct for assistance, but there was no mention of it in the cold case file. Unless the squad car that showed up was from the 109th.

FORTY

The next morning, I drove to Flushing Hospital and found several police vehicles parked out front. Inside, a few patrolmen stood near the front desk, eyeing me. I nodded and showed identification to a middle-aged woman, mentioning my relationship to Bobby Larkin, and asked for a visitor's pass.

She made a call, nodding to the phone a few times. She hung up, then handed me a pass. "Room 202." She pointed at the elevator doors.

On the way over, I bought Bobby a chocolate bar from Walgreens. He loved Godiva. Reaching the floor, a uniformed policeman in his early twenties nodded as I approached.

"He's sitting up, a good sign. The receptionist told me you were his nephew. I didn't know Bobby had one."

"So, you know Bobby?"

"Only by reputation. I'm told he's a great guy. Too bad I didn't get a chance to work with him back in the day."

"I'm actually his godson," I said. "He and my father were best friends."

"Oh. Anyway, you're his first visitor."

213

Bobby was barely sitting up. His face was drawn, and he looked pale. His glazed eyes were facing the TV, but I doubt he was paying attention to the news. He was clearly on heavy drugs.

He blinked when I stepped in front of him, holding up the Godiva's chocolate bar.

"Hey," I said. "You look great for a guy who just went ten rounds."

He studied me for a moment then nodded. "Say, Hank."

"I can imagine what the other guy looks like." I smiled and placed the chocolate on his tray table next to a glass of water and a thermos.

Bobby attempted a laugh but got into a coughing fit. He recovered and motioned me to sit on a nearby chair.

I nodded at the door. "The uniform outside said you haven't had any visitors yet. No detectives asking for statements?"

He shook his head slowly. "The nurse told me I've been out until a little while ago," he said stumbling on his words. "It was quick."

"The attack?"

A nod. "Guy who opened the door was covered in blood. Looked really angry." Bobby stopped, wiped his mouth with his tongue, and took a breath. "I grabbed something, don't remember what and swung." He looked down at his bandaged hands. "Knife kept slicing at me."

He took a breath. "I...pushed him into the door, but he jus' came back and..." Bobby touched his neck, also bandaged. "Then he took off."

"I found you in Conor's bedroom."

At first it didn't register. "I wanted to help. When I saw him, he was on the bed bleeding. That's all I remember." A longer pause. "Is he...?"

I tightened my lips. "I don't know. He lost a lot of blood. If you hadn't been there..."

He nodded absently.

"You told me when I found you the attacker had scars. That sounds about right? Maybe it was the guy who confronted Conor at the bar."

Bobby closed his eyes for a moment, then nodded. "Scary guy."

I didn't expect Bobby to answer in his condition, but I had a theory. The attacker had been in prison, only not for Annie Baxter's murder.

"Hank?"

I looked up, and he pointed to the thermos.

"Thirsty."

I poured a glass and helped him sip through a straw. After swallowing, he nodded, and I returned it to the tray.

I said, "What were you doing at Conor's place anyway? I thought you were going to the bar."

Bobby blinked. "Wasn't there so I went to his house."

"Could have been a tragic mistake." I said, "Conor told Finn he saw Lee Jensen with the killer that night. Turns out Jensen had a nephew who lived with his mother in Whitestone." I paused, let him digest it. "It's possible the nephew killed Annie Baxter and now attacked you and Conor. Did you know him? His name's Danny Caruso."

A blank stare. "Think he died."

"Those were the rumors. What if Danny didn't die? What if he killed Annie and Jensen helped him escape?"

I didn't expect Bobby to answer, as he stayed almost frozen.

The door opened and a nurse popped in with a tray of food.

She greeted me, then to Bobby, she said, "It's nice that you have company, Mr. Larkin, but it's time to have lunch." She was about to place a tray of something including Jell-O on the table and smiled. She lifted the chocolate bar. "My favorite. Are we going to share this?"

Bobby nodded slowly. "Sure."

215

I stood, grinning at the nurse, a thirty something black woman with a monotone voice.

"Okay, then," I said. "I'll come back later." I kissed Bobby's forehead and whispered, "Enjoy your lunch."

I returned to my car, wondering about Danny Caruso. If he were still alive and responsible for attacking Bobby and Conor, I knew I was next. That meant I would go on the attack.

I glanced at my buzzing phone—Lisa. I wondered if she was going to continue accusing me of interfering in her personal life. Instead, she babbled about something totally different.

"I told you I was taking Mom to my place and started packing her clothes. That's when I found something. I can't make heads or tails of it. Can you come over?"

I was curious about the 'heads or tails' thing and told her I'd be right over. It must have been important because Lisa was standing outside the front door. No smiles, kisses, or hugs this time, just a confused expression as she waved papers at me.

"Settle down," I said, holding her hand. "Let's discuss whatever this is inside."

She perched next to me on the sofa as I removed documents from a plastic cover. The first page was headed: Whitestone Life Insurance Company. I looked over at her, my brows arched.

"It's an insurance policy."

"Keep reading."

I got to the middle of the page and stopped. My eyes narrowed on the insured and beneficiary. Now I was confused.

"It says Luca took out a life insurance policy in the amount of ten thousand dollars. Your mother was the beneficiary. It was issued a few days before he disappeared." I scratched my chin. "Any idea why Luca would take out a life insurance policy? And where would he get the money to pay the premium? He worked only part-time." I shook my head. "Makes no sense." I peered up from the document. "And you found it where?"

"I began gathering my mother's clothes and when I searched her closet, I discovered it in a corner above a strong box. It was among other papers." She paused. "You can imagine my surprise. I don't remember my mother mentioning an insurance policy, especially that one. Believe me, Hank, I would have remembered if she had. It's not like we were suddenly rich. Nothing changed. What do you make of it?"

I read the attached pages, but it was too legal for me. All I assumed was Luca obtained a policy to help his mother and Lisa in the event of his death.

Lisa kept shaking her head. "Was Luca concerned he might disappear or god-forbid be killed?"

I looked up. "Did you ask your mother?"

"Of course, but she doesn't have a clue. Mom can't remember too much these days. She says maybe our father took it out. But that's impossible; he'd been dead for five years."

I crossed my legs. "Has your mother taken her pills today? Maybe that's why she can't remember."

"Who knows? She was quiet and distant when I arrived, the way she gets when she hasn't been medicated. I was too busy reading the policy to take notice. She's upstairs sitting on her bed. I'll check for her pills, get her dressed, and bring her down. Maybe you'll have better luck."

When Lisa left, I studied the policy again, wondering if I'd missed something. But I hadn't. I dropped it on the table and got up to stretch. It helped me think.

I walked to the window and peered out. Nothing suspicious.

"Here's Hank, Mom."

The scent of her perfume wafted over me, and I turned and smiled.

"Hank, it's so nice of you to drop by." She took a few steps, hands outstretched, face beaming. I returned it and looked at Lisa, who was following her mother. At least she remembered me.

We embraced.

"I missed you." She looked down at the table, and I assumed she was looking at the insurance policy. Instead, she turned to Lisa, "Honey, get Hank some coffee. I have a few treats somewhere on the table." She pointed at the sofa. "Come, let's sit."

She took a breath. "There's been a murder in Whitestone." She held my arm tightly. "I'm going to stay with Lisa a while. Terrible. You and Bobby have to watch yourselves. How is Bobby?"

Marie obviously hadn't heard. "He's fine."

She nodded, but there was sadness in her eyes. She was still hooked on my godfather, despite their short-lived relationship years ago. "Say hello for me."

I squeezed her slight arm. "I will."

Lisa returned with coffee, jam, and croissants, which reminded me of Mrs. Haviken's Danish at the rectory.

After two bites of the croissant and a swallow of coffee, I peered at Lisa who had brought a chair over and sat facing us. I nodded for her to start the conversation.

She picked up the insurance policy. "Mom, I found this among your things this morning. Remember, I asked if you were familiar with it. I found it in your closet. How could Luca afford a life insurance policy?"

We waited. Marie glanced at the policy and shrugged. "That was so long ago, Lisa."

"Yes, but ten thousand dollars. I don't remember you having that kind of money. You were struggling to get by, and I worked part-time to attend college. And Luca was still missing. If we had that kind of money...anyway, what happened to it?"

Marie sat quietly for a moment, then turned to me. "Bobby helped us financially. Maybe that was it."

I could see Lisa getting worked up.

"Marie," I said touching her hand. "Bobby was very kind, but he would have told me if he bought a policy in Luca's name."

She blinked. "Luca worked part-time for Lee Jensen. Maybe he took it out as a…you know, one of those things they give employees."

"Benefits," I said.

"Yes, benefits. Now I remember, he took one out on everyone who worked for him. Nice man."

"Lee Jensen told you that?" I said.

"Yes, I remember now. He came over after…Luca disappeared, and said he bought it for Luca and wanted me to know the money would be coming at some point." She stopped, closed her eyes. "There was something else, but I can't remember, Hank. Sorry."

I searched Lisa's face and mouthed, "Lee Jensen."

"Can we go now, Lisa? I'm afraid to stay here until they find the killer."

"We're leaving now Mom."

Marie rose slowly and smiled. "You take care, Hank."

With the 109th guarding Bobby and Conor twenty-four-seven, I decided to work out of Bobby's house. I sat in his favorite chair near the living room window and collected my thoughts. My previous conversation with Matt hadn't gone well, but I needed information on his father and hoped now he'd be receptive.

I held my breath and punched in the number. Matt answered after a few rings sounding friendly. He apologized for being abrupt last time but wanted Tara's pregnancy to remain in the past.

"No need to apologize," I said. "It was insensitive of me to ask. Sometimes my line of questioning is uncomfortable for people. That's the nature of the business." I paused, peering out the window.

A young couple holding hands walked past heading to the park. I smiled, remembering those days.

"I don't know if you heard that Conor and Bobby were attacked in Conor's house. The assailant got away. Bobby's recovering, but Conor's condition is grave."

"Hank, that's terrible. Are you thinking it had to do with your investigation?"

"Has to be." I told him about Conor's encounter with Annie Baxter's killer at the bar, and Bobby being in the wrong place when Conor was attacked. "You're not going to like this, but Conor witnessed your father near Annie Baxter's crime scene. He didn't think your father was directly involved but knew the killer. And it appears it's the same person who attacked Conor and my godfather."

When Matt finally responded, his voice was subdued. "My father was there? Gee, Hank, this is a serious allegation. It's not that I don't believe Conor, but he could have been mistaken. Who was he, the killer?"

"Your cousin, Danny."

A snort. "No way. He's been dead for years." He stopped, realizing the murder had occurred years ago. "Danny?" he breathed.

I said, "He was a handful and constantly in trouble as a teen. What if Conor is right?"

"I'm having a hard time taking this in. I admit, Danny was trouble—"

"You said he's dead. Was there ever a funeral?"

"Well, not that I'm aware of."

"When did you last see him?" I asked, watching a jogger run by.

"Oh, God, a long time ago. Probably at a family dinner at our house. Before the murder. Hank, it's not like we hung out. Like you said, he was trouble. Even though we were related, I didn't want anything to do with him."

Matt paused. "I do remember asking my father about him maybe a year after the murder. He said Danny died tragically traveling abroad. Something like that."

I waited for Matt to work out the kinks. "Thinking about it, I wonder why my father hadn't mentioned Danny's death until I brought it up." He paused. "And Conor definitely identified my cousin as Annie Baxter's killer?"

"He did the other night when Danny confronted him at Fillmore's. Why he showed up after all these years is anyone's guess. Except, someone must have told your cousin about my investigation. Maybe that someone was your father."

"Oh, God. Where the hell has Danny been for the past twenty-five years? And how did my father find him?"

I walked to the kitchen and poured a glass of water. "My guess is he'd been in prison. I have no idea how your father found him." I chugged down the water and returned to the living room. "Look, I know it's a lot to take in, but Danny attacked Conor for a reason. And my best guess is he knew or found out Conor witnessed the crime. Bobby was probably collateral damage."

I heard Matt sigh.

"Should I call my father and tell him I know what's going on? Maybe he can stop Danny before he plans…"

Matt had to be naïve. "Your father will deny everything. In fact, I suspect he's given Danny the green light to finish the job, which means your cousin is coming after me."

"My father," he said, his tone sullen. "I suspected he was into dirty stuff but never murder."

"There's something else. Did you know your father took out a life insurance policy for Luca not long before he disappeared? His mother thought it was an employee perk. She was the beneficiary."

A soft chuckle. "You're joking, right? My father wouldn't spend a dime on perks, especially an insurance policy." He stopped. "Hank, if my father had anything to do with Luca's disappearance, I swear…"

"You won't be first in line."

Matt called later that night. He'd called his mother and discovered his father had been in New York. She wasn't happy about it, given his history of cheating.

"It's too coincidental, him being here while people are attacked and killed. After I got off the phone, I went to their house here in Whitestone and looked around. It doesn't look like anybody's been there lately. The sofa and chairs in the living room were covered in sheets." Matt took a long breath. "This is so bad."

FORTY-ONE

Danny grabbed a few slices and a Coke from Renaldo's Pizzeria in Whitestone. He took an enormous bite and downed it with his drink. Wiping his mouth with his hand, he searched the restaurant and spotted a young woman sitting by herself. She looked Latina: long black hair, dark features, and ripe red lips. His loins screamed for her, and as she peered over at him, he smiled, widening his scary facial scars. She turned away quickly, and he could tell she was frightened by his appearance.

"Bitch," Danny muttered. If he had the time, he'd follow her. She'd be real sorry she dissed him. He wolfed down his food and slipped off his stool, then took a long look at the woman, who kept staring at her meal. She was lucky, Danny thought. There was always tomorrow.

On the way out, Jensen buzzed him.

"Hey Uncle, I'm heading to Long Island."

"He's not there."

"Okay, where then?"

"His car is parked in Bobby Larkin's driveway, so I assume he's staying there while Larkin is in the hospital." He stopped. "I'm still upset with you. I told you to go after Reed first. I hope this doesn't come back to bite us in the ass."

Danny smirked to himself. So much fun. "You worry too much, Uncle Lee. By tonight, Reed will be dead and the investigation over."

Alex remained in a coma from the fall, Conor was near death, and Bobby was scheduled to be discharged in a day or two. Jensen would be talking to Danny, and Danny would be looking for me.

At Bobby's, I made myself at home. Except for a few cans of Bud and leftovers from one of his female friends, Bobby's refrigerator was near empty. I didn't bother to unwrap the plate. At least he had coffee, and I made a pot. It was almost nine, and I called out for a pizza. That would hold me over for a while.

In less than an hour, a car pulled up, and a young man walked toward the house, carrying the pizza box. That eased my concern, and I opened the door.

After devouring several slices of pepperoni, I sat back in Bobby's favorite chair, overlooking the street. Before hanging up with Matt, I asked for his father's cell number. I fidgeted, contemplating the conversation, then dialed out.

Jensen picked up on the second ring.

"Who is this?" he asked, his tone anxious.

I knew Lee Jensen as Mr. Jensen, and I addressed him as such.

"Who is this again?" he asked.

Good answer. I hadn't seen him in over twenty-five years.

"Hank Reed, Mr. Jensen. You probably don't remember me, but I was a close friend of your son, Matt, and Luca Falcone. You're probably wondering why I'm calling."

"Well, I am a bit…curious."

Another good response.

"Lots of bad things have been happening in Whitestone lately. Murder and attempted murder. You might have heard from Matt."

"Yes, it's terrible. Matt's very upset. He told me the bartender, Conor, I think, died or is near death. And your godfather, how is he?"

"They're both recovering," I lied. "Thanks for asking."

"Wonderful news."

Bullshit.

"Fortunately, Conor was able to provide the forensic sketch artist with a detailed description of his attacker. The guy had multiple jagged facial scars, making it easier for Conor to identify him."

I paused. "Turns out, the attacker was the same guy who showed up at his bar the night before. Dumb, don't you think? I mean, if you're going to kill someone, why show your face sooner? The real question is why did he go after Conor in the first place?"

I paused again, letting Jensen take in his potential problem. "And Conor, while not the strongest guy around, must have sensed his attacker would act soon, and he wasn't taken by surprise. Otherwise, the scar-faced guy would have finished the job. It's just a matter of time before the police find the guy."

Jensen appeared to be searching for air. "That's hopeful news," he said weakly. "But, I'm at a loss as to how I fit into this."

"Oh, right, I should have mentioned that sooner. I'm a private investigator. Lisa Falcone, she's Pisano now, asked me to investigate her brother's disappearance based on a letter she received informing her that Luca didn't kill Annie Baxter. The contents of the letter were eye-opening. It seems a witness saw the real killer." I paused, smiled to myself. "I'm frustrated that he hadn't come forward sooner, but at least now, I have something to go by."

Jensen coughed. "Did the letter identify the person?"

"Good question. He claimed he didn't know the guy, only that he'd see him around the neighborhood. So, he had to be local. What do you think?"

I heard a hard swallow. "Gee, Hank, I haven't a clue. Outside of the detectives questioning me and my daughter, Tara, there's nothing new I can offer. I'm so sorry."

I bet.

Jensen then rattled on about him being a councilman in good standing with the community. I thought his head was about to explode when he finished. "Is that it?"

"Let me check my notes." Another smile. "Oh, right. I believe Luca worked part-time for you. Again, I'm just verifying a few things. And that he and Tara were dating at the time of his disappearance."

"Well, yes, that's true," he blurted.

"Did I catch you at a bad time? I can call back."

"No, no, now is fine. I just returned from…a business meeting and then a round of golf, so I'm feeling a bit fatigued."

I'm sure.

"I hear they have terrific courses in Hilton Head," I said not having a clue. "Lucky you."

"Yes, terrific is one way of describing the courses here. You golf, Hank?"

"Never took up the game, I'm afraid, Mr. Jensen."

"Please, don't be so formal. You're not a teenager anymore. Please call me Lee. Anyway, golf is a strategic sport, and, among other things, requires concentration."

"So, I heard."

"What else can I help you with now that we're finished talking golf?" He laughed guardedly.

"I was wondering if you recall anything else about that night. You said the detectives questioned you and Tara. I spoke to her before, and she confirmed that. But any little nugget you might have overlooked would be helpful."

"I'm afraid not," he answered too quickly. "Sorry, it was so long

226

ago. I'm older now and my memory isn't what it once was. You'll get there one day."

"Sure, I understand." I added, "If you recall at the time, Luca was the prime suspect."

"Unfortunately, that's true."

"But now, according to a witness, Luca was walking toward Fort Totten at the time of the murder, so he couldn't have killed the woman. It's in the letter. The witness left before Luca disappeared from the fort. I'm working that angle."

I paused. "Anyway, the police have their sights on the real killer, so it's just a matter of time before they pick him up. And now, with the attack on Conor, there could be a connection between the two. I'm guessing, of course."

Jensen cleared his throat. "Well, I never believed Luca killed her. He and my daughter were involved at the time, and I saw a bright future in him, and them. So sad."

More bullshit.

"And since you're not here in Whitestone, you might not have heard about another murder a few days ago. A retired detective. Seems the killer used the same weapon on Conor Mulcahy and Bobby Larkin. Detectives are canvassing the area as we speak."

When he didn't respond, I said, "Lee?"

"Yes, I'm here. Do the investigators know who the victim was and what he was doing in the area? Sounds like it could be an isolated case," he said.

Good try.

"Possibly. It's just that everything happened within days of each other. So crazy. Anyway, that's about all I have. If you remember anything, please call me."

"Yes, of course. The number you called from, is that good?"

"Yes, the one and only."

He asked, "Do you still live in Whitestone, Hank?"

He should ask his nephew. "I've always lived on Long Island, but

I'm staying at my godfather Bobby's place a few days. It's close to the investigation."

"Yes, makes sense. Give my best to Bobby."

"I will. And good luck with your golf game. Remember to concentrate."

FORTY-TWO

Darkness made it easy. Danny parked around the corner from the park, a few blocks from old man Larkin's house. He knew the neighborhood from his youth and snuck through backyards until he reached his kill. He was especially pleased the lights inside the house were off.

It was after midnight, so he figured Reed was asleep. Danny removed a four-inch switchblade from his pants pocket, snapped it open, and kissed the blade for good luck.

He wasn't in a rush and pulled on a few windows until he found the kitchen window unlocked. Stupid Reed. He slithered over the sink, and onto the floor. His eyes shifted about until they adjusted to the darkness. He snapped open his blade, then slowly moved about. He wasn't familiar with Larkin's house, but he'd been in others similar and walked into the living room.

No sign of Reed.

He crept into a bedroom and wiped his right hand on his pants to get a better grip and stood over the bed. It was empty. He continued down the hall and stopped at another bedroom.

Danny's sneer suggested he reached the right room, as a body bulged from underneath a bed sheet. He approached with caution, his knife settling over his head.

Reaching the bed, Danny plunged the knife into the body like he was tearing up a rag doll.

"You're a dead man, Reed."

He heard a moan, then a cry, and a plea, only it wasn't coming from the bed. He jerked his head around to a shadow standing near the closet.

"Hello Danny."

<hr>

Lee Jensen should have been happy when his son called. They'd been estranged for years. Matt hated him for being a serial wife cheater and a crook, which his father vehemently denied.

But when his son charged the conversation with vitriol, swearing his father had done the unthinkable, including faking a life insurance policy, his mouth went dry.

"Was it blood money?" Matt demanded.

Jensen's stomach tightened and he denied it vigorously. "Life insurance policy on Luca's life, that's crazy. Who's feeding you this bullshit? Reed?"

"How do you know about Hank Reed? I never mentioned him."

Jensen stuttered. "He called me. He's a troublemaker and causing a rift between us. I've given you nothing but love—"

"The way you gave Mom love by screwing everyone in sight."

When Jensen failed to answer, Matt said, "First of all, Whitestone Insurance Company doesn't exist. The ten thousand you gave Mrs. Falcone came from your campaign money. You didn't even pay the full amount at once. Your records show you paid her over a year. That must have hurt, paying anything, and I ask you again: Was that blood money for killing Luca? He was my good friend and your daughter's boyfriend."

"You went through my confidential records? You have no right—"

"So, you don't deny it."

Jensen was grateful he was home and alone. "You have it all wrong, Matt." He stopped. "Where are you?"

"At your house. I know you were in New York. How come you didn't stay at the house?"

"What?"

"Forget it. You'd only lie."

"Matt, please don't do anything crazy with my files. They're personal."

"Always about you. I'm sure the authorities will find them interesting and incriminating," he said, and disconnected.

Jensen struggled to breathe. He needed a solution and fast. Was Matt just angry or was he willing to hand over his secret documents? He tried pushing aside the unthinkable.

FORTY-THREE

Savage slammed on his brakes as he turned the corner. He counted four squad cars in front of Bobby Larkin's house, and backed up slowly hoping he wouldn't be discovered, then made a U-turn and drove down the next street and parked.

He took a deep breath and called Jensen. "It's done."

Jensen was too wound up with his conversation with Matt to sleep, so when the call came in at 1:00 A.M., he was wide awake.

"Where are you?"

"Around the corner from Larkin's house. The cops are all over the place. I'm guessing your nephew escaped. This would be the time to make an anonymous call and send the cops to Danny's motel room."

"Wait! How do you know he killed Reed?"

"What do you mean? I saw the cops outside—"

"You're assuming Danny did the killing. What if it was the other way around?"

Savage stared through the dirty windshield. "I guess I was getting ahead of myself."

"He was quick," I said, holding up my bandaged left arm, sitting on a hospital chair across from my godfather at eight the next morning. "He nicked me with his knife, then slammed me with a pillow, knocking my gun to the floor." I shook my head. "The bastard took off before I had a chance to catch him." I gave Bobby a drained smile.

"It was Jensen's nephew, wasn't it?" Bobby groaned. "The guy's a psychopath."

"I'm sure Jensen tipped him off after our conversation. I told him I'd be staying at your place a few days." I paused. "Oh, by the way, I owe you a new set of sheets and a pillow."

"Not funny, Hank. He could have killed you. Now let the police do their job."

I nodded to appease my godfather.

"Or, at the very least, park your car around the corner from the house." Bobby was sitting up looking healthy with rosy cheeks and a tough demeanor.

"I'm getting out of here later today, so the bastard will have to deal with me next time he pays another visit."

"Easy," I said. "They won't release you if your blood pressure is through the roof."

"Yeah, yeah. Any news on Conor?"

I shook my head. "No real change."

Bobby shook his head. "Poor Finn. I'll check in on him after I'm discharged. Conor is all he has, and vice versa."

We sat quietly for a moment. "By the way, Father Charlie called back. He now remembers his brother telling him a police car showed up at Fort Totten the night Luca disappeared."

"A squad car?"

I nodded. "I'm guessing the 111th got involved, but I don't remember reading about it in the case files. Do you?"

He shook his head.

"If Charlie's brother saw a local squad car pull up and grab Luca, the cops would have contacted the 109th. That didn't happen."

Bobby thought for a moment. "Unless it wasn't the 111th squad car that showed up."

I walked to the window and looked below. Two local squad cars were parked outside.

"What if the car that pulled up was one of ours?" Bobby suggested.

I turned. "The 109th?"

Bobby's expression turned dark. "Possibly."

My heart raced. "That former detective who was killed across from Jensen's sister's house, Kip something or other, wasn't he involved in the Annie Baxter investigation?"

He nodded. "I'm beginning to get a bad feeling about this, Hank."

"You said you never trusted the guy. What if he was working for Jensen at the time? Maybe he drove to Fort Totten that night." I stopped, meeting my godfather's gaze. "We assumed Jensen was calling the shots back then. It's likely the guy was still on his payroll, helping his nephew finish the job."

"I don't know, Hank," Bobby said. "If Kip was involved with Danny, why did he kill him?"

Good question. "Maybe Danny didn't know whose side he was on."

FORTY-FOUR

My guess was Danny regrouped to figure out his next move. Mine was to head home and I told Bobby I'd call him in the morning.

Traffic was light after midnight, and I arrived home in forty minutes, exhausted and drained. I needed to sleep and dropped onto the sofa.

My car alarm wrenched me out of a deep sleep, and I leaped off the sofa, my head in a fog. I fumbled for my Glock on the end table and checked the time. It was just past 2:00 A.M., so I'd slept no more than an hour.

I drew the living room curtains back and watched my car create a carnival-like effect: headlights in concert with the horn blowing like crazy. Grabbing the key fob, I was about to turn off the alarm but stopped. If anyone lay in wait, they'd figure I'd walk out the front door. Instead, I stepped out the back and circled around to the front.

The carnival ended and I peered into near-darkness. Nothing moved, but I was certain the alarm hadn't gone off by itself. If Danny was close by, he'd be hiding. I took a breath and inched around the car, stopping at the sagging passenger rear tire.

Someone had punctured it. Danny's trademark. Was Scarface close by? Or was he just taunting me? I couldn't stay out all night and edged to the back of the house. I was about to enter the kitchen for a glass of water then stopped.

Except for a nightlight in the next room, the interior was dark, but I sensed something was out of place. I'm neat and keep my closet doors closed. The one in the living room was open.

I coughed and a shadow leaped out.

Danny charged, his knife ready to strike. I swung my Glock, but he dodged, partially blocking its impact on his jaw. He managed to smack my wrist with the butt of his knife, sending my weapon flying. No chance to regain it with his knife flashing in front of my face. I swiped at his arm, the blade missing my face by inches.

He dropped into a crouch and ranted incoherently about not killing me the last time. I feinted, trying to avoid that gleaming blade and dove into him low, knocking him off balance. He cursed and staggered back but didn't fall, and we broke free and began circling each other again, looking for an opening. Then he darted in, slashing back and forth with his blade. I leaped aside and snatched at his wrist. With a quick turn, using body leverage, I managed to spin him to the floor.

Danny rolled to his knees and sneered, seemingly unfazed. His lips twisted into a snarl, the ugly scars on his face red and inflamed, and he jabbed at empty air with his switchblade still firmly in his grasp.

"Fuck you, Reed," he growled and leaped into a crouch as he yanked on the throw rug where I stood, sending me on my ass. He leaped at me, his knife in both hands and struck at my chest. I rolled away, but the blade caught my shirt and nicked a rib as it buried into the floor.

I kicked him in the ribs, but he hung onto the knife. His left hand latched onto my ankle, trying to pull me into striking distance as he tried to free his blade.

I tried to wriggle free and scrambled frantically for my Glock. Luckily, one finger hooked the trigger guard. I drew it to me and struggled to sit up. When Danny saw me gaining control of the weapon, his eyes flared. He leaped up and charged for the door, screaming.

I staggered to my feet and dashed after him, but before I reached the front door, I heard a gunshot then another.

I paused, then realized Danny didn't have a gun. I dropped to my hands and knees and crawled out the open door as I heard a car engine fire up in the distance. It couldn't be Danny Caruso's: he was sprawled out on the ground, not moving.

I called my former boss, Suffolk County Lieutenant Jimmy Stanton, whose jurisdiction included Huntington. I generally called Jimmy when I was in trouble. And I was definitely in trouble. He was surprised to hear from me so soon and reminded me I was on his shit list.

"What the hell, Reed, do you realize what time it is? It's a good thing I'm at work. I wasn't expecting to hear from you for at least a year." He laughed guardedly. "I'm guessing it's not social."

My eyes remained on Danny Caruso. "Not this time."

My neighborhood lit up from the sirens. Their lights on, neighbors in whatever they wore to bed, stood anxiously in front of their homes staring my way. I didn't realize I was so popular.

Despite his rhetoric, my lieutenant came through and called a contact at the Suffolk County Police Department – 2nd Precinct, who sent out a team. They found me alone, near Danny Caruso's body. So much for my neighbors' curiosity.

237

I glanced from my slashed tire to Danny and wondered who I should send a thank you card to. Certainly not Lee Jensen: he was back in Hilton Head, though I suspected he had a hand in it. And it certainly wasn't the deceased corrupt cop, Kip.

Detectives checked my house, my unfired Glock, Danny's knife, and questioned me about the incident. I provided a short version, which seemed to satisfy Detective Eric Kashdin, a guy I'd known for years. He suggested I should be on the lookout for Danny Caruso's killer in the event I was the target. Great advice.

I didn't go back to sleep but waited until seven in the morning to break the news to Bobby.

"Danny Caruso is no longer a problem," I told him. "He was killed in front of my house, only not by me."

"You're okay, though, right?"

"After three strong cups of coffee, yeah, I'm fine."

"It had to have been one of Jensen's guys. I'm guessing his nephew became too volatile. Unless…the bullet was meant for you."

I peered out the window. The sun began to rise, and my tire still had a gash in it. Last night wasn't a dream. Okay, maybe a nightmare. "Hopefully not," I said. "But I'm not taking any chances."

"So, you're not quitting the investigation."

I blinked and turned away from the sun. "Not until Jensen is dealt with. Any ideas?"

"Funny you should ask. I got in touch with a cop I know, Harry Pitts, who retired at the same time I did. He was a detective at the 109th. Very straight guy. Happily married, with a son about your age. Also, a cop. He heard about the recent murder in Whitestone. Crazy times, he said."

I needed more coffee and walked into the kitchen.

He continued. "I told him about the witness who followed Luca to Fort Totten and the squad car that showed up. He was aware of the disappearance but not much more. Certainly, nothing about a car showing up. I told him it wasn't in the cold case files.

"We got to talking about the Annie Baxter case. From what Harry heard, he believed the detectives in charge worked the case too quickly, as though someone wanted it closed ASAP."

"Interesting." I lifted the top of the coffee container, counted four scoops, then added water, and turned on the coffeemaker.

Bobby said, "It didn't surprise him because, like me, he wasn't crazy about the detectives in charge. He called them the shady detective team. Years later, when one of them retired, he gave himself a retirement party at his house. We were invited, but I made up some bullshit story about having a prior engagement.

"Harry went, and when he arrived at the guy's house in Lloyd Harbor, not far from your Huntington office, he couldn't get over the place. He said it had to be at least three thousand square feet with a sprawling backyard that ended at the sound."

"Damn," I said, waiting for my coffee to finish brewing.

"Right. Ostentatious is what Harry called it. Where did the newly retired get the shekels to buy a one-point-five-million-dollar house back then, especially when he lived in a modest place in Bayside while on the job?

"Disgraceful bastard." Bobby spit. "Sorry, Hank, I get worked up every time I think about the guy. At first, Harry figured he came into money when his parents died. Or maybe he won the lottery. Neither happened, so Harry assumed the retired detective got his money elsewhere."

"Illegally," I suggested, hearing the coffeemaker chime.

"Had to be. What I don't get is why he'd boldly show off his dirty wealth to other cops. Of course, there was talk later and, according to Harry, the guy became a pariah."

I poured a cup of Java and took a sip, waiting for Bobby to identify the dirty cop. But when he remained silent, I asked him, "This crooked cop, does he still live in Lloyd Harbor?"

"As far as Harry knew, but like I said, after the retirement party, the rest of the guys stayed away."

"Are you going to keep me guessing?"

"Right, his name. Jimmy Savage. And the guy killed near Jensen's sister's house was his partner, Arnie 'Kip' Lefkowitz."

FORTY-FIVE

Jimmy Savage made it home without incident and needed a stiff drink. He'd never killed anyone before, but he had no compunction about his victim. The guy was venom, a murderer, and needed to be dealt with. At least, that was how he justified his actions.

He downed a Dewars neat, then another, then called Jensen. "It's done."

He imagined Jensen's wide smile. "Good job, Jimmy. Danny or Reed? Or both?"

"I didn't see Reed, only Danny. He came charging out of Reed's house without his knife, so I assumed he left it in the P.I.'s gut. Either way, your nephew won't be a problem anymore."

"I hope Danny didn't talk to Reed. I mean, why would he? The kid would only implicate himself."

Savage poured another drink. He didn't like what Jensen was getting at. "Look, Lee, the confrontation was quick. I'm guessing they weren't into conversation, so let's leave it at that."

"No, you're right. I guess I'll have to comfort my sister and insist on paying for the funeral. A small distraction before getting back to my golf game."

Savage knew Jensen was a cold-blooded bastard.

"Maybe I'll play it cool with my wife and try getting back into Matt and Tara's good graces."

"Sounds like a win-win situation," Savaged mocked.

"Great news for sure. Oh, and Jimmy, you're entitled to a free vacation. I'll throw in a cruise for you and the wife. Not a world cruise, of course." He chuckled. Jensen was in a jolly mood.

"Thanks." He suddenly envisioned dark thoughts. "I just hope no one saw me. If I'm caught…"

"Nothing's going to happen," Jensen assured. "Pour yourself a drink and relax."

Savage gazed at his glass and chugged the liquid down. "Yeah, but what if—?

"Then we'll deal with it," Jensen said, sounding annoyed. "Just enjoy the moment."

Savage didn't trust Jensen, and if he tried to screw him, he had a backup plan. More than informing the police that Jensen helped his dead nephew escape after killing Annie Baxter. Much more. One that would put Lee Jensen away for life.

The following day, I called Bobby around 5:00 P.M. He generally answered my calls immediately unless he was entertaining one of his lady friends. Given his recent release from the hospital, I assumed he wasn't quite ready for a romantic evening. So, I was surprised when my call went to voicemail.

"It's about five o'clock. Call me," I said.

When he didn't get back by six, I called again. No Bobby. I suddenly felt like a concerned parent and wondered if I should call one of Bobby's girlfriends, only I didn't have their phone numbers.

By eight o'clock, I started to panic. If he was on his meds, he might have fallen into a deep sleep. But given what had been happening lately, I decided to pay him a visit.

When I arrived, the interior lights were out, but his car wasn't in the driveway. With a spare key, I let myself in and searched around, calling out his name. My heart pounded when I reached the only door closed: his bedroom.

I opened it slowly. Bobby's end table light was on, but the room was empty. My gaze caught a Sticky, and I peeled it off, attempting to read his handwriting. Something about going after the dirty cop, and he was up to it.

Bobby would probably assume I'd eventually stop by, but why go after this guy alone? I swallowed hard and hoped he was up to it, whatever that meant.

It had to be Jimmy Savage. I speed-dialed Bobby and wasn't surprised when he didn't pick up.

"Don't do anything foolish," I demanded. "I'm on my way."

I Googled FIND A PERSON and found Savage's address. He lived close to my office, so I was familiar with the area. From Whitestone, it would take less than an hour, hopefully in time to stop whatever situation my godfather was involved in.

The Northern State Parkway was the quickest route, and I sped until reaching the Huntington exit, then turned north on Route 110. When I reached Main Street, I continued to West Neck Road, passed the old Marshall Field Estate, now Caumsett State Park, and reached Sound Bay Drive. I swung left and stopped in front of Savage's house. Bobby's car was parked on the gravel driveway blocking a three-car garage. At 9:00 P.M., all was quiet and dark.

I followed the slate walkway to the back, where I heard an altercation, voices escalating, followed by accusatory threats, and then a pop. I ran to the backyard deck with my Glock out and pointed it at Jimmy Savage who was standing over Bobby, pistol in his hand, mumbling.

"Drop your gun, Savage, and stand back. I have my weapon on you."

He turned, lifting his gun in my direction, his eyes narrowed.

"I'm a perfect shot and a former detective. Don't make me convince you."

He paused, gazed down at Bobby, dropped his gun, and stepped away. "It was an accident. He made me."

"Bullshit." I heard Bobby mumbling as he shifted his body and struggled up.

Savage stepped back. "I missed?"

Bobby sneered, unzipped his windbreaker. "I came prepared, asshole," he said, exposing a Kevlar chest protector. His smile was weak, but he looked okay. He stared at Savage's handgun and kicked it over to me. "You tried to kill me, you bastard."

"You made me," Savage complained. "It's your fault. Why did you have to bring up the past?"

"I should call this in," I said.

Savage's eyes begged me not to. "Please don't, Reed. It was a mistake. Tell him, Bobby, we had too much to drink."

I scooped up the revolver, looked it over. "This isn't Florida, Savage. Guns are illegal here."

"Come on, you know I'm a retired cop. I have a permit to carry. Besides, I need it for protection." He stopped and averted his eyes.

"From whom?"

"Just in case," he said too quickly. He pointed at Bobby. "No one got hurt, so can't we just forget what happened?"

"How do you know my name? I asked. "I've never seen you before. If I checked your phone, would my number show up as a recent call?"

He said nothing.

"You called the other day, warning me not to continue the investigation. Whose idea was that yours or Jensen's?"

He shrugged. "Jensen didn't know I called. I was trying to protect you from someone."

"Danny Caruso," I said. I held up Savage's revolver. "If this is tested, would it match the slugs that killed him? Don't get me wrong, you probably saved my life, but it's still murder."

Savage shot a look at his patio slider, then back to me. "I know you're interested in finding out if I killed Luca Falcone. I told Bobby I didn't and swore on my life."

"But you know who did?"

He wiped his lips. "I could use some water."

"Not until I get answers."

He turned to my godfather. "Bobby, I swear, I don't know."

Bobby glared. "You know something, Jimmy. That's why we got into an argument. You're shielding someone, maybe your former partner, Kip, who was killed across the street from Jensen's sister's house?"

"Dammit, no! And for the record, Jensen's psycho nephew killed Kip. He was my friend. That shouldn't have happened."

I glared. "But dealing with murderers can backfire. At least, the only person left to deal with is Jensen. I doubt he killed anyone; he always called the shots."

Savage scoffed. "So, you say."

I side-glanced Bobby and he shrugged.

"Did Jensen kill Luca?" I said, my gaze holding his.

He shook his head.

"Then who?" I demanded.

Savage said nothing.

I pointed a finger. "It was you who drove to Fort Totten that night. Why? That wasn't your precinct?"

Savage closed his eyes and took a breath.

"Tell me, goddamn it!"

He spoke softly. "Jensen said he only wanted to talk to Luca."

"At four in the morning?"

Savage shrugged. "He didn't say why."

"That's bullshit. You grabbed Luca and took him to Jensen. One or both of you killed him."

"Luca took off," he blurted. "That's the truth."

I turned to Bobby who was deadpan. "You expect us to believe he escaped and never once called his mother or sister?"

Savage swallowed hard. "If he's dead, it wasn't me who killed him." He turned to Bobby. "I swear. Can't we fix this, one cop to another?"

Bobby sneered. "You were a cop in name only, but you were never a decent one. You're gonna spend the rest of your days wishing you'd never met Lee Jensen."

Savage looked panicked, as though he'd never escape the situation. He charged for the patio door and ducked inside, slapping the lock shut. I chased after him, my hands banging on the slider. Savage turned, staring at me like he was in a trance. He then trudged toward a wooden cabinet, bent down, and removed a handgun.

"Savage, no!" I screamed. "Help us get Jensen."

For a moment, I thought he might relent. He hesitated, then looked at me squarely through the glass slider. But then his expression turned calm, and his decision was clear. As he placed his pistol under his chin, the sound of the gunshot echoed through the peaceful neighborhood.

I called in Savage's suicide, not to my former lieutenant, who would surely place me on his permanent shit list. We provided statements tying Danny Caruso's attempt on my life with Savage's confession he killed him before offing himself.

We returned to Bobby's house in separate cars. Sitting in his living room, each holding a Bud, I asked how he managed to get invited to Savage's house.

He shrugged. "Easy, I told him I'd been looking at precinct photographs and became nostalgic. I mentioned I had an unopened bottle of Blanton's Gold Edition that someone had given me for my birthday. He wished me a happy birthday and told me to bring it over. His wife was out of town." Bobby paused. "The stuff cost me three hundred bucks, but it was worth it."

"Your birthday was April first."

"April fool's day, right, but it was the only excuse I could come up with. Remember, I'm retired and not as quick on my feet as I used to be." He laughed softly. "Come to think of it, you never gave me a birthday present."

I smiled. "Okay, I owe you three hundred dollars."

Bobby was enjoying this, and I could tell he missed the uniform.

"We had a couple of shots, and when Savage relaxed, I started questioning him about Annie Baxter's murder and Luca's disappearance. He wouldn't budge, said it was old news, and he couldn't remember that far back. I told him that was bullshit.

"One thing led to another, and I pushed hard, accusing him of still working for the crooked Jensen. I told him he was a disgrace to the uniform." He paused. "By then we both had plenty to drink and that's when he grabbed his gun from under his sofa and shot me."

Bobby's hand shook as he snapped open the can and took a sip. "I guess Jensen is the only one left who can answer for the past."

"Looks that way," I said. "But if Savage was telling the truth that Luca took off, where did he go?" My eyes met Bobby's. "Something's not adding up."

FORTY-SIX

Hilton Head

Jensen felt liberated. Now that his nephew was dead, he was a free man. Danny couldn't talk from hell. The bartender was probably dead, but if he survived and discovered his attacker was killed, he'd have no reason to help Reed's investigation. Let sleeping dogs lie.

Jensen was ready to celebrate victory, and by five that afternoon, he arrived at his club. A local oldies band called the Sharks were in full swinging, blasting out, "You Give Love a Bad Name." Very apropos.

Club members knew Jensen's reputation as a lady's man and ignored him. He could care less. He ordered a scotch and water, took a large gulp, and scanned the dance floor.

Out of the corner of his eye, he noticed a woman in her early forties dancing solo. She looked his way and smiled. What luck. He finished his drink and slid off his bar stool, making his way around the other dancers to the woman. Her hips were moving in a fluid motion, her arms loose and comfortable. God, her body was calling him.

By the time he reached her, Bon Jovi ended, and he frowned. "Too bad I missed the dance," he said, grinning. "You looked like you were enjoying dancing solo."

"A shame there was no one to dance with. You dance?"

Did he. And more. "I do. I'm Lee."

She extended her hand. Soft and warm. "Tara."

Jensen blinked and took his hand away too quickly. That was his daughter's name. He suddenly felt odd. He was at least twenty years older than she. But then he recovered.

"Tara, a beautiful name." He realized he and Tara were the only ones standing on the dance floor, and as he looked around, disapproving stares followed them. Screw them. This was *his* day.

"How about a drink?" he said. "It looks like the band is taking a break."

She nodded. "Sounds good."

Jensen pointed to a table in the back and followed her. Damn, she had one hell of a sway. Jensen hated small talk, but if he was going to get lucky, he'd have to listen to her babble.

A familiar server arrived. Jensen knew Gary, a guy his age who retired from the fishing industry and decided to leave his boring sofa and find a part-time job.

Gary knew Jensen's reputation with women but remained discreet, not mixing his business with his client's.

He smiled at Tara. "What can I get you?"

"The house cabernet, please."

He nodded. "Mr. Jensen, the usual?"

So formal when he was with a woman. "Please."

After Gary left, Jensen leaned into Tara. "So, tell me about yourself."

She didn't back off and touched his hand. "Well, first of all, this is my first time at the club." Her hand went to her mouth to stifle a giggle. She looked around. "I lied to get in. I told the front desk I was moving to Hilton Head and wanted to join this fancy club. They were delighted and let me check it out."

Jensen grinned. Probably something he'd try. Already, he liked her. "So, you're not interested in becoming a member," he said. "That's too bad."

She tapped his hand lightly. "The truth is I'm on vacation and got bored sitting on Coligny Beach all day. Don't get me wrong, I love its wide sandy beach. But after a while, I got tired of hanging out alone. I heard about this club. I love to dance and meet interesting people. Are you interesting, Lee?"

He considered himself an interesting storyteller, but he wasn't about to regale her with murder, infidelity, and corruption. "I like to think so. But I'm interested in you, Tara. How about you start first?"

She leaned back against the high-cushioned chair and watched as Gary arrived with their drinks. They toasted to having fun. "Before I discuss my boring life, tell me what brought you here to Hilton Head. You're too young to retire, so you must work here."

He touched his immaculately cut brown mustache. She thinks I'm younger. Hell, he was in love, especially now that she settled her hand on his thigh.

"You must have won the lottery," Tara said. "You seem so content."

Jensen moved her hand farther up his thigh, just south of little Lee. "Better than that." He surveyed the bar, then downed his drink. "I beat the system." He put a hand to his mouth. "There's nothing like being totally free." He leaned in for a kiss, but Tara put up a finger. "I never kiss without knowing a man. I learned that years ago from my former husband. I should have never kissed him." A giggle. She downed her wine.

That was quick. Jensen called over the bartender and asked for another round. He was vulnerable when it came to young, beautiful women. He wanted to get laid and began bragging about being a councilman, a successful businessman, and a very wealthy guy.

Tara smiled. "Wow, keep talking. You're getting me excited." She kissed him on the cheek.

Oh, God!

The band returned for the next set.

Tara said, "How about we celebrate this perfect day with a song?"

He glanced at the group. "A song?"

"Why not? I have one for the occasion." She got up and swayed to the band. After a few moments, the singer nodded, then looked through his digital sheet music.

Tara returned. "You're gonna love this, Lee. It's one of my favorites."

The lead singer tapped the microphone. "Lisa Falcone dedicated this next song to Lee Jensen. I'm sure you'll remember 'Another One Bites the Dust' by Queen."

At first, Jensen thought he hadn't heard right. She said her name was Tara. Lisa Falcone was the name of a kid he knew from Whitestone. She was...Luca's sister. Christ, what the hell was happening?

He glared at her. "What's going on?" he said, his tone threatening. "You said your name was Tara. Is this a joke? I'll have you kicked out of here." He stood and was about to yell at the band to stop singing, but it was too late.

Lisa scowled. "Murderer," she yelled. "Soon, you'll bite the dust."

She reached inside her bag and Jensen edged back. Was she going to kill him?

She withdrew a sheet of paper and waved it at him. "This is just a sample of your secret files Matt found in your house," she lied. The paper was the first page of the fake insurance policy that Jensen supposedly took out on Luca.

"Matt?"

"It'll be going to the authorities, so enjoy your freedom while you can."

Thank God the band was loud. Still, people stared as he attempted to calm her down.

"Money is not an object, Lisa. Just say how much?"

She picked up her drink and splashed it at him, the red dripping down his mustache and onto his clothes. "Do you seriously think you can buy me off? Maybe you didn't kill Annie Baxter, but you helped your nephew escape. And your cop friend who killed himself told Hank Reed it was your idea to meet my brother." She sneered. "You had Luca killed." She stopped to catch her breath. "And Hank Reed isn't going to stop until you're arrested."

He grabbed her arm, but she shrugged off his grip, slapped his face, and stalked off.

Lisa begged me to pick her up at LaGuardia Airport at ten that evening. She'd be flying in from Savannah and said it had to do with Lee Jensen.

"What the hell were you thinking?" I demanded as she entered my car. "You should know by now what Jensen is capable of. And you were alone." I continued admonishing her until I ran out of breath.

Lisa averted her eyes. "I needed to do this," she protested. "I wanted Jensen to know we're after him."

"No, dammit, *I'm* after him." I pulled out of the spot, trying to calm down until we entered the Grand Central Parkway. I shook my head, side-glanced her. "Look, I was nervous when you called from the airport. I'm sorry I let out steam."

She touched my hand. "That's sweet."

I pulled back. "Still, I don't know if Jensen has anyone left in his corrupt organization to do damage. You need to take a few days off from your job, go home, and take care of your mother. She must be wondering what happened to you. And Chuck, where did you tell him you were going?"

A sigh. "He doesn't know anything. I made up a story about sorting out things at my mother's place for a few days. He believed me."

"And Matt?"

She huffed. "I told you we're done."

"Not what I mean." I reminded her that Matt was helping with his father's files.

She rolled her eyes. "Oh, why didn't you say so? I called him from Hilton Head. He knows his father is guilty of lots of things. But not murder. I'm sure Jensen called his son, begging him to purge his confidential files, which Matt assured me he wouldn't."

I softened my tone and told her that despite putting herself in danger, she did great. What else could I say?

"Leave Jensen to me," I added.

We reached her mother's house. "Please, go back to Connecticut. I'll call you when I have something. And be careful."

She nodded, peered over at her mother's place. "Wanna come in for a bit? Maybe celebrate with a glass of wine." She gave me a young Lisa look.

I sighed. "I really need to continue the investigation."

Her lips turned down, and she stepped out of the car.

Conor died without providing a statement witnessing Jensen and Danny at the crime scene. It was his father's hearsay anyway that probably wouldn't hold up in court. As for getting Jensen, I was back to square one.

FORTY-SEVEN

Meeting up with Lisa Falcone the day before was bad enough. Now, he had to deal with his carelessness, leaving his files unprotected. He should have shredded them years ago. But, as he continued having dark thoughts, he realized those files were over twenty-five years old. What could they pin on him now? Some misstep handling in campaign funds?

And, as for Luca, who might have witnessed him committing a crime, Savage took care of him after pulling up in a squad car at Fort Totten. Savage claimed it was an easy kill and buried him out at sea.

Jensen was dressed in Alex Mill chino shorts and a white Lacoste T-shirt, a scotch and soda in his hand, sitting on a cushioned Adirondack deck chair overlooking his pool. He hadn't been ready for a round of golf in some time. But after reconsidering his seemingly unwarranted troubles, he looked forward to a game tomorrow.

He took a sip and shook his head. What was that silly charade with Lisa Falcone or whatever her married name was? If she thought he'd confess to a crime, she was sadly mistaken.

His thoughts were interrupted when his wife stepped outside, a glass of merlot in her hand. She wore a sun dress, with her face made up as though she were going to dinner, though it was only one in the afternoon.

"You look tired, Lee," she said almost sympathetically. "Your recent trip must have been stressful. Or maybe, you were having too much fun."

She was obviously mocking him. He studied her for a moment. She looked unusually attractive, and he wondered what she was up to. Hopefully, not sex. That was the last thing on his mind.

"What's the deal?" he asked, taking another sip of his drink. "Got a date?"

She smiled. "Not yet." She took a seat across from him. "I've been thinking lately. Actually, for a while. You've treated me like crap over the years, and I put up with it. First, holding the family together, then helping in your campaign, even now in retirement." Her eyes searched the pool area, then returned to him. "I don't know why I didn't divorce you years ago."

Here we go, another bullshit threat. He couldn't care less about a divorce. He had enough money hidden beyond her reach. She knew nothing about his past dealings; he was smart enough to close the door on that possibility. Still, he wasn't in the mood for confrontation.

"Look, Carol, I wasn't the greatest husband, but I tried. It's just that between work and—"

"Stop!" she demanded. "I knew you'd start with a ridiculous excuse. I already filed for divorce." She nodded with a smirk. "I have a very capable attorney who thinks I'm attractive. I'm meeting him for lunch to discuss further options."

He held a snort.

"Go ahead, laugh. I expect you to leave *my* home soon. You can keep the house in Whitestone. It's old and doesn't have a pool. And, as far as playing your stupid golf, you can get a membership at the Trump Golf Links. It's just over the Whitestone Bridge in the Bronx."

He downed his drink and threw the glass in the pool. "I know where it is." He paused and composed himself. "Come on, Carol, can't we work this out? I promise I'll change."

She checked her watch and stood. "Sorry, Lee, it's too late for phony promises. Besides, it's me who's changed."

FORTY-EIGHT

A few days later, Monsignor Valencia called. He sounded upbeat.

"Alex is out of a coma and resting comfortably at the Colorado Hospital Trauma Center. He's not very talkative, but he wants to speak to you. He's in Room 306."

"That's great news, Monsignor. I'll call him now."

"And Hank, thank you for all you've done. If you're ever in the neighborhood, please stop by."

We disconnected and I buzzed Alex. He immediately picked up, which was a good sign. After a few moments of reminiscing, I asked if we could Facetime. "It's been years since we last saw each other. What do you think?"

"I'd like that very much. I've changed over the years as I'm sure you have. But I looked in the mirror this morning and still have a bandage wrapped around my head."

I chuckled. "No problem. I was hit on the head recently, but fortunately my bruise didn't require stitches."

When we connected, Alex looked haggard but he was alive. He

propped himself up with the help of a nurse and adjusted his iPhone.

We studied each other for a long moment.

"Hank, you look almost the same, just older." He looked weary.

That was a humble and loving priest talking, and I thanked him. "Considering what you went through, you don't look too bad yourself. It's great we have this moment. Congratulations on becoming a priest. Can I still call you Alex?"

"Yes, of course. I was Alex when we hung out."

I waited for him to share his past and, given his pained expression, I knew it would be difficult.

"I had a breakdown," he finally admitted. "The past caught up with me. This whole thing with Luca. I tried prayer and…anyway, God didn't want to take me just yet. I guess he figured I'd been doing good work for him. At least, I hope I have."

"We're all grateful," I said, and told him Lisa and Tara, and the other Whitestone boys, were praying for him, although a few admitted they don't pray very often.

"Jesse," Alex said. "If it wasn't for him…you're probably wondering why Jesse." He sighed. "We have a lot in common. Tough upbringings. To be honest, we've kept in touch over the years. I knew he had a drinking problem and I tried to help him. He, in turn, helped assuage guilt about my family."

He stopped, adjusted his position. "We're very similar, both coming from fractured families. We were good for each other. And then, with my breakdown, Jesse flew out to Colorado immediately, no questions asked."

He paused. "But you want to know what happened that night, and I'm going to tell you. But please, be patient."

After a moment of silence, Alex took a deep breath. "It started before that night. I haven't spoken about this before, not even with Jesse. Please understand I'm not proud of what I'm about to tell you." He paused. "As you know, Luca and I worked part-time for Lee

Jensen at his law office, which was also his political headquarters. We also worked at his factory.

"We didn't make much money, just enough to save for a rainy day. Jensen's factory was set up as an injection molding process for making stuff. That's pretty much all I knew about the company. Anyway, Jensen had a partner, one of his wealthy constituents, who later sold his share to Jensen." He paused. "There were rumors about the deal, and I'll leave it at that."

Alex blinked into the phone. "Luca and I worked after school mostly at the factory, where Jensen's nephew was the manager. He had the title and thought he had the authority to do whatever he pleased. He bullied us around, and it became very uncomfortable being there, but we needed the money and put up with him."

"You're talking about Danny Caruso."

Alex's eyes widened. "You know him?"

"Sort of. He tried to kill me at my house. Only he dashed out and was shot and killed."

"Oh." Alex made the sign of the cross, then continued. "Danny had a bad temper and could be cruel at times without reason. A few days before Luca's eighteenth birthday, he told us to leave and clean up his uncle's law office. We knew what he was up to. Danny had plans with a woman at the factory."

He paused, took a breath. "When we arrived, Jensen's office lights were out. We were about to leave when we heard arguing from his inner office, which was set up for clients.

"We froze. It didn't sound like he was entertaining a client. In fact, Jensen did most of the yelling, and it appeared it had something to do with his wife."

"His wife?" I asked. "She was there?"

Alex closed his eyes for a moment. "No, no, it wasn't her. He was threatening someone *if* she called his wife. The woman had a Spanish accent, so it was difficult to understand her. I took Spanish in high school, and the one word I remembered was *bebé*.

259

"Baby," I said. "The woman was pregnant?"

"Or, already had a child. Either way, it sounded like it was Jensen's."

We stared at each other for a long moment. I was beginning to get the picture and asked, "What happened next?"

Alex took his time. "I told Luca we needed to leave and that whatever we heard should be kept to ourselves. But he refused and pressed me to take off without him. I was scared, Hank, and left in a hurry."

"Without him?" I said, holding back my temper.

Alex buried his face in his hands, and I lost facial contact. He started crying, clearly reliving that night. I heard footsteps, and a moment later a voice interrupted our conversation.

"Alex, you need to rest."

A nurse removed the phone from his hand and appeared on the screen. She wasn't happy. "Sir, this is not a good time." With that, she disconnected.

FORTY-NINE

A few days later, Alex returned to the parish and called me.

He greeted me with an apology. "Sorry about the break-down at the hospital. I'm better now. A lot has changed since my fall and concussion. Coming out of the coma, I realized if I were to lead a normal and healthy life, I would have to break the silence. That's why I believe we need to talk in person. Are you up for the trip?"

"You bet. I'll see you in a few hours. And Alex, thanks. You're my last hope in finding the truth."

As I crossed the Whitestone Bridge on my way to the Poconos, lightning strikes fired in every direction. I struggled to see through the torrential rain that followed, and I arrived at the rectory a half-hour late.

Monsignor Valencia opened the door. "Hank!" He gave me a big hug and whispered, "Thanks for coming." He looked over his shoulder. "The patient is doing great."

"I'm glad to hear it. I know it's been a long and painful struggle."

He looked beyond me at the dark sky. "I heard the rain was horrible."

"A bit crazy."

The monsignor patted me on the back and ushered me inside to the study, where Alex sat across from a young woman at a table. He looked better than when we Facetimed. Dressed in a full-collared shirt and cassock, he stood and we hugged, lingering a bit.

"Hank, I'm so grateful for everything you've done. Thanks for coming."

I chuckled. "I think you call it divine intervention."

"Yes, exactly."

The monsignor added, "And *He* sent Jesse to the rescue."

I stepped back and looked Alex over.

"What?"

"I must admit, I never thought this would be your calling. But I'm happy you chose the priesthood." I then glanced at the young woman whose infectious smile radiated. I knew it was Emily from the photograph I'd seen on Alex's screensaver.

"Emily, so glad to finally meet you."

"You too, Hank."

We sat around the table like old friends and waited for Alex to start.

A quick breath, then, "Hank, I wouldn't have asked you to drive all this way, but I felt we needed to share the information in the privacy of the church. Monsignor and Emily are my rocks and know some of what I'm about to reveal." His eyes shifted to the others and he grinned. "I hope that's okay with you."

"As long as our conversation remains here."

He nodded. "Yes, of course."

The monsignor spoke first, his eyes meeting mine. "As I mentioned when you were here last, we're a small parish. Most parishioners know each other. They worried about Alex's disappearance and were relieved when he returned in one piece. I tried to put the incident in perspective, not hurting the parishioners or Alex. I resorted to a white lie or venial sin, and I pray that I'm forgiven for it."

Monsignor Valencia didn't mention the reason given, and I had no reason to ask.

"But he's back, and everyone is happy again, especially me. I told Alex I was getting too old to take over his duties." He laughed lightly.

"Anyway, this meeting has to do with your investigation."

I began. "I'd like to continue where we left off. You and Luca happened to be in the wrong place at the wrong time. You fled Jensen's office and then what?"

He took his time. "Maybe an hour later, Luca found me by the bridge. The Whitestone boys had an agreement that if anyone got lost or into trouble, we'd meet up under the bridge. When he arrived, I was shaken, confused, and felt guilty for not being brave enough to stay. I felt like a traitor."

My eyes shifted to the others. Alex had their attention.

"Luca was scared, but he tried not to show it. He told me he was okay, but his face showed a different story. He was clearly rattled by what he'd witnessed."

Alex adjusted his position and continued. "After hearing a thud, Luca was afraid the woman was hurt and pressed his ear against the door. He heard footsteps and was about to pull back when Jensen yanked the door open.

"Jensen started screaming, admonishing him for sneaking up on him. Luca didn't have a chance to explain that Danny ordered him there."

Alex paused, swallowed. "Luca never mentioned that I'd been there, too. Had he..."

Alex stopped, took a breath. "He saved me from Jensen's wrath."

My mind worked overtime. "Did Luca know who Jensen was arguing with?"

He shook his head. "It happened so quickly. Like I said, the outer room was dark, but Luca glimpsed inside and saw a woman lying face down. He told me there was a pool of blood next to her."

Definitely a crime.

"Luca said Jensen threatened him if he revealed anything that happened. He then said, 'I'll deal with you later.'"

My eyes widened. "Jensen used those words: 'I'll deal with you later'?"

Alex scowled. "Verbatim, according to Luca.

"Soon after, Jensen picked up the phone but held off dialing. He demanded Luca leave immediately and again threatened him, saying he'd be in touch soon."

I side-glanced Emily. She'd been crying, and her expression of grief made me wonder why she was personally involved in Alex's experience. Was their relationship more than just friendship?

Alex continued. "I couldn't sleep and certainly didn't want to go to the party. But how would it look if I didn't show up? So, I went and had a beer."

"Two, according to Kyle." I smiled.

He nodded. "I was consumed with guilt when Luca disappeared. Honestly, Hank, I didn't know what to do. I was afraid if I went to the police that Jensen, being a councilman, had connections and would deal with me, maybe the same way he might have had with Luca."

He stopped, shook his head. When he faced me, tears trickled down his cheeks. He couldn't speak, and Emily touched his shoulder lightly.

The monsignor sat frozen, staring at me.

After recovering, Alex took a breath. "Sorry about that. For weeks afterward, I checked the newspapers, searching for a murder in and around Flushing. That's where Jensen's factory was located. But I found nothing and figured … no, I hoped Jensen didn't kill her, that he only hurt her, treated her, and it ended there. Still, my brain started playing tricks, and I realized I needed to withdraw from everyone."

He wiped his eyes and drew a breath. "At some point in college, I met a priest not much older than me, and we became friends. He

THE BRIDGE TO MURDER

had a wonderful approach to life. Thanks to him, I decided to become a priest. I realized I had to deal with my failure to help Luca. Over the years, my faith has helped me, and I continued to pray for guidance."

"Until I started investigating Luca's disappearance," I said. "And the demons returned."

He fell silent.

I asked how Luca's knife wound up in his cigar box. "Everyone knew he'd never part with it," I said sternly. "And yet, you have it. What's your explanation?"

He threw a quick glance at the monsignor as though it was his fault I'd found it.

Alex's breathing became erratic, and he hesitated. "The night of his party, when everyone but Luca and I were asleep, he handed me the knife and said if anything happened to him, I should give it to Tara. Of course, innocently, I asked what he meant, but he dismissed my question.

"Luca said he was happy for our friendship and would miss me and the others. God, Hank, I was so frightened for him. Would Jensen actually harm him? But then Luca vanished, and I was certain he had. Oh, Hank…"

I waited for Alex to continue, but when he wavered, I scoffed, "But you kept the knife and never told Tara." I shook my head. "I'm sorry Alex, but this is very unsettling. Especially since I believe Jensen got away with murder. Maybe twice."

Alex sensed my irritation and folded his hands in prayer. "I knew Tara would demand to know how I got it. But I was more concerned she would tell her father, who, I was sure, would figure Luca told me what happened that night and come after me." He stopped, his hands still in prayer. "My home life was in shambles, but I didn't want to die."

"A Catch-22," I offered.

"After that, life became a blur. I had to get out of Whitestone, far away from everything and everybody. The guys must have wondered why I never participated in Luca's disappearance theories. How could I?" He stopped, caught his breath. "For days, I kept praying Luca would return…"

I held back my fury. Blaming Alex wouldn't solve anything. He'd been living with his guilt. That was punishment enough. Emily continued to console Alex and gave me a narrow look.

Definitely more than friendship.

I stood. "Thank you, Alex. I know how painful it was to reveal the past and hope you can continue in peace."

We hugged, and he whispered, "Thank you."

I peered out at the threatening weather. It was time to go.

The monsignor walked me to the door. "I hope you can bring justice to the situation." He looked back. "I pray Alex can now live in peace."

We shook hands. As I settled in the car, I watched black boulders rumbling across the sky. I was grateful Alex managed to share his past, but would it help my investigation after twenty-five years? All I had was a missing woman, probably dead. What bothered me was Lee Jensen escaped a crime, and I couldn't prove it.

I left the rectory wondering if I'd ever find the truth. Going back and looking for a missing or dead person in Flushing would be a monumental task for me, but I knew someone who had access to a missing persons database.

A thin smile crossed my face as I thought of that person: my good friend, Senior Homicide Detective JR Greco.

I hadn't spoken to him in months, soon after I solved another case involving his cousin and a missing person in Florida.

I had him on speed dial, and he answered immediately.

"Don't tell me you're in trouble again, amigo." JR laughed

lightly. "Or are you asking me to save you a seat at my cousin's wedding?"

"Both. I'm looking forward to catching up. But——"

"Here it comes."

"I need your help on a case." I gave him the information.

"It could be vital," I pleaded.

"I like it when you grovel. No problem. Give me the name of the missing person."

I swallowed. "That's the problem. I only know the victim was a woman, probably murdered in Flushing, Queens."

"Oh?"

"But I have an approximate date. The end of June 1996. Possibly the beginning of July."

"Old."

"I know. It's related to another missing person, a good friend. I believe he was abducted and killed by the same person who killed the woman in question, if she was killed."

"I see. So, you're looking for a body, or possibly just a missing person."

"Correct."

"I'll see what I can do. How soon do you need the information?"

"What are you doing now?"

FIFTY

T he Whitestone Bridge from the Bronx side was slowed by
traffic. Cars crawled as lightning strikes opened the skies on
both sides of the bridge. I'd never witnessed such a violent storm,
and my wipers fought to keep the pelting rain in check.

When I crossed to the Queens side, the air horn blasted from a
fire truck heading toward Whitestone. I exited at Fourteenth Avenue,
then swung around toward the park. The rain finally subsided, and
as I turned down Bobby's block, I saw him walking north and pulled
over.

"Hey, are you lost?"

He turned. "Hank. There's something going on a few blocks
away."

"No kidding. Hop in."

We stopped where the block was cordoned off by the 109th
precinct assisting firefighters.

"Park here," Bobby said excited as though he were entering an
amusement park. "Let's see what's going on."

I looked. "I already know what's going on. That house is on fire."
I pointed to a Cape Cod, or what was left of it.

The local engine company, along with its rescue squad and ladder truck, stood in front of the house fighting furiously to put out the flames. I was perfectly happy standing at a safe distance, but my ever-curious godfather ran over to a patrolman.

I let them chat for a moment then joined them.

"Hank, this is Seth Marshall. He was one of my recruits. Straight A student."

"Pleased to meet you," I said, my eyes shifting between Seth and the fire. "I'm Bobby's godson. I don't think I ever got an A in anything." I winked at Seth. "It looks bad from here."

He nodded. "First time I've seen a house burn down." He looked around. "If you wanna get closer, go ahead. Just not too close."

That was all Bobby needed to hear. We edged to within fifty feet and stopped.

"Damn, that's Lee Jensen's house."

My stomach tightened as I peered over at the all-consuming fire.

Firefighters blasted Jensen's house with pressure that would have stopped almost anything, only they must have arrived too late. I didn't want to stay, but Bobby was in a hypnotic trance. Great entertainment. He turned and waved at the neighbors across from Jensen's house like they were having a block party.

The fire was put out in less than two hours, enough fun for me, and I was about to suggest we head back for a beer when my godfather, now a fire expert, said, "See that? It's a pike pole. You must have seen them. They're used for removing another object. Looks like they're pulling something out of the crawl space."

I said, "Looks like a metal barrel. A big sucker."

"They must have seen something on the Thermal camera that piqued their interest."

I rolled my eyes.

"Hell, there could be anything in there." We watched two firefighters roll the blackened barrel onto the street. Twenty feet from us, a voice called out, "Be careful, guys."

We turned. "That's the Battalion Chief. I know him." He waved. "Hey, Anthony."

He recognized my godfather and waved us over. "Say, Bobby."

Anthony DuBois was around fifty. Bobby introduced us and we shook hands.

"We haven't seen too many houses destroyed like this in a long time. Glad the owners weren't home." He pointed. "It appears the strikes hit the roof, which, in turn, started the fire in the attic space."

We watched a firefighter pry open the now upright barrel.

"That's a Halligan bar," Bobby said, and I wondered if my godfather missed his calling.

The firefighter peered inside. He turned our way and shook his head.

"Hey, Chief, something weird is going on. I think we have a crime scene."

My immediate thought was it was Luca's body. All these years, and my good friend was buried in plain sight. And there could only be one suspect: Lee Jensen.

What made no sense was the burial ground. Literally underneath Jensen's house. What was he thinking? I guess criminals don't think.

The container must have weighed several hundred pounds, plus the body. From my vantage point, the blackened industrial barrel didn't have an insignia or name on it, but my guess was it came from Jensen's plastics factory.

I thought of Jimmy Savage who swore he hadn't murdered Luca. That left Danny Caruso.

Bobby interrupted my thoughts. "I don't get it, Hank. That would be the last place I'd bury a body. The East River is just down the street. Why not dump it there?"

My eyes steadied on the container, and I shook my head. "I can't imagine Lisa and her mother taking it well."

"Or Matt, and especially Tara," Bobby added. "I think the crawl space was under her bedroom. How cruel."

I was about to call Lisa and break the bad news when JR called.

"Today's your lucky day, amigo. I think I found your missing woman, and it didn't take as long as I thought."

I stepped away and held a hand to my ear. "She have a name?"

"She does. It's Marta Reyes, born in Guatemala. She moved to New York at seventeen and disappeared at the beginning of July 1996, at age twenty-two, so your timeline is right. Her roommate told me Marta never returned home."

"She had a roommate?"

"Correct. A woman by the name of Sonia Molina. She reported her missing."

I looked back at the barrel. "Did the cops follow up?"

"Not according to the NYPD missing persons report. They claimed Marta had been missing only a day and that her friend needed to wait a few days to make a report. Only, Sonia never followed up."

"Marta could have returned to the apartment," I said.

"She never did."

"You know this for a fact?"

"Hey, you know I follow through. I called Sonia. Seems she has the same phone number and apartment. How's that for luck?"

"You'd make a great detective," I said with a chuckle. "Please tell me the rest of the story."

"I saved the best part for last, Hank. The good news is New Yorkers don't often move. I identified myself and asked about Marta Reyes. I must have hit a nerve because she started crying like it had happened yesterday. She told me she got frustrated with the police and never called back. Turns out Marta Reyes is still missing."

"Or dead," I added, my gaze staying on the barrel.

"I have more info if you're interested."

Such a tease. "Go on."

"Marta was working at the time she disappeared. And, according to her roommate, she was five months pregnant."

I thought about Alex's explanation at Jensen's law office. The argument, the thud, the *bebé*. Could the victim in the barrel be Marta Reyes?

"Where did she work?" I asked, my fingers crossed like a kid.

"J Plastics Company. It's in Flushing."

J for Jensen.

"Hank, I hope that helps."

"Oh, yeah, JR. You did good. I owe you."

"That I know," he said with a chuckle. "Now let me ask you a question. Where the hell are you? And what's that commotion in the background?"

Bobby and I weren't going anywhere. I felt numb waiting for the crime scene specialists to examine the contents of the barrel. In typical fashion, they set up parameters and cordoned off the area. The lead investigator peered inside and delicately moved some of its contents around. He approached Detective Jeff Eisman with a confused expression. They spoke briefly, then called over his crew.

Eisman approached us outside the perimeter. "Bobby, I can only reveal that the person you expected is not in the barrel. It was a woman."

I sighed in relief knowing it wasn't Luca.

"You sure?" Bobby asked scratching his pate.

"Definitely a female, and she was pregnant. She'd been preserved. The barrel was filled with material that kept her body intact and made it airtight. They discovered a bruise on her fore-head, most likely from a blunt instrument."

The thud Luca heard at Jensen's office.

Eisman said, "You might consider searching elsewhere for your missing person."

FIFTY-ONE

Lee Jensen was in a fun-loving mood. His wife was filing for divorce, but he wasn't concerned; his assets were beyond her reach in an offshore account. Let her keep the house. Hell, he'd throw in a new car.

Jensen studied his face in the bathroom mirror. He needed to color his mustache. He'd been under a lot of pressure lately, but that was past. His son, Matt, texted that he wouldn't send his files to the FBI, to spare his mother the humiliation. Another betrayal, Matt added.

Jensen snickered. Good boy, Matt. He removed the Just for Men tubes from the box and mixed the ingredients, then *voilà*.

After finishing the five-minute process, he showered, splashed on his favorite cologne by Bvlgari, a real woman-getter, especially the young ones, and dressed in casual dark denim navy jeans, a button-down collar piqué shirt, and a linen sports coat. He was pumped.

With his wife away—not that it mattered—he'd drive to the club, meet a young woman—not Lisa Falcone, and bring her back for a night of sex.

His erotic thoughts were interrupted by the cell phone. It was Matt.

"Hey, son."

Matt rambled about a lightning strike at their house. "I got a call from Mr. Mason, one of your neighbors. He said the house took a direct hit. It looks bad. Firefighters are everywhere." He stopped. "You might have lost everything."

Jensen stood frozen. He gasped and almost gagged on the cologne. "The entire house?"

"That's what Mr. Mason said. I'm on my way now. I'll fill you in when I get there."

Jensen rubbed his chin. "That's awful. No one got hurt, I hope."

"I won't know until I get there."

Jensen sat on the sofa and thought about the fire. He was covered by homeowner's insurance, so that wasn't a problem. As far as the contents, he and his wife took the good stuff with them when they moved to Hilton Head. If his house was completely leveled, it meant his delicate files were gone. That brought a smile to his face.

"Dad, you there?"

He'd forgotten about Matt. "Yes, son, I am. So sad." He faked a sigh. "We'll manage, thanks."

"Mom will be real upset."

"I'm sure she will. I'll let her know when she returns."

"She's out?"

Who the hell knew? She was probably shtupping her attorney. "Not sure where she went, but I'll let her know. Thanks for calling. Terrible news, just terrible."

"Sorry I had to be the bearer of bad news."

A broad grin. Great news! "We had fond memories, didn't we, Matt?"

He heard a sigh. "Despite everything, we did."

Jensen checked his watch. He was eager to get to the club.

"So, I better go, Matt. I have a lot to think about."

"Of course. Oh, and by the way, Mr. Mason mentioned something about the firefighters removing a steel drum from the crawl space. I told him I had no idea what it was.

"Do you?"

FIFTY-TWO

Perspiration dripped from Jensen's forehead. He'd forgotten about the damn drum. He opened the top button of his shirt and searched for air. Stupid decision back then.

He put on his legal hat. Okay, they found a barrel, but after twenty-five years, what would they discover? A decomposed body? They'd never be able to identify her.

Jensen was outside pacing the lanai and stopped in front of the barbecue grill. He suddenly got the chills despite the warm, sunny day.

He closed his eyes, recalling the incident. His mistress told him she was pregnant, though she didn't show. She threatened him if he didn't leave his wife for her. She wanted her baby legal.

Fat chance. His wife would have taken him to the cleaners. The woman—he wouldn't even admit her name—claimed she would call his wife and tell her she'd been his lover for over a year. Jensen would never let that happen.

He sucked in air. Of course, it never happened. Jensen glanced over at his neighbor's house. Jerry Klein was watering his lawn. He peered over and waved.

"Great day, huh, Lee."

Asshole. He waved back then trudged inside. His wife had given him less than a week to vacate. She'd be staying with a friend until then. Right, friend. He wondered if her attorney was racking up billing hours while screwing her.

Where was I? Right, the altercation. Why didn't he and Danny toss the barrel into the East River? Okay, it weighed three hundred pounds, and his nephew kept bitching about the weight. Said he was afraid of getting a hernia. So, they settled for the crawlspace. Christ, what an idiot!

FIFTY-THREE

Jensen hadn't slept in days. He was too busy planning his next move. He had two days before his wife returned and tossed him out on his ass. He hadn't thought of a destination. Too busy wondering if he, the former councilman, successful lawyer, and businessman, would do time for accidentally killing someone.

Jensen scanned a copy of the list of non-extradition countries: the Maldives, Morocco, or Indonesia. He was considering one when the doorbell rang. He checked the time. It couldn't be his wife.

He fingered back the curtain. Two guys in street clothes. They looked like cops. Maybe they weren't. But if they were, they'd only return later, or maybe sit in that black car out front until…

He opened the door and presented a wide smile.

"Hi, can I help you?"

The men, both lean and over six feet tall, returned it. They held up their shields and identified themselves as detectives Mario Benitez and John Plato.

Jensen looked around. "I didn't call the police."

"We're not local, Mr. Jensen," said Plato with a New York accent. "We're from the 109th precinct in Whitestone, New York."

"Oh, God, was my house burglarized? My son would have called if it was. Maybe I should call him."

"No need. It wasn't a burglary. There was a lightning strike, and your house went up in flames. Are you sure your son didn't call you?"

He shook his head quickly. "Destroyed? Oh my God, I had expensive heirlooms. Maybe I should call my insurance company." He fished in his pants pocket for his cell.

"Sure, but not now."

"Okay," he said, wiping an eye. "We had so many memories there: birthdays, anniversaries, and well, you understand."

"And a murder," added Benitez, with an equally New York accent.

Jensen's head snapped up. "Sorry?"

"That's the reason for our visit."

When he failed to respond, Plato said, "We have a few questions regarding a body discovered in your crawl space. A pregnant woman. Shouldn't take very long."

Right, flying down from New York for a short interview, not likely.

Jensen said, "Do you have the right Lee Jensen, officers? There aren't any dead bodies anywhere in my house as far as I know. How—?"

"I think we should discuss this inside," Plato said, glancing at the street. "You don't want neighbors wondering what's going on, do you?"

He surveyed the area, nodded, and stepped aside. "Please." He brought them to the living room. "Can I offer you a drink? I have beer, wine, the hard stuff."

Benitez checked his watch. "It's only ten in the morning."

He slapped his head. "Of course, what was I thinking?" He exchanged looks with the slightly taller detective with a shaved head and dark brown eyes. "I do have coffee."

He nodded. "Coffee's good. I take mine black."

He turned. "And you, Detective?"

"Plato. If you have half and half, that would be nice."

Half and half would be nice. What is this a fucking restaurant?

"Great. Be right back." He left and put on a pot of coffee. While waiting, he thought about charging out the back, but they'd probably hear his footsteps. Those guys looked in great shape and would catch him before he made the subdivision guard house.

"Mr. Jensen?"

"Almost finished," he called out. Scratch that idea. He could lie. He was good at that. Hell, he lied to everyone.

A few minutes later, Benitez stood at the doorway. "You need help with the mugs and coffee?"

Lie, lie, lie. "I was just thinking about the body you found. When I was running for councilman, my opponent tried everything in the book to discredit me. Could he have killed the woman? He died suddenly before the election, so his plan obviously didn't work."

Benitez scratched his pate. "Interesting theory. I'll discuss it with John."

"John?"

"My partner. He likes theories." The coffee maker made a ready ping, and Jensen turned. "Coffee's done."

They returned to Plato. Jensen set the coffee and mugs, along with the half and half, on the table. Jensen's hand trembled, and he asked the detective to do the honors.

They sat quietly, sipping coffees, until Jensen said to Benitez, "How about we tell your partner, John, about my theory?"

A smile. "Maybe after we leave. Right now, we need your statement, and we're requesting a DNA sample."

Jensen froze. "Why? I didn't do anything."

"Maybe, but we have to eliminate you as a suspect. Makes sense. You're an attorney, you know the process. A quick swab and we're out the door." He settled his coffee mug on the table. "What do you say, Mr. Jensen?"

Jensen was afraid to move, afraid he'd spill his coffee on the table, and held the mug tightly. He stifled a deep breath. "Detectives, as an attorney, you know I won't provide a sample without a court order."

The detective named John side-glanced his partner and got up.

Oh, shit.

"Okay, Mr. Jensen, we'll be back tomorrow."

Jensen knew the detectives would return the following day with a court order and demand a swab sample. Once tested, it would surely connect him to the woman and the DNA proof from the fetus.

There'd be almost a hundred percent chance he was the father. That wasn't enough to prove he had killed her. The only witness was Luca, and he was dead. That probably didn't matter since the body was discovered under *his* roof. He should have been more forceful and ignored Danny's bitching about dumping the barrel in the river.

Jensen took a breath. He had a day or two before his wife expected an empty house. And now, this. Over twenty-five years ago, he screwed the wrong woman. She was young, pretty, and flirtatious. He should have seen it coming.

He'd continued to want her, and when she got pregnant, begged her to get an abortion. She was a good Catholic girl and refused. But she was also manipulative, and the rest was history.

They argued and...that damn marble lamp he grabbed off the table. Those thoughts tightened his chest, and he was having a hard time breathing. He gave his eyes a good rub. Was that...Marta—that was her name, sitting by the pool, sipping a drink and waving?

He needed to distract himself and only one place provided relief. He ran to the garage, grabbed his golf bag, and tossed it into the trunk. Opening the garage door, he now realized the weather turned dark, like his mood. He laid his head on the steering wheel and began to weep.

FIFTY-FOUR

My investigation was over. At least when it came to Luca's fate. While Jensen would hopefully be convicted of murder, he'd never admit to killing Luca. Without that, I had nothing further to go on. Conor, the only eyewitness to Annie Baxter's murder, was dead. And as far as Lisa and her mother's hope of finding peace, that was now improbable.

It was early evening, and my drive home from Bobby's was filled with anguish. The expressway traffic was light, not that it mattered. I wasn't in a rush.

I pulled up to my house, parked the car, and took a breath. A dark, empty house awaited me, and I regretted not having someone to share my life with. Divorce was the beginning of my loneliness, followed by short relationships that never panned out. I was feeling sorry for myself. I was plain tired.

Inside, I turned on the lights and was about to grab a beer from the fridge when I heard movement behind me. When I turned, I was staring at a pistol.

"Sit down, Reed."

I recognized Jensen's voice from our phone conversations. Lisa had described him in Hilton Head as impeccably dressed, with pricey designer clothes. Could this be the same Jensen? This disheveled mess staring at me? He looked homeless!

We glared at each other, and I refused to sit. Jensen's mouth upturned into a sneer. His voice was harsh and angry, and his expression demonic.

He brandished the gun. "Goddamit, Reed, I said sit, or I swear I'll shoot you where you're standing."

He was going to kill me either way but I sat, hoping for time to think.

"After all these years, you had to get involved," he said, his tone grating and accusatory. "The case was over—"

"What case?" I demanded. "Marta Reyes's, Luca Falcone's, or Annie Baxter's?"

Jensen waved the gun. "Don't be a smart ass. I didn't kill Luca or Baxter. And as far as Reyes, that was an accident."

I kept staring at him. "I had nothing to do with the fire, so the barrel they found in your crawl space is on you. Pretty dumb, don't you think?"

He wiped a hand on his jeans, then held his weapon in both, probably to hide his trembling. "Still, you had to keep pressing, opening doubts. My nephew killed Annie Baxter, okay? And Savage killed Luca."

"At your direction. That makes you an accessory."

He sneered and took a step closer to me. "Savage is dead. Prove it."

My mouth went dry, but I managed, "So is your nephew, but before Savage killed him outside my home, Danny swore you had Savage kill Luca. Check the accessory box again."

Jensen's eyes widened.

"Guess he never let out that secret. And, by the way, before Conor died, he signed a sworn statement to that effect," I lied.

Jensen stepped back, I assumed, to assess this latest revelation. I doubted he'd ever used a weapon. He hired others, and his trembling suggested he was afraid or angry, meaning he was unpredictable. Either way, it wasn't good.

I looked directly at him and asked, "At least answer one question: Why did you have Savage kill Luca?"

He waved his gun. "I'm not telling you anything."

My hands perspired. "I already know the answer. Luca witnessed you kill Marta Reyes in your office." I nodded. "I have proof from a witness who was there with Luca, only he didn't stick around. He's now a priest and a solid witness."

I added. "But I don't need proof. Your DNA will match Marta's fetus. You're going down for murder." I pointed at him. "And, when Luca wouldn't agree to keep your secret, you had him killed."

His eyes blazed and he stepped closer. "I just wanted to talk to him—"

"Bullshit! Luca never had a chance."

When he didn't respond, I said, "Do I have that right, Councilman?"

"Fuck you, Reed."

He looked tired, lost.

"Before you kill me, at least tell me where Luca's body is buried. I need closure."

Jensen's silence suggested he was mulling over my request. "I really liked Luca," he said quietly. "He and Tara were great together. As you know, she got pregnant. A mistake that caused grief for our family. We had no choice but to give her up for adoption."

Her.

"But that had nothing to do with his...demise."

"But you must have considered it when you decided to have him killed." I stood slowly, and he backed off.

"What are you doing?" he said, his weapon aimed at my head.

"My leg fell asleep," I said rubbing it.

"Fix your problem, then sit."

I looked beyond Jensen. "I think that's all the evidence we need. You can come out now, Detective Oliver."

Jensen jerked his head, and I dove at his feet, knocking him to the floor. He was older and not very strong, but the adrenaline kept him fighting to hold onto his weapon.

He slammed his arms down and elbowed my nose and, for a moment, I was dazed. That was all he needed. Jensen angled the gun at me, and I saw fear in his eyes. He turned it around, and I realized he wasn't going to kill me.

FIFTY-FIVE

A few days after Jensen killed himself, I met Bobby at Fillmore's. He wasn't very talkative. In fact, he struggled for conversation, which, for my godfather, was rare. I extended my arm with a bottle of Peroni, and, with effort, he held up his with a neat scotch.

"To Lee Jensen. Gone forever," I said.

It wasn't a celebration, just a relief. Though Luca's presumed death was anything but a celebration, I hoped in the end, my good friend hadn't suffered.

I said, "Let's celebrate Luca's life."

Bobby swallowed hard and nodded.

I took a slug. "Jensen fell for the oldest trick in the book," I said with a grin. "There was no detective in my house, but I had no other way to distract him."

He smiled faintly.

I looked around. Fillmore's was near-empty, typical for a Wednesday night, but Finn didn't seem to care. After losing Conor, he'd been in a justified funk, tending bar indifferently. He told Bobby he was putting it up for sale. Made sense since he had no one to leave it to.

"Years of corruption had finally caught up with Jensen," I said. "He knew he'd probably be found guilty and sentenced to life in prison. He must have added up the years and realized he couldn't do the time. I suppose he wanted to take me down first, but after our skirmish, he had little choice."

Bobby nodded absently, and I could tell his mind was elsewhere, probably mulling over his recently announced move.

"Are you serious about moving to Florida, old man?"

He chucked softly. "It's time, Hank. I don't need a big house, the cold winters, or the murders. Mary's moving to Port Saint Lucie." He met my gaze. "I really like her."

My godfather had liked many women over the years, but his expression suggested he was serious about this one. At least enough to follow her to Florida.

"I'll miss you," I said sadly. "You've been my surrogate father for years. Will you make room for me when I visit?"

He patted me on the shoulder. "Of course. Maybe you'll decide to move your business south."

He sounded serious. "Gee, Bobby, I'd have to think about it. I'm not against the idea. And you're my only family."

Bobby returned to his drink, took a sip, and sighed. "We're a match made in heaven, you and me. I'm serious about you heading south. Maybe you'll find a nice woman."

I checked the time. It wasn't late, but I was ready to leave. "Let me take you home."

He shrugged. "Sure."

We drove in silence, and when we arrived, he turned. "Thanks for everything, Hank." He got out and trudged up his sidewalk, then disappeared without looking back.

The following morning, Bobby called. "I'm looking around my house and feel a bit overwhelmed. Do you have time to help me get rid of some junk?" He paused. "Besides, I can use the company."

"Sure, nothing's going on here, so I'll see you in an hour."

Arriving, I peered at Bobby's house. I would miss this place. Inside, my godfather approached, spreading his arms and leaning in for a hug. He appeared cheerful, unlike the night before.

"I guess I needed to make a decision about moving," he said. "I spoke to Mary, and she's excited we'll be neighbors."

"Neighbors? So, you're not jumping into the moving-in thing?" I grinned.

"We talked about it and realized we should take things slowly. What do you think, my boy?"

He was asking me for romance advice.

"Gee, Bobby, I'm no expert, but I think that's a smart idea. What if…?"

"Go on," he said when I hesitated.

I smiled. "Mary seems very nice, and she's a terrific cook. I think she's good for you, but only time will tell."

He nodded. "That's my Hank, playing it safe. My same sentiments."

I glanced around the living room. My godfather had already begun tossing stuff in a pile. "Lots of memories," I said with a sigh. "I started coming here when I was about fourteen and made lots of friends over the years. The Whitestone boys. And Lisa." Another sigh.

He met my gaze. "Youth. The best of times. But for me, it's time to move on. Anyway, how about you start in the basement? If you find anything you want, it's yours."

"You mean junk," I said with a chuckle.

"You never know what you might find," he said. "I'll be up here if you need me."

Downstairs was one big, cavernous room that looked like a

dumping ground. It reminded me of the TV show, *Sandford and Son*, a seventies sitcom that I'd seen on reruns. Old small tools, haphazardly thrown in boxes, a broken backdoor window, a lawn mower that had to be fifty years old. No wonder he asked me to start down here.

Oh well. In one corner, I noticed an old, rusty file cabinet. Good thing I didn't need a tetanus shot. Rather than remove the entire cabinet, I opened one of the drawers where I found old files, mostly police stuff, and assumed Bobby would want to shred them. I placed the files on a wobbly table, it too, would be tossed out.

The bottom drawer was much the same, and I removed a thin file containing old newspaper articles from the night of the murder. I was about to place it in a personal file when an unopened envelope slipped out and landed at my feet. I retrieved it and glanced at the front. The postage stamp was from Lisbon, Portugal, and addressed to my godfather from Carlota Abreu.

Carlota, Bobby's girlfriend? I scratched my head and hesitated to open it since it appeared personal. I gazed at the postmark date, then closed my eyes and recalled it being a few days after Luca had disappeared.

I turned to the basement staircase. Bobby was upstairs. I took a breath wondering why he hadn't opened the letter. And, why I should now. Something about the date, the sender, and that it was unopened told my gut to go ahead. I was willing to apologize later if it was too personal.

I carefully removed the letter and began reading. Carlota addressed it as 'My Dearest Bobby.' I took a breath then continued. I again questioned why Bobby hadn't read the letter. It was brief but to the point, possibly hedging in the event it fell into the wrong hands. I knew for certain: Carlota Abreu was on a mission.

I was stunned by what I'd discovered and debated whether to show Bobby the letter. I decided to hold off until I returned from my own mission, which, after twenty-five years might wind up being a fishing expedition.

Arriving in Lisbon the following morning, I waited for a connecting flight to the Island of Madeira, known as the Pearl of the Atlantic, a Portuguese Island 300 miles from Morocco. I'd never heard of the island but read it was a perfect place to unwind.

Madeira was known for its stunning views and perfect weather year-round. But also, a mecca for more adventurous activities: sailing, scuba diving, surfing, and paragliding. And, for its levadas, a myriad of networks of paths or trails alongside man-made irrigation systems, and great for hiking.

I read the typical tourist stuff while flying to Funchal, the capital of Madeira, located on the main island's south coast.

I'd gone through customs in Lisbon, so once I landed at Madeira Airport, I took a taxi to the Sé Boutique Hotel in the heart of the city. Not having much time to choose a place, I had hopped onto Booking.com and loved the hotel reviews.

Andre, the manager, greeted me. I'd emailed him before leaving the States and told him my plans. He was eager to help.

"Welcome to Madeira," he said, extending his hand. "I trust your trip was pleasant." A friendly smile crossed his face.

"Very."

Andre's English was perfect. We chatted about Madeira, and after a few minutes, he asked if I'd like to check in early. "I have a room available. Maybe you'd like to nap before venturing out."

"Thanks. I need a nap, but I'm anxious to begin my search. I could use a cup of coffee."

"Of course. We have coffee at our restaurant, but how about you settle inside, and I'll have a member of my staff bring it to you?"

I liked this place already.

Andre pointed to a small sitting area beyond the check-in desk. "You'll be comfortable there. It's quiet."

"Thanks." I had previously requested a driver for the day and told Andre I'd need him in about a half hour.

He nodded. "I'll text him."

"Again, thank you," I said.

Inside, I sat on a mustard-yellow chair facing a green sofa. The room was tastefully decorated with a mix of cohesive, different colored chairs and several old paintings on the walls. Very traditional and authentic yet sophisticated at the same time.

Five minutes later, a twenty-something woman with a friendly smile brought over a coffee and something that looked like a custard tart.

"That looks delicious," I said. "What do you call it?"

"I see you've never visited Portugal before, Sir." Another smile. "It's *Pastel de Nata*, our traditional dessert. Enjoy."

After she left, I indulged in the egg tart pastry dusted with cinnamon. Quite tasty. I sipped my coffee and gazed around. I felt relaxed, if only temporarily. The room reminded me of a small Parisian hotel I stayed in a few years back on police business to identify a dead perp. An easy gig.

As I looked around at several elegant photographs on the wall, I stopped at one of a woman near a street market, perhaps Morrocco. I rose and walked over to it. She appeared to be looking beyond the photographer when it was snapped. Though it looked digitally enhanced, creating a slight blur, her eyes and features reminded me of Patrice, a woman I'd met inside a local Paris café. She had asked me to help find her fiancé. The investigation turned out to be life-changing for me and almost cost me my life.

Andre interrupted my thoughts. "Do you like the photo, Sir?"

I turned to him. "Very much. Do you know the photographer?"

Andre beamed. "I am the photographer. All the photos in the hotel are mine. It's my passion when I'm not working."

"This one is quite exquisite," I said. "It looks like you captured her off guard."

Andre said, "Thank you for the compliment. I was visiting Fez, Morocco, at the time, I guess about a year ago, when I noticed she was looking in my direction for someone or maybe a store. The sunlight was perfect, and I took a few of her. This was the best one."

He looked at the photo and laughed softly. "She must have guessed I took her picture and ran off. When I got home, I tweaked it a little. Her eyes were sparkling, and her features beautiful."

"Do you mind if I take a photo from my iPhone?" I asked.

Andre smiled. "It would be my pleasure."

Ten minutes later, a white Peugeot model 2008 pulled up in front. The driver, a short man in his mid-thirties with dark brown hair and a friendly face, held open the back door for me.

"*Olá.*" He kept smiling as I approached, and we shook hands. He introduced himself as Cesar, and said he was at my disposal for as long as I needed him. According to Andre, Cesar knew the island as well as anyone. I hoped so.

We entered Avenida do Mar, the main road in downtown Funchal, and headed up the coast, the North Atlantic Ocean on my left. I leaned back and attempted to relax, but the thought of being disappointed kept me from enjoying the vistas.

Cesar glanced at the rearview mirror. "If you would like to stop for coffee or whatever, let me know, though the drive is only about an hour."

"Thanks, I'm good."

"You will enjoy the countryside. Everyone who visits our island does."

Cesar was proud of Madeira, and as I took in the view, I understood why.

"I'm already enjoying it," I said. "I know Andre told you about my search for a farm. I could be mistaken since the information is quite a few years old."

He nodded. "Once we reach Ribeira Brava, we turn and follow the road into the mountains and then make our way to the coast. It's a spectacular drive. From there, we head inland to Lagoa do Fana." He paused. "And your destination." A hopeful smile.

I was exhausted from the two flights and closed my eyes.

"Sir."

I heard a voice from a distance and opened my eyes.

"We are here." Cesar pointed to a long dirt driveway leading to a modest farmhouse. "My GPS says we are at your destination."

I yawned, then stepped outside and stretched.

Cesar's window was open. "Good luck," he said. "And don't worry about time. I will be here as long as you need me."

I nodded nervously. "Thanks."

The path leading to the farmhouse was quiet and lonely. The sign near the entrance read Goncalves Quinta. I hesitated. That wasn't the name I'd hoped to see. I looked back at the car, then started down the path. The farmhouse sat on my left, about two hundred feet away, and as I approached, I noticed a teenager walking my way carrying fruits or vegetables in a basket. When she saw me, she froze and looked around. Please don't bolt on me.

I waved and she continued toward me, not smiling, but not appearing frightened. Maybe curious.

"*Olá*" I said, in my limited Portuguese.

She looked beyond me, saw Cesar's car, and probably assumed I was lost, which in a way, I was.

She was about thirteen and answered in Portuguese.

"Do you speak English?" I asked.

She nodded. "Are you lost, sir?"

I pointed to the name on the farm sign I'd passed. "I hope I have the right place. I'm an American looking for a friend?"

She squinted and laid down her basket. "Here?"

My heart sank. "His name is Luca Falcone. Does he live here?"

She held my gaze and shook her head. "Maybe my dad can help you."

I followed her back to the house and asked her name.

"Gabriela," she said over her shoulder.

I smiled. "Pretty name."

I watched from a distance as she pointed to a citrus tree. The man, his back to us, was dressed in overalls, a white straw hat, and appeared to be inspecting the fruit.

"*Pai?*"

He turned to his daughter, then saw me and froze. His head shifted from side to side as though he might run.

I waved. "It's me, Hank. You're safe now."

We hugged, we cried, but most of all, we were friends again. Like me, Luca had changed over the years. His face had a mature look, with a few days of facial growth. His dark brown eyes sparkled, like they had years ago. His lean body was tight, and I suspected physical work had something to do with it.

"How did you find me?" he asked, nervously looking over my shoulder.

Good question. "It wasn't easy." I told him about my godfather's sudden decision to move to Florida and needing to clean up his basement. I reached into my back pocket, produced Carlota's now-opened letter to Bobby, and handed it to Luca. "I found it unopened in a basement cabinet. Thank God, I was curious."

Luca read it over then looked up at me. "No wonder Bobby never got in touch with me. I agonized for months." He rubbed an eye and sighed. "But then I thought it probably had to do with Carlota dying in a car accident soon after she brought me here and her not reaching him."

He sighed. "I think about her often."

Luca looked around, suddenly in a panic. "What about Jensen? He—"

"He's dead," I assured him. "Along with everyone involved with him from that night, including his nephew, Danny."

Luca's shoulders sagged, and he closed his eyes.

I touched his arm. "It's true," I said. "I witnessed their deaths. You have nothing to worry about."

He looked at me. "You?"

"I'm a private investigator. We'll talk about my involvement in time." I smiled. "Let's just say I'm the bearer of good news."

Luca studied me. "I don't know what to say. It's been so long since I felt safe."

"Twenty-five years."

He nodded. "My birthday party." He sighed. "I got so caught up with you being here, I forgot to ask about my mother and sister. Are they okay? God, I miss them so much. You don't know how often I wanted to call and tell them I was okay and safe, but I was worried Jensen might find out." He paused. "If my whereabouts leaked out, they could have been in danger. Hank, I couldn't risk it."

I touched his arm and smiled. "They're doing fine. We'll figure out a way for you to see them. Right now, nobody knows I'm here."

I nodded at Carlota's letter still in Luca's hand. "What happened that night?"

His eyes welled up. "God, what a night. Actually, my life changed before that night when I went to Jensen's law office a few nights before my party. There was a commotion in the inner office. Alex was with me, but he was too nervous to stay, and I told him to leave. Hell, I should have gone with him. But I was curious, and when

Jensen opened the door, I saw a woman covered with blood sprawled out on the floor."

He paused, took a breath. "Jensen was angry and scared and pleaded with me to help get rid of the body. I refused, of course, and that's when he threatened me if I told anyone about what I saw. Before I dashed out the door, Jensen demanded I meet him the night of my party, just outside Fort Totten. He said with a sneer, 'Have a good time at your birthday party. We'll talk afterward.' When I think about his comment, it sends shivers down my spine."

Luca looked at me, fear on his face. "It still haunts me. Jensen knew I was a liability, and I was afraid he'd kill me. The night of my party, I figured he'd send Danny to do his dirty work."

Luca stopped and caught his breath. "I arrived at the fort early and waited on a bench. Sometime around four in the morning, I noticed headlights coming from Bell Boulevard. I was confused because it was a cop in a patrol car, not Jensen. Had he sent someone from the local precinct? At that point, I thought I'd be arrested. Or killed. Either way, I knew I was screwed. Before the car entered the lot, I skirted the fort's perimeter and took side streets until reaching the Cross Island Parkway. There's a bike and pedestrian path leading to Little Neck. I never ran so fast in my life, and when I reached Northern Boulevard, I found a phone booth and called Bobby."

"Bobby?"

He nodded. "I didn't know who else to call."

"Only Bobby wasn't home," I said. "Carlota was."

Luca nodded. "He'd gone fishing for the weekend with friends. Thank God she was there and picked up the phone. She didn't hesitate to help."

Luca gazed over at his daughter who was still sitting near the door and waved. "*Meu amigo,*" he called out. "We're going for a walk. Tell Mama."

She nodded, picked up her fruit basket, and disappeared inside.

Luca patted me on the shoulder. "Come."

"Okay, but I have a question." I thumbed to the sign out front. "It says Goncalves Quinta. Is Goncalves the owner? Or did you change your name?"

He smiled warmly. "It belonged to Luiz Goncalves, a wonderful person who took me in, no questions asked. He's kind and generous. And he introduced me to my wife, Anabela. He's my daughter's godfather. When Luiz retired, I bought the farm from him. Me, Hank, a farmer." He paused. "I didn't change the name for obvious reasons, though my passport reads Joseph Salerno. I go by Joe. It's the same in Portuguese."

"What do I call you, Mr. Salerno?"

He smiled. "I'll always be Luca to you. God, I can't believe you're here."

I gave him an affectionate hug. "I missed you, buddy. We all did."

As we strolled along a path, fruit trees on either side, it was easy to imagine Luca and Kyle as partners.

Luca stopped short, his expression dark.

"What?" I said.

He looked over his shoulder. "Carlota told me the police were looking for me about the woman killed under the Whitestone Bridge. It had to be Danny. I bumped into him in the woods as I was leaving the park. His shirt was covered in blood."

Luca shook his head. "He was one crazy bastard. I thought maybe Jensen sent him to kill me. Instead, he wanted to become blood brothers and jabbed me with his knife." He paused. "Hank, I'm not making this up."

"I know. The detectives found your DNA on the knife. It was in the bushes."

"I don't doubt it. I threw it there. Danny wanted me to poke him with it. I just tossed it and ran."

It now made perfect sense. "The detectives assumed you disappeared after killing her."

"I didn't," he defended.

I touched Luca's shoulders and squeezed lightly. "Of course not. Before Jensen killed himself, he admitted it was Danny who killed her, and when I return to the States, I intend to clear your name."

Luca took a breath. "Thanks, but it could get complicated. I'd rather the authorities not know I'm alive. I could still be arrested if I gave myself up. And you know how long a trial can take after an arrest. Even if I'm found innocent, that could mean a year or more." He spread his arms. "I have a life, a family. I can't chance it."

Luca was right. "I get it, but I'm not giving up. There must be a way to avoid the process."

Luca smiled wearily. "I'll be here waiting."

Luca looked out at the field, then at me. "My wife knows very little about my past. I didn't want her involved."

We stopped by a pond. "Anabela and I built this. Just for fun. See the fish?" He pointed, then turned to me. "I love it here. She and my daughter gave me a second chance."

"Your daughter, Gabriela. We met. She's very pretty."

"She, too, is my life."

We continued down the path and stopped near an orange grove. Luca picked a few off a branch and handed me one. I ripped into it and sucked down the juice.

I licked my lips. "You're one hell of a farmer. Did you know Kyle owns a farm on Martha's Vineyard? He and his wife grow organic fruits and vegetables. He said you and he might have been partners."

A smile crossed my friend's face. "I always knew he'd go into farming. Good for him. And the other Whitestone boys? What are they up to?"

I told him about the others.

"Alex a priest. Who would have guessed?" He turned serious. "Do you know if he ever gave Tara my knife? I trusted him because I didn't know…"

I shook my head. "Alex has been going through a rough time

299

over the years. He blames himself for not sticking around the night he left you at Jensen's office. The priesthood helped somewhat."

"I'll have to have a heart-to-heart with him. The last thing I'd want is for him to feel guilty."

We finished our oranges. "It's beautiful here, Luca. You're very lucky."

He looked around. "I am. I have found true happiness here. How about we go inside, and I'll introduce you to my family?"

"I'd like that very much."

FIFTY-SIX

Jimmy Savage hadn't lied. He never told Jensen that Luca got away. It probably saved my friend from being killed. Whether Savage had a conscience or was afraid to tell his boss he'd screwed up, was anyone's guess.

Those thoughts stayed with me as Luca, and I drove along Madeira's coast. I didn't want to leave, but Luca had to get back to work. He kiddingly asked if I'd like to change professions and get my hands dirty. I was almost tempted. Oranges or searching for missing people? While I'd probably give it some thought, I had nothing to keep me in Madeira. No wife or family. Not that I'd ever marry again or have children, but I wasn't ready to make a commitment. Luca understood.

As for Luca returning to the States, that wasn't possible. The threat of incarceration loomed over him. But we managed to figure out a visit. It turned out that Luca was a Portuguese citizen through marriage. And so, he decided to travel back to the States under his Portuguese name: Joe Salerno.

Before I left, I called Bobby. There was a five-hour time difference, Madeira later, and I reached him at 2 p.m. his time.

"Hank, where have you been? You left a note telling me you were going away for a few days, but you didn't say where or why. I got worried and called a bunch of times, but your damn voicemail kept kicking in. What's going on?"

I looked at my phone. Of course. "Bobby, I'm sorry. I had my phone on airplane mode."

"Airplane mode? Where the heck are you?"

"Portugal. I was in a hurry."

My godfather remained quiet for a moment, and I suspected he was mulling over my response. "I don't understand. What's so important in Portugal?"

"Not what, Bobby, who?" I passed the phone to Luca.

He smiled. "Hello Bobby, it's Luca."

FIFTY-SEVEN

A week later, after deciding to make a quick trip to the States, Luca caught a TAP flight to JFK from Madeira via Lisbon. I had parked in the airport parking facility, and with an hour to kill, called Lisa. She and Bobby had planned the reunion for Luca and invited the Whitestone boys. All promised to attend.

We hadn't spoken in a while, and she was grateful again for me finding Luca. I insisted it was Carlota, beyond the grave, who came through.

She said, "Hank, I need to get something off my chest. When I saw you after all these years, my feelings toward you resurfaced. I'm sorry if I led you on as though nothing had happened since then. The truth is my life had been going downhill, and I'd hoped you'd be my savior. I now realize only I can make my own happiness."

She paused. "I started AA meetings not long ago, and the fog is beginning to lift from my brain. I'm working hard to put my life in order. That...time with Matt at the hotel was a mistake. We haven't been together since." She paused. "Please don't think badly of me."

I took a much-needed breath. "Thank you for trusting me. Crazy things happen in life, but we won't be judged by our mishaps. I appreciate you sharing your story and look forward to seeing you later."

My conversation with Lisa left me with mixed emotions. I was happy she'd begun to find peace. As for me, I felt I was on a perpetual merry-go-round, waiting for my life to slow down so I could smell the roses.

I checked the dashboard clock. Time to go. I headed for international arrivals and wondered what Luca was thinking as he stopped at immigration.

The Terminal 4 arrivals area was abuzz with passengers, and I found a corner on the side and waited. And waited. Panic struck. Had Luca been detained for murder? Maybe he shouldn't have come.

Almost an hour later, my friend appeared through the exit doors leading to the arrivals hall. He looked bewildered until he spotted me.

We hugged, and I took his carry-on.

"Sorry about that. The agent kept staring at my passport, and I began to panic. Turned out it was nothing. He asked a bunch of questions, and I answered with a Portuguese accent. He told me to enjoy my stay."

He added. "And like you suggested, I gave him your address where I'd be staying." He looked around anxiously. "I'm not used to crowds. Let's get out of here."

Luca was pensive throughout the ride to Whitestone, and when we reached his childhood home, he peered out and smiled wistfully.

"It hasn't changed much. Just as I remembered it. I used to dream about this house, my bedroom, my mom, and my sister. And, of course, Tara. Here I am, back twenty-five years later." He took a deep breath and turned to me. "I'm nervous."

I touched his shoulder. "You'll be fine, but the reunion is else-where. I was afraid with all the cars and people showing up at your mother's house, one of the neighbors from that terrible night might still live here. I didn't want to take a chance that one might get nosy."

He nodded. "Good thinking."

"Bobby arranged the reunion at Fillmore's. It's been locked up since Finn put the place up for sale. Without Conor, he had no reason to keep it open."

Luca sighed. "Another tragedy, thanks to Jensen and Danny."

When we arrived, a half-dozen cars were parked in the lot. The same Fillmore's name flashed across the bar like it had every night before. It was always considered a neighborhood bar.

I turned to Luca. "You ready?"

He nodded. "I think so."

———

Emotions flooded Luca as he stepped inside like Lazarus returning from the dead. In a sense, Luca had.

As he scanned the bar, he must have felt he was in a different universe. My friend knew everyone, yet after all these years, it was almost like meeting them for the first time.

His mother was back on her meds regularly since she discovered her son was alive. She rushed to him, and tears flowed everywhere. Even the Whitestone boys cried. I stood in a corner, watching the reunion. They were older but acted like teens again.

Matt, whose father was responsible for Luca's disappearance, would surely seek Luca's forgiveness for his father's past doings.

Kyle would try lining up a farming partnership. Jesse might have an awkward moment being married to Luca's first love, but years had passed, and Luca was happily married.

Father Alex, who was dressed in street clothes, seemed more seri-ous. I was certain he would ask for Luca's forgiveness for not being stronger the night Jensen killed Marta Reyes. Before leaving Madeira, Luca assured me he wasn't angry with Alex.

Bobby and Luca had spoken while I was in Portugal, and they emotionally celebrated Carlota's life. It turned out a friend of Carlota's, another flight attendant, knew about her and Bobby. She called my godfather soon after the accident. When Carlota's letter arrived a few days later, Bobby was too distraught to open it, and there in the basement it sat until I found it twenty-five years later. Poor Bobby, he never knew Carlota saved Luca.

Tara stood to one side, waiting for Luca to approach her. They'd been sending each other glances since he arrived. When Luca approached, he kissed her on the cheek and held her hand. They spoke briefly.

Alex approached them. Being a priest, he was probably offering blessings to them and their families. But as the discussion continued, they became serious, looked shocked and confused. Luca and Tara turned to each other dazed.

I looked around at the others for their reaction, but the gang was too busy drinking and laughing to notice.

Something was going on as Tara covered her face and cried. Luca appeared stunned. Alex held their hands, appearing to comfort them. For what? I focused on their expressions, which went from numbness to joy.

Luca and Tara hugged. I guessed while the past would always remain in their hearts, their lives belonged with different people.

And then the reunion was over. Unlike Luca's eighteen birthday party, this event ended on a positive note, with hugs and smiles.

Two days later, while driving Luca back to the airport, I side-glanced him. He appeared in deep thought. "What are you thinking?"

He looked at me and sighed. "Hank, I'm overwhelmed. My brain is churning with everything that has happened since I returned."

"I can imagine."

Luca hesitated. "More than you think. I learned from Alex that Tara and I have a daughter together. I didn't know she was pregnant when I disappeared." He took in a breath. "You're not going to believe this but, our daughter is one of Alex's parishioners."

"Emily," I said without hesitation.

His eyes widened. "You knew? Alex said he hadn't told anyone but us."

"He didn't have to. I just now guessed." I explained that I met Emily while investigating. "When Alex spilled his guts about the night he left you, Emily was there, along with his monsignor. She was physically upset, as though your disappearance and presumed murder were personal."

"Damn." Luca looked shocked.

I entered the Van Wyck Expressway and not in a hurry, stayed in the right lane. "I observe a lot in my business. Anyway, congratulations. So, what's next?"

Luca stared out the window. "With Emily? I haven't met her yet. Well, not in person. We Facetimed. Tara and me. As weird as it appeared, we had a wonderful conversation. Emily promised to fly to Madeira and visit me as soon as she could. In the meantime, she and Tara are meeting next week."

Luca paused. "I guess I have a lot of explaining to do. But given the circumstances, I'm sure my wife and daughter will welcome Emily with open arms."

"You're a lucky man, twice," I said.

He nodded and smiled. "I am."

We stayed quiet for a while, Luca still processing his new life. He turned as I entered Airport Road.

"So, Mr. P.I., what's next for you?"

"Good question. I haven't figured that out yet."

He elbowed my side playfully. "I can use a strong back on the farm. I'll teach you how to plant crops," he said with a chuckle.

I rolled my eyes. "Is this a job interview? Seriously, while it's tempting, my roots are here in the States. No pun intended. But I promise to visit often and bring Bobby."

"Can't forget Bobby. And his girlfriend, of course."

I laughed. "Girlfriend of the month. As my mother used to say, Bobby changes his girlfriends more often than his socks."

We both laughed.

I pulled up to a departure gate curb at JFK International Terminal, shifted into park, and turned to Luca. "This is your stop, Whitestone boy."

He sighed and smiled. "No matter where I live, Hank, I'll always be a Whitestone boy."

We hugged, then Luca exited the car. Before disappearing inside, he turned and gave me a thumbs up. I waved.

Good luck, my friend.

I remained at the curb a few minutes longer staring at travelers entering the terminal. Lucky them.

Where to next, Hank?

Unlike Luca, I had nothing to go home to. I didn't even have a pet. Maybe I'd take Bobby's advice and move to Florida. I removed my cell phone from the glove compartment and scrolled through my photo app until reaching the picture I downloaded from Andre in Portugal.

Maybe not.

Those piercing eyes. Could she be Patrice? In Morocco? Andre suggested she ran off not wanting to be photographed. Why? If it was Patrice, she'd probably be running from the law. And me.

I pulled out of the spot and drove toward my office, wondering if I should take a chance and find out. What could possibly happen?

THE END

AFTERWORD

Writing this book was a personal journey. I wanted to write about the place where I grew up: Whitestone, New York. I have fond memories as a teenager hanging out at Francis Lewis Park, below the Whitestone Bridge. While I don't believe there was much crime near the bridge, a fourteen-year-old girl was murdered in a deserted lot near my house, a few miles from the iconic Whitestone Bridge. The killer was caught thanks to one of my friends, who identified the guy and informed the police. He later went on to become a police officer.

I still maintain friendships with several childhood companions, though, like Hank Reed, most have moved away from Whitestone and settled in the New York suburbs. Several old buddies were instrumental in jogging my memory for the book: Bob Marchant, Frank Kelly, Bob McMahon, and Tom Eirman. Yes, Whitestone was the ideal place to enjoy a life filled with friendships, personal growth, and imagination.

MURDER BY CHANCE
A HANK REED MYSTERY, BOOK 5

In *Murder by Chance*, the fifth installment of Hank Reed's mystery series, Hank is drawn into a high-stakes investigation on the open seas. He accepts a favor for his friend, Homicide Detective JR Greco, by boarding a European cruise to keep an eye on JR's niece and her questionable boyfriend. As the luxurious ship sails towards Italy, the boyfriend mysteriously vanishes, presumed lost at sea, leaving the niece as a prime suspect.

With the clock ticking, Hank must navigate a web of secrets among the ship's passengers to find the truth. From the glitzy casino to the opulent dining rooms danger lurks at every corner. As Hank races to solve the mystery, he must untangle the complex motives of a ship full of suspects who might have wanted the boyfriend dead.

Can Hank unmask the real killer before the ship reaches Italy and the chance for justice sails away? *Murder by Chance* is a gripping mystery where danger, deception, and intrigue collide on the high seas.

Available in Paperback and eBook from Your Favorite Bookstore or Online Retailer

ABOUT THE AUTHOR

Fred Lichtenberg is a native New Yorker who resides with his wife in Jupiter, Florida. After spending a career as a Senior Field Agent with the IRS, Lichtenberg changed gears from crunching numbers to creating fictitious villains and heroes. *The Art of Murder* (formerly *Hunter's World*), the first in the Hank Reed Series, starts with the murder of an outside celebrity living in a small community on Long Island.

Lichtenberg's second book, *Murder on the Rocks*, takes Hank Reed (now a Suffolk County Detective) in search of a missing person presumably involved in a whistleblower investigation.

The Edge of Murder, Lichtenberg's third book, shifts Hank from a detective to a private investigator, where he searches for a missing woman.

Hank Reed's latest addition (*The Bridge to Murder* #4) is his most personal and challenging, when the sister of his childhood friend, who disappeared twenty-five years ago and was charged with the murder of a young woman under the Whitestone Bridge, in Queens, New York, receives an anonymous letter claiming her brother's innocence.

Another hoax? Maybe, but as Hank plunges into the cold case, he quickly realizes there is more to the story. As he relentlessly investigates, past sinister players are working against him. Will Hank find them before they shut down the investigation? And Him?

Lichtenberg's stand-alone novels include: *Double Trouble*; *Deadly*

Heat at The Cottages: Sex, Murder, and Mayhem; *Murder 1040: The Final Audit*; and the humorous, *Retired: Now What?*

Lichtenberg also wrote *The Second Time Around…Again,* a one-act play about finding love in a nursing home, performed at the Lake Worth Playhouse.

Lichtenberg is an active member of the Mystery Writers of America and International Thriller Writers.

www.fredlichtenberg.com

 facebook.com/fredlichtenberg

www.ingramcontent.com/pod-product-compliance
Lightning Source LLC
Chambersburg PA
CBHW020538020726
47494CB00006B/1816